OLAF THE

A STORY OF THE VIKING AGE

BY ROBERT LEIGHTON

PREFACE

The following narrative is not so much a story as a biography. My hero is not an imaginary one; he was a real flesh and blood man who reigned as King of Norway just nine centuries ago. The main facts of his adventurous career--his boyhood of slavery in Esthonia, his life at the court of King Valdemar, his wanderings as a viking, the many battles he fought, his conversion to Christianity in England, and his ultimate return to his native land--are set forth in the various Icelandic sagas dealing with the period in which he lived. I have made free use of these old time records, and have added only such probable incidents as were necessary to give a continuous thread of interest to the narrative. These sagas, like the epics of Homer, were handed down from generation to generation by word of mouth, and they were not committed to writing until a long time after Olaf Triggvison's death, so that it is not easy to discriminate between the actual facts as they occurred and the mere exaggerated traditions which must surely have been added to the story of his life as it was told by the old saga men at their winter firesides. But in most instances the records corroborate each other very exactly, and it may be taken that the leading incidents of the story are historically true.

The Icelandic sagas have very little to say concerning Olaf Triggvison's unsuccessful invasion of England, and for this part of the story I have gone for my facts to the English chronicles of the time, wherein frequent allusion to him is made under such names as Anlaf, Olave, and Olaff. The original treaty of peace drawn up between King Ethelred the Second and Olaf still exists to fix the date of the invasion, while the famous battle of Maldon, in which the Norse adventurer gained a victory over the East Anglians, is described at length by a nameless contemporary poet, whose "Death of Brihtnoth" remains as one of the finest of early English narrative poems, full of noble patriotism and primitive simplicity.

I have given no dates throughout these pages, but for the convenience of readers who may wish for greater exactness it may be as well to state here that Olaf was born A.D. 963, that he started on his wanderings as a viking in the year 981, that the sea fight between the vikings of Jomsburg and the Norwegians took place in 986, and the battle of Maldon in the year 991. Olaf reigned only five years as King of Norway, being crowned in 995, and ending his reign with his death in the glorious defeat at Svold in the year 1000.

ROBERT LEIGHTON.

CHAPTER I: THE FINDING OF OLAF

It happened in the beginning of the summer that Sigurd Erikson journeyed north into Esthonia to gather the king's taxes and tribute. His business in due course brought him into a certain seaport that stood upon the shores of the great Gulf of Finland.

He was a very handsome man, tall and strong, with long fair hair and clear blue eyes. There were many armed servants in his following, for he was a person of great consequence, and was held in high honour throughout the land.

He rode across the marketplace and there alighted from his horse, and turned his eyes towards the sea. Before him stretched the rippling, sunlit bay with its wooded holms. A fleet of fishing boats was putting out with the flood tide, and some merchant vessels lay at anchor under shelter of the green headland.

Nearer to the strand a long dragonship, with a tall gilded prow rising high above the deck tent, was moored against a bank of hewn rock that served as a wharf. At sight of the array of white shields along this vessel's bulwarks his eyes brightened, for he knew that she was a viking ship from his own birth land in distant Norway, and he was glad. Not often did it chance that he could hold speech with the bold warriors of the fiords.

Close by the ship there was a noisy crowd of men and boys. He strode nearer to them, and heard the hoarse voices of the vikings calling out in loud praise of a feat that had been performed by someone in their midst. Sigurd joined the crowd, and saw a boy step out upon the vessel's narrow gangplank, and there, standing between the ship and the shore, begin to throw a knife high up into the sunny air, catching it as it fell.

It seemed that the lad was of good station, for his clothing was of finely woven cloth, and there was a gold neckband to his kirtle, and his long black hair was well combed and curled. Thrice he threw up his glittering knife high above his head and deftly caught it again. But soon, thinking perhaps to excel those who had gone before him, he took a second knife from his belt, and juggled with them both with such skill that the shipmen watching him from under the awning swore by the hammer of Thor that the feat could never be surpassed.

"Well done, well done!" they shouted. And the boys on the bank cried out, "Well done, Rekoni!"

At this the youth put fuller strength into his arms and flung the knives yet higher into the air. But his ambition for the praise of the warriors was greater than his caution, for, in reaching forward to catch one of the weapons, he lost his balance and fell headlong into the deep green water beneath. And as he swam to shore the vikings laughed aloud, and some who had thought of giving him a reward put back their gold into their wallets and turned away.

Now, very close to where Sigurd Erikson was there stood two boys, whose close cropped hair and dress of coarse white vadmal showed them to be slaves. One of them was a tall, gaunt youth, with pale thin cheeks and large sad eyes. He was fair of skin, and by this Sigurd knew that he was not an Esthonian. His companion seemed about twelve winters old, sturdy and broad backed, with very fair hair. His neck and bare strong arms were burnt by the sun to a ruddy brown. Sigurd could not see his face, and might not have noticed him had not the elder lad urged him forward, bidding him step upon the plank and show his skill.

"Not I," said the younger, with an impatient toss of his cropped head. And he thrust his thumbs into his belt and drew back. "Too much have I already done in bidding Rekoni try the feat. Well is it for me that he is not hurt by his fall into the sea, else would his father's whip be about my back. Even as the matter stands, my master will surely stop my food for having left his sheep to stray upon the hills."

"I had but wished to see you succeed where your master's son has failed," sighed the elder lad. And at this the boy turned round and said more softly:

"Well, Thorgils, for your pleasure will I do it, and not for the vikings' praise. Lend me your dirk."

So he took the knife from Thorgils' belt, and, leaving the crowd, walked boldly to the end of the gangplank. Here he rubbed the soles of his bare feet in the dust and then stepped to the middle of the narrow board.

"Now what thinks this child that he can do?" cried one of the vikings.

The boy turned sharply and looked at the man who had spoken. He was a tall, red bearded man, whose nose was flat against his scarred, bronzed face. At sight of him the boy drew back a pace as if in fear.

"Ay. What thinks the babe that he can do?" echoed another of the warriors. But those who were nearer made no answer, for they saw that the boy was very agile and strong beyond his years.

Sigurd watched him as he took his stand on the plank. The sunlight shone upon his fair young face. His clear blue eyes flashed like stars under his knitted brows. He ran his fingers over his short yellow hair, and then, turning with his back to the sun, flung one of his knives high up into the air. As it turned in its descent he flung a second knife, then

2

caught the first and again threw it high--higher even than the vane on the ship's tall mast. He stood with his bare feet firmly gripping the plank, and his head thrown back, and his lithe, well balanced body swaying in regular movement with his arms. Then as the two gleaming weapons were well in play, rising and falling in quick succession, one of his hands went to his belt, and he drew yet a third knife and plied it in turn with the other two.

At this there was a murmur of praise from both ship and shore, and the vikings declared that never before had they seen one so young display such skill. And all the while Sigurd Erikson kept his eyes upon the lad's glowing, upturned face.

"Who is this child?" he asked of the tall youth at his side. But the sad eyed Thorgils paid no heed to the question, but only crept nearer to the end of the gangboard, and stood there earnestly watching. As he looked at the ship's bulwarks he caught sight of the man with the red beard and broken nose--the chief of the vikings,--and he cried out to his companion:

"Enough, Ole, enough!"

Then the boy caught his knives and thrust them one by one into his belt, and, turning shoreward, strode quickly down the plank and made his way through the cheering crowd, followed by Thorgils. Many of the vikings called him back with offers of reward, and Sigurd Erikson tried to arrest him as he passed. But the young slave only gave a careless laugh and ran swiftly away.

Now it seemed that Sigurd had a mind to go after him. But as he was leaving the crowd he met a certain rich merchant of the town, and he said:

"Tell me, Biorn, who is this yellow haired lad that has just proved himself so skilful at the knife feat? And whence came he into Esthonia?"

The merchant shook his head and said:

"He is a wild and wilful loon, hersir, and of no account to any man. As to his feat with the knives, had I my will I'd have it instant death to any thrall who should so much as touch a sharpened weapon."

"By his looks I would judge him to be Norway born," said Sigurd.

"That may well be," returned the merchant, "for it is true that he came with the west wind. It was I who bought him from the vikings, with another of his kind--one Thorgils, who is to this day my bond slave. I bought them in exchange for a good he goat from Klerkon Flatface. Very soon I found the younger lad was worthless. There was little that I could do with him; so I sold him to a dalesman named Reas, who gave me a very fine rain cloak for him; nor do I rue my bargain, for the cloak is still in use and the lad is scarcely of the value of his food and shelter."

"How do men name the lad?" inquired Sigurd. "And whose son is he?"

"Whose son he may be is no concern of mine," answered the merchant. "Some viking's brat, it may be; for he has the viking spirit in him, and the salt of the sea is in his veins. No landman can tame him. As to his name, if ever he had one, 'tis certain he has none now, and is only known as Reasthrall, for he is the thrall of Reas the bonder."

"If it be that Reas will sell his thrall," said Sigurd, "then I would willingly buy the lad, and take him back with me into Holmgard as an offering to the Queen Allogia."

"Think twice ere you act so unkindly towards the queen," said the merchant. "A goodlier gift for Allogia would surely be the jewelled brooch that I showed you yesternight; and you shall have it very cheap. The price is but twelve gold marks."

But before Sigurd could reply a heavy hand was laid upon his shoulder, and a gruff voice called out his name. He turned and saw at his side the tall red bearded viking chief,

3

whose broken nose and coarse scarred face were now shielded from the sun's rays by a wide hat made of dry reeds.

"Well met, Hersir Sigurd!" said the warrior. "And what lordly business brings you north to the coast? 'Tis long since last we met--not since the yuletide feast at Holmgard, two winters back, when we had the horse fight. How fares the Flanders mare that won such glory at that time?"

"A sickness killed her," answered Sigurd. "But I have a foal in training that will soon beat any horse in Holmgard; ay, even in Norway. So if you have a mind to see a good horse fight, come when you will with the best horses you can find. I wager you that mine will beat them all."

"If I meet not my death before the end of the cruising season," said the viking, "then will I engage to bring you the best horse in all the Norseland to fight against." He looked among the crowd of boys that still loitered near the ship, and added--"Where has the youngster gone who stood just now upon the plank? He has in him the makings of a good war man. Such lads as he are scarce, and I would buy him if he be for sale."

And then the merchant spoke.

"Why," said he, addressing the viking, "'tis but six summers since that you sold that self same boy, here on this marketplace. 'Twas I who bought him from you, Klerkon. Have you forgotten the white haired he goat that you got from me?"

"Life is too full for me to keep mind of such small events," answered Klerkon. "But since the lad is yours, what price do you now put upon him?"

"Nay, he is no chattel of mine," said the merchant. "He is the thrall of goodman Reas, over in Rathsdale--a morning's walk from here. If you would deal with him a guide will soon be got to take you over the hill."

"Young flesh will keep," returned the warrior. "I will buy the lad next time we come to Esthonia."

Sigurd said: "It may be that ere that time he will already be sold, Jarl Klerkon; for it chances that I also have taken a fancy to him."

"In that case," said the viking, "we may make him the stake to be fought for in our coming horse fight. And if my horse overcomes yours, then the lad shall be my prize, and I will make a viking of him."

"And how if the victory be mine and not yours?" asked Sigurd.

"You shall have value equal to the boy, be assured of that, hersir."

"Agreed," said Sigurd. "And now, what news have you from west over sea?"

"Ill news and good. There has fallen a great famine in Norway. In Thrandheim the folk are dying for lack of corn and fish, and in Halogaland the snow has lain over the valleys nigh until midsummer, so that all the livestock have been bound in stall and fed upon birch buds. Men lay the famine to the account of Gunnhild's sons, who are over greedy of money and deal hardly with the husbandmen. There is little peace in the land, for the kings are for ever quarrelling over their jointures; but it seems that Harald Greyfell is having the upper hand over his brothers. Little joy is there in ruling over a realm these days. I had rather be as I am, an honest sea rover."

"Doubtless the viking life is, after all, the most joyful that a man can live," said Sigurd. "How fare our friends at Jomsburg?"

"Right well, as always," answered Klerkon. "Sigvaldi has built himself a fine new dragonship of five and twenty seats, and the Jomsvikings now number in all seven times ten hundred men. They speak of making a sally across the sea to Angle land, where there is corn and ale in plenty, with fine clothes, good arms, and vessels of silver and gold to be won; for these Christian folk are very rich, and there is abundance of treasure in their churches, with many a golden bowl and well wrought drinking horn as booty for those who are bold enough to make the adventure."

"But these Angles are good fighting men, I hear," said Sigurd. "And they have many well built ships."

"They are ill matched against the vikings, with all their ships," returned Klerkon. "And I am told that their king is a man of peace; Edgar the Peaceable, they name him. And talking of kings, how fares King Valdemar?"

"As sunny as a summer's noon," answered Sigurd.

"Come, then, on board my ship, and let us pledge to him in a full horn of mead," said the viking. And he drew Sigurd with him across the gangplank, and they went below and sat drinking until one of the shipmen standing on the vessel's lypting, or poop deck, sounded a shrill horn as a sign that the ship was about to leave the harbour.

Then Sigurd came ashore and went about the town on the king's business, and he thought no more of the yellow haired slave boy until the evening time.

It chanced then that he was again beside the sea.

Down there on the shore he stood alone, idly watching the white winged seabirds--some floating in their own reflections on the calm pools of water left by the outgoing tide, others seeking food amid the green and crimson weeds that lay in bright patches on the rocks--and often he turned his eyes in the direction of the setting sun, where, in the mid sea, Jarl Klerkon's dragonship moved slowly outward, with her wet oars glistening in the rosy light.

Suddenly from behind him there came a merry childish laugh, and he turned quickly round, and saw very near to him the white clothed slave boy of the gangplank. The lad was standing at the brink of a deep pool of seawater, and had, as it seemed, started a fleet of empty mussel shells to float upon the calm surface. He was dropping pebbles from his full hand into the water, to give movement to the tiny boats.

Sigurd stepped quietly behind him, and then said:

"Why do you thus set these shells to sail?"

The boy looked up in surprise, and his blue eyes rested for a long time upon the tall strange man. Then he answered:

"Because, hersir, they are my warships, setting out upon a viking cruise."

At this Sigurd smiled.

"It may be, my boy," said he, "that you will yourself command great ships of war in time to come."

"That is what I should wish," said the boy, "for then I might take blood vengeance upon my enemies."

"Not often do I hear one so young thus speak of enemies," said Sigurd. "What is your age?"

"Ten winters."

"And your name?"

The boy looked up once more into the stranger's face, and at his large crested helmet of bronze and gold. He glanced, too, at the man's great sword and his cloak of rich blue cloth, and guessed rightly that he was of noble rank. There was a smile upon his lips, and his eyes were tender and kindly, winning confidence.

"My name is Olaf," answered the boy.

"Whose son?" asked Sigurd.

At this question Olaf turned aside, threw his pebbles away into the water, and wiped his wet hands on his coarse kirtle. Then stepping nearer to the stranger he stood upright and said, almost in a whisper, as though fearing that even the seagulls might overhear him:

5

"I am King Triggvi's son."

Sigurd drew back with a little start.

"King Triggvi's son!" he echoed in surprise. And then he looked yet more keenly into the boy's face, as if to seek some likeness there.

"Even so," returned Olaf. "And what of that? Little good can it do me to be a king's son if I am also a slave, made to work hard for my daily portion of black bread and tough horse flesh. Triggvi is in Valhalla, with Harald Fairhair and the rest of them, and he cannot help me now. But Odin be thanked, he died not like a cow upon a bed of straw, but with sword in hand like a brave good man."

"A brave good man in truth he was," said Sigurd. "But tell me, boy, what token have you to prove that you are indeed the child of Triggvi Olafson? You are but ten winters old, you say; and yet, as I reckon it, Triggvi was slain full ten winters back. How can I know the truth of what you tell?"

"No token have I but my bare words," answered Olaf proudly.

Sigurd caught him by the hand and led him up the beach to a ledge of rock, and sat him down before him, bidding him tell how it came about that he was here in bondage in a foreign land.

So Olaf answered him thus:

"I came into the world an orphan," said he, "and never heard my father's voice. But my mother bade me ever remember that I was a king's son, and to make myself worthy. Astrid was the name of my mother. She was the daughter of Erik Biodaskalli, who dwelt at Ofrestead, in the Uplands, a mighty man. Now, after the slaying of Triggvi, Queen Astrid was forced to fly from the realm of Viken, lest she too should fall into the hands of Gunnhild and her wicked sons and be slain. And she travelled as a fugitive through many lands. In her company was her foster father, Thoralf Loosebeard by name. He never departed from her, but always helped her and defended her wheresoever she went. There were many other trusty men in her train, so no harm came to her. And at last she took refuge on a certain islet in the middle of Rand's fiord, and lay hidden there for many days. On that islet I was born, and I am told that they sprinkled me with water and named me Olaf, after my father's father. There, through the summer tide she stayed in safety. But when the days grew short and the nights weary and long, and when the wintry weather came upon us, then she left her hiding place and set forth with her folk into the Uplands, travelling under the shelter of night. And after many hardships and dangers she came to Ofrestead, her father's dwelling, and there we abode through the winter.

"Little do I remember of these matters, which befell while yet I was a babe in arms. This that I tell you was taught to me by Thorgils, my foster brother, who is the thrall of Biorn the merchant; and he can tell you more than I know, for he is older than I, and the son of our faithful Thoralf. Thorgils has said that when Gunnhild got tidings that I had come into the world she sent forth many armed messengers, and bade them fare into the Uplands in search of this son of King Triggvi, that they might prevent my growing up to manhood and claiming my father's realm. But in good time the friends of Erik were aware of the messengers; so Erik arrayed Astrid for departure, and gave her good guides, and sent her east--away into the Swede realm to one Hakon Gamle, a friend of his and a man of might, with whom we abode in all welcome for a long while."

"And what then?" urged Sigurd. For the boy had paused, and had pulled a tangle of brown seaweed from the rock where he was sitting, and was cracking the little air bladders between his fingers.

"Now it chanced," continued Olaf, "that even again Queen Gunnhild secretly learned our hiding place. So she sent a goodly company east to the Swede king with good gifts and fair words, asking that he might send Olaf Triggvison back with them into Norway, where Gunnhild would foster me, and bring me up as became a king's son. And the king sent to Ofrestead. But my mother Astrid knew that there was treachery in this-- for in like manner had Gunnhild beguiled my father,--and she would by no means let me go into the care' of my father's murderers, and so Gunnhild's messengers went back empty handed.

"By this time I was full three winters old and strong of limb, and my mother took me on board a trading ship that was eastward bound for Gardarike; for in that land her brother was a great man, and she knew that he would gladly succour us until I should be of an age to avenge my father's death and claim my rightful heritage."

At these words Sigurd grew very grave, and he put his hand gently on Olaf's arm, and asked to know what ill had befallen Queen Astrid, and whether she had reached her journey's end.

"Alas!" answered Olaf. "You ask me what I cannot tell. Would that I knew her to be still living! But never once have I seen her or heard tidings of her since the dread day when we were brought into this land and sold into bondage."

As he spoke the lad looked sadly over the sea to where the viking ship was slowly drifting into the shadow of the holms. Sigurd's eyes dwelt upon him with curious intentness.

"We set sail across the Eastern Sea," Olaf went on "and there were many merchants on our ship with great store of money and rich merchandise. And, as always, Thoralf and his son Thorgils were with us. Now, scarcely was our vessel beyond the sight of land when we were met by a great viking ship, that bore down quickly upon us, and attacked our seamen, first with arrows and stones, and then with spear and sword, and there was great fighting. So the vikings killed many of our people, and took our ship and all that was in it. When we had been made captives the rovers took and shared us among themselves as their bond slaves, and it befell that my mother and I were parted. An Esthonian named Klerkon Flatface got me as his portion, along with Thoralf and Thorgils. Klerkon deemed Thoralf over old for a thrall, and could not see any work in him, so he cruelly slew him before our eyes and cast his body into the sea. But he had us two lads away with him, and he sold us here in the marketplace in exchange for a white goat. Then, being companions in our misfortune, Thorgils and I swore foster brotherhood, and we took an oath in handshaking that when we grew strong enough we would go out upon the sea and take vengeance upon the man who had slain old faithful Thoralf."

Sigurd pointed outward to the ship that was afar off upon the dim horizon.

"Jarl Klerkon, of whom you speak," said he, "is now upon yonder ship."

"And well do I know it," returned Olaf. "Today when I stood upon the vessel's gangplank I saw him standing on the lypting; and I knew him by the token that his nose was flat against his face. I had a mind to throw one of my knives at him, but there were over many of his men around, who would soon have overpowered me had I been so rash. And now," the boy added, as he glanced up at the darkening sky, "it is time that I go back to the hills to gather my master's sheep into the fold, for the night will be dark, and wolves will be about. Too long already have I tarried here."

And before Sigurd could put out his hand to detain him Olaf had bounded up the rocks, and was soon lost to sight.

CHAPTER II: SIGURD ERIKSON.

On the next morning, as the red sun rose above the mist capped hills of Rathsdale, Olaf was at work among his master's swine, cleaning out the styes and filling them with new straw. As he worked he asked himself who the tall man could be who had spoken

7

with him last night upon the beach, and he began to regret that he had told so much, believing now that the stranger might be an enemy--perhaps even a spy of the wicked Queen Gunnhild, who had so often sought to add to her own security by clearing her path of all who had power to dispute her rights. Gunnhild was a very wily woman, and it might well be that she had secretly discovered the abiding place of the young son of King Triggvi, and that she had sent this man into Esthonia to entrap him.

"Never again shall I be so free in telling my story to a stranger," said Olaf to himself. "Thorgils was wise to counsel me to keep secret my kinship with Triggvi Olafson. When I am a man, and can fight my own battles, then it will be time enough to lay claim to my father's realm; and it may be that if I remain in thraldom till that time no one will guess who I am. As a thrall, then, I must work, even though that work be no better than the cleaning of my master's stables and pig styes--Get back, you greedy grunter!"

This last command was addressed to a great bristly boar that brushed past the boy and made its way to the bed of new straw. Olaf caught the animal by its hind leg and struggled with it for a moment, until the boar was thrown heavily on its side, squealing and kicking furiously. Then three of the other pigs rushed forward, and one knocked against the lad with such force that he fell on his knees. This made him very angry, and he rose quickly to his feet and wrestled with the pigs, driving them back with blows of his clenched hands. But the boar was not easily turned. It stood stubbornly glaring at him with its small bloodshot eyes, then suddenly charged at him with a savage roar. Olaf leapt up, but too slowly, for his left foot was caught by the boar's high back, and he rolled over in the mire. And now his wrath got the better of him, and he leapt at the boar with a wild cry, seizing its ears in his two hands. Then they struggled together for many minutes, now rolling over, now breaking asunder and again returning to the charge. But at last Olaf gained the mastery, and his adversary lay panting and exhausted on the coveted straw. Olaf sat upon the animal's side with his bare foot upon its snout. His arm was bleeding, and there was a long scratch upon his cheek. But he did not heed his wounds, for he had conquered.

As he sat thus a shadow moved across the yellow straw. He raised his eyes, and beheld the faces of two men, who looked down upon him from over the barrier of the pig sty. One of the men was his master, Reas. The other he quickly recognized as the tall man who had spoken with him last night. Sigurd Erikson was seated on a beautiful white horse, and he was arrayed as for a long journey.

"This is the boy you mean," said Reas, as Olaf rose and went on with his work--"an ill favoured loon you will think him. But had I expected you I should have seen that he had been well washed and decently clothed. If you would have him for hard labour, however, he is at least strong, and I will warrant you that he is healthy, and has no bodily faults. It may be that he is a little wild and wilful, but you can tame him, and a sound flogging will do him no harm, as I have ofttimes found. What price do you offer for him, hersir?"

Olaf looked up in anxious surprise, wondering if in truth the stranger had come to buy him, so that he might carry him off to the wicked Queen Gunnhild.

"I will give you two silver marks for him," said Sigurd, "and that is the value of a full grown man slave."

Reas demurred, looking at Olaf as if regretting that the lad was not more presentable.

"No," he said at last. "You will not find such a thrall as he in every day's march. If he were but a little cleaner you would see that he is a very pretty boy. Look at his eyes-- keen as a young snake's! Why, no woman's eyes are more beautiful! Look at his skin, there where his kirtle is torn. Is it not fair? And he is skilled in many feats. My own son Rekoni is not more clever than he. He can run for half a day without being wearied. He can climb the highest pine tree in Rathsdale--as he did last seed time to harry a bluejay's nest; and no seamew can swim more lightly on the water."

"As to his climbing," said Sigurd, with a curious look in his blue eyes, "I do not doubt that he will some day climb much higher than you list. But swimming is of little avail where there is no sea. And if he runs so well there is all the more danger of his running away. I think you will be well paid if I give you two silver marks. But since you set so high a value on him for his beauty and his skill, then I give you in addition this little ring of gold for your good wife's wearing. What say you?"

"It is a bargain!" said Reas, eagerly grasping the ring that Sigurd took from his belt pouch; "and you may take the lad at once."

Olaf drew back to the far corner of the pig sty. There was a frown on his brow, and his blue eyes flashed in quick anger.

"I will not go!" he said firmly, and he made a rapid movement to leap over the barrier; but he forgot the wound in his arm, and the pain of it made him so awkward that Reas caught him by his wrists and held him there until Sigurd, springing from his horse, came and put an iron chain round the lad's neck. Then the two men forcibly drew him to the gate of the pig sty. So, when Reas had opened the gate, Sigurd, who was a very powerful man, caught Olaf in his arms and carried him to the horse's side, and, holding the end of the chain, mounted. Olaf struggled a little to free himself, but finding the chain secure about his neck, resolved to await a better chance of escape. Then Sigurd gave Reas the two silver marks in payment of his purchase, and urged his horse to a quick walk, dragging Olaf behind him.

Very soon Reas and his straggling farmstead were hidden from sight behind a clump of tall pine trees. Then Sigurd halted at the side of a little stream.

"You have done well," he said to Olaf, "in thus coming away with seeming unwillingness. But do not suppose that I value you so lightly as did your late master, who thinks, foolish man, that you are no better than many another bond slave whom he might buy in the marketplace. Had Reas exacted an hundred gold marks instead of two paltry marks of silver, I should willingly have given him them."

"And why?" asked Olaf with a frown. "Is it that you think to take me west to Norway, and cast me like a young goat among wolves? I had thought when you so blandly spoke to me yesternight that you were a man of honour. Haply Queen Gunnhild would reward you well if you should deliver me into her clutches. But this you shall never do!"

"Rash boy," said Sigurd as he stroked his horse's mane, "do you not recognize a friend when you meet one? Or is friendship so strange to you that you take all men to be your enemies?"

"Enmity comes so often in the guise of friendship," said Olaf, "that it is well to be wary. I had been wiser last night if I had refused to speak with you."

"The time will soon come," said Sigurd, "when you will not be sorry that you so spoke. But I will warn you that it may go very ill with you if you tell your story to all strangers as you told it to me."

Olaf was perplexed. He looked into the man's face and saw only kindness there, and yet there was something very suspicious in the stranger's eagerness to possess him.

"If you are indeed my friend," said the boy, "why do you keep this chain about my neck? Why do you drag me after you like a dog?"

"Because I am not willing that you should escape me," answered Sigurd. "But if you will shake my hand and tell me that you will not run away, then I will take off your chain and you shall ride in front of me on my horse. You are King Triggvi's son, and I know that, once spoken, your word will be sacred."

Now, Olaf had never taken any man's hand since he swore foster brotherhood with Thorgils Thoralf son. He looked upon handshaking as a most solemn covenant, only to be made when great matters were at stake. Also, he had never yet told or acted a lie, or been false to anyone. He answered promptly:

"No, I will not take your hand. Neither will I give you my word that I shall not escape from you very soon. You may keep the chain about my neck. It is more easily broken than my promise."

Sigurd looked at the lad and smiled.

"I think," he said, "that I would admire you even more if you were a little cleaner. Here is a stream of water. Get in and wash yourself."

"I cannot take off my clothes without removing the chain," said Olaf, "and if the chain be removed I shall run away to where even your horse cannot follow me. But if you will give me one boon I will promise you that I will wash myself clean and then come back to the chain."

"What is your boon?" asked Sigurd.

"It is," said Olaf, "that since I am now your lawful thrall, and must go with you wheresoever you wish, you will go to Biorn the merchant and buy from him my foster brother Thorgils."

Sigurd leapt from his horse and at once unfastened the chain from Olaf's neck, and even helped him to draw off his kirtle and woollen sark. And when Olaf stood before him naked, Sigurd drew back amazed at the pure fairness of his skin, the firmness of his well knitted muscles, and the perfect beauty of his form.

In the stream near which they had halted there was a deep, clear pool of water, with a high cascade tumbling into it in creamy foam. Olaf ran lightly over the mossy boulders and plunged into the pool, as though he knew it well. Sigurd watched him rolling and splashing there in childish delight. Sometimes the boy seemed lost in the brown depths of the water, but soon his white body would be seen gliding smoothly along under the surface, and then emerging amid the spray of the waterfall, where the shafts of sunlight made a rainbow arc. And at last Olaf came out and ran swiftly backward and forward on the grassy level until he was dry. Then returning to his new master he took up his woollen sark. But his kirtle was gone.

Sigurd said: "I have thrown it away, for it is not well that a king's son should wear a garment that is sullied by the marks of slavery."

He took off from his own shoulders a riding cloak of scarlet cloth and added, "Take this cloak and wear it. And when we reach the town I will buy you more fitting clothes, with sandals for your feet, and a cap to shield your head from the sun."

Olaf blushed, and took the cloak and put it over him, saying nothing. Then he caught up an end of the chain and signed to his master to fasten it about his neck. Signed fastened it and then remounted his horse.

They had gone a little distance seaward down the dale when they were met by three armed horsemen, who seemed to have been waiting for them. Sigurd gave Olaf into their keeping, bidding them guard him well, and himself rode on in advance. Soon from the top of a hill they came in sight of the blue sea, and then the little town with its wooden huts nestling at the foot of the cliffs.

When they entered the town, two of Sigurd's servants took Olaf with them to the house of a certain merchant, where they gave him some roasted eggs and wheaten bread,

10

and there they kept him until after noontide, never speaking to him, but only watching him while they played countless games of chess and drank many horns of ale.

Now Olaf, as he sat on the floor, chained to the door post, set to wondering where his new master intended taking him to, and he could think of no likely destination but Norway. Why else should this man have bought him but to deliver him to Gunnhild? So thereupon he began to question how he could escape. And he determined in his mind very quickly, that when they were on the sea he would free himself from his chain and jump overboard and swim to land. But then came the thought that if he did this he would be quite alone in the world, and no one would ever believe him if he told them that he was the son of Triggvi Olafson, and perhaps he would again be taken into slavery. If Thorgils were with him they might do very well together, because Thorgils was full of the world's wisdom, and could by his wit earn food and shelter until they were both old enough and skilled enough to join some viking ship and win renown and power. But if Thorgils was to be left behind in Esthonia then it would not be so easy. Nothing could be done without Thorgils. So then Olaf thought it would be much wiser in him to try to escape at once, before he should be taken on board ship.

The chain was tight about his neck and it was fastened behind, so that he could not loosen it without arousing the men's suspicions by the noise it would make. He looked at the other end of it, and saw it was so fastened that he might easily undo it. Little by little he crept nearer to the post as the men went on with their game. Before he could do more, however, there was the sound of horse's feet outside. The two men sprang up from their seats. One of them went to the door and presently returned with a bundle of clothes, which he threw down on the floor, bidding Olaf dress himself. Olaf saw at once that the garments were of very fine woven cloth, and he wondered much. Even his old master's son Rekoni had never worn such rich attire as this, and it was passing strange that he, a bond slave, should be told to clothe himself in such finery.

He was dressing himself--albeit with great trouble, for the things were strange to him who had hitherto worn naught but a poor slave's kirtle--when a shrill horn was sounded from without. Then one of the men came and helped him to lace his sandals and to don his cloak, and hurried him out into the courtyard. Here were three horses waiting. The men pointed to one of them, a shaggy brown pony, and told Olaf to mount.

"I cannot ride," said the boy.

"You will be able to ride long before you reach our journey's end," returned the man. "And, lest you should be afraid of falling off, you will be tied with strong ropes to the horse's back."

"I had rather walk," objected Olaf.

"Slaves must obey their masters," said the man; and he took hold of the boy to help him to mount. But Olaf drew quickly aside with a flash of rebellion in his eyes.

Now at that moment a company of horsemen came in sight, led by Sigurd Erikson, and followed by many mules that were laden with bags of food and merchandise. All the men were well armed with swords and spears, bows and arrows. The sight of so many horses at once showed Olaf that the journey, whatever its destination, was to be made by land. As they came nearer and halted, his eyes quickly searched among the men for Thorgils Thoralfson. Yes, there indeed was his foster brother, mounted on one of the pack mules, with the sunlight falling on his white kirtle and downbent head! Then Olaf grew calm, for his master had kept his promise, and it mattered little where he was to be taken now that Thorgils was to be with him in his bondage. Sometime--not today, perhaps,--they would have a chance of speaking together and of contriving an escape.

11

Sigurd, seated on his beautiful white horse, looked like a king surrounded by his bodyguard. He watched Olaf springing on the pony's back, and saw the men securing the boy with ropes. One of the men took the end of the chain, while the other held the pony's halter; and thus, with a mounted guard on each side of him, the young slave was led out through the gates.

Very soon the little town in which he had lived in bondage for seven long years, and the sea that he loved so well, were left far behind. Sigurd and his followers rode southward over the hills, and then through long dreary dales, that were strewn with large boulder stones that made travelling very difficult. There was only a narrow horse track to guide them, and soon even this was lost in the rank herbage, and the land became a wild desolate waste without sign of human dwelling, but only the bare rugged hills, with here and there a thread of water streaming down them into the lower land. Olaf began to feel very weary, and the jolting of the pony over the rough ground became painful to his untrained limbs. But at last the hot sun sank in a blaze of gold, and the first day's journey came to an end.

A halt was made within the shelter of a vast forest of pine trees, at the side of a wide, deep stream. Here the horses and mules were unburdened and allowed to wander, with dogs to watch them lest they strayed too far. Some of the men then set to raising tents, others gathered cones and dry twigs to build a fire, while two mounted guard over their master's moneybags. When all was ready, food and drink were served round to all alike.

At nightfall, Olaf and Thorgils, still chained, were put to sleep on a bed of dry ferns. Near them was another slave, a young man who seemed to be of a foreign land. They watched him silently until he was asleep, then as they lay there with the stars shining down upon them through the dark tree branches, they questioned one the other concerning what had happened to them that day. Olaf asked Thorgils if he had heard the name of their new master.

"No," answered Thorgils. "Nor can I guess why it is that he has bought us. All that I know is that he is a Norseman, and that he is very rich."

"I can only think," said Olaf, "that he intends some treachery by us, and that he means to take us west over sea and deliver us into the hands of Gunnhild's sons."

"There is little cause to fear such a thing," said Thorgils. "To him we are but as any other slaves that he might buy in the marketplace, and I think he has only chosen us because we are of his own country. Had he discovered that you were your father's son he might indeed design to take us to Norway. But that is not possible. There are none but our two selves in all Esthonia who know that you are Olaf Triggvison, and this man could not by any means have discovered it."

Olaf was silent for many moments, then at last he said:

"Thorgils, I cannot deceive you. This man knows full well whose son I am, and it was I who told him."

Thorgils drew in his breath, as if he had received a blow.

"You told him?" he cried. "Oh, rash that you are! Have I not always bidden you keep this secret close in your heart? What need was there to tell your story to the first inquiring stranger who crossed your path? You are over ready with your tongue, and now, alas! our misfortunes must only be greater than before."

"He spoke kindly to me," explained Olaf, "and I could not refuse to answer him when he asked me how I came to be a bond slave. I little thought that he was an enemy."

"You are unskilled in the knowledge of men, Ole," returned Thorgils. "There is a look in his eyes that might soon have told you that there is evil in his heart, and such smooth tongued men as he are not to be trusted. But there is one good thing that your thoughtlessness has done: it has brought us again under one master, so it will go ill if, working together, we cannot contrive to run away, and join some viking ship."

"That will not be easy if our new master should take us to an inland place," said Olaf. "None of his men have the marks of the sea upon them; they are landmen."

Thorgils glanced up into the sky and searched for the polar star.

"We are journeying southward," he said presently.

"And what country lies to the south?" asked Olaf.

Thorgils could not tell. But he remembered that on a time some merchants had come to the coast from a great city in the south called Mikligard--which was the Norseman's name for Constantinople,--and he guessed that that might be their journey's end.

Then Olaf crept nearer to their sleeping companion and wakened him.

"Tell me," he asked, "who is this man, our master, and whither is he taking us?"

"I cannot tell," answered the youth. "It is but three days since that he bought me, and I can ill understand the tongue these men speak, for I am not of this land. My home is far across the seas."

"In what realm?" asked Thorgils.

"In England."

"That must be far away indeed," said Olaf, "for never have I heard of such a land."

"It is an island, out across the Western Sea," explained Thorgils; "often have I heard it named. In that same land it was that King Erik Bloodaxe lived and died. Many vikings out of Norway have crossed the seas for the sake of the wealth they can win from the Angles. And if I were a viking it is to England I would steer my course."

"Gladly would I go with you," said the English youth; "ay, even now, if we could but escape. But it seems that we are journeying away from the seacoast, and there is little hope that we can win our way on board a ship."

"There is hope enough if we do not delay our escape," returned Thorgils, looking out to where the campfires burned. He was silent for many minutes, then, laying his hand on the stranger's arm, he asked:

"What name have you?"

"Egbert," the lad replied.

"And how came it," inquired Thorgils, "that you were brought into Esthonia?"

Egbert then told his story. He was born, he said, in Northumberland. His father, a wealthy armourer and silversmith, had been slain by one of the Northmen who had made a great settlement in that part of the country, and his mother, whose name was Edith, had then wedded the man who had made her a widow. The man was named Grim, and he was a warrior in the service of Erik Bloodaxe, the ruler in those parts. On the death of King Erik, Grim and many of the Norsemen went back to Norway in the train of Queen Gunnhild and Erik's sons, and with him he took his wife and young Egbert. Edith did not live to reach Norway, and Grim, unwilling to be burdened with her son, had sold Egbert into slavery. For ten years the boy had suffered in bondage under different masters, the last of whom--Klerkon Flatface--had brought him into Esthonia.

"My one wish during all these years," said Egbert, "has been to return to England, where the people are Christian, and do not worship your heathen gods. Many times I have tried to escape, but always without success; for I have had no companions, and it is not easy for one so young as I am to make his way alone through foreign lands."

"What is your age?" Olaf inquired.

"Fifteen summers," answered Egbert.

13

Thorgils stood up and leaned his hand against the trunk of a tree, looking down at his two companions.

"I think," said he, "that it would be a very good thing if we three should run away from this new master of ours--now, while the darkness lasts,--and, keeping in company, try to get back to the coast. There we might take possession of a small sailboat, and so make our way over sea to the land of the Angles. What say you, Ole?"

Olaf was silent for a while. At last he said:

"It were much wiser in us to wait until we are old enough to fight our way in the world."

"And you will not try to escape?" asked Thorgils.

"No," answered Olaf firmly. "We have a good master. Why should we leave him?"

"It is because he has given you that fine cloak that you think him good," returned Thorgils tauntingly; "but, believe me, he has his private reasons for so bribing you. I can well guess what he means to do with you, and I tell you that you will surely rue it if you do not escape while we may; for, if men bear their true nature in their faces, then this man who has bought us has an evil heart."

"And what would it avail if we were to escape?" asked Olaf. "Boys as we are, we should be of little use in the world, I think."

"You are afraid!" cried Thorgils.

"Yes," echoed Egbert, "you are afraid." Then turning to Thorgils, he added: "But why should we urge the lad against his will? He is but a child, and would only be a burden to us. Let us leave him and go our ways without him."

"You are not of our folk, Egbert," returned Thorgils, flinging himself down upon the dry leaves, "and you do not know what the vow of foster brotherhood means. You ask me to do that which I would sooner die than do. Ole and I will never part until death parts us. And if either should be slain, then the other will avenge his death. If Ole wills to remain in slavery until he is old and gray, then I will always be his companion in bondage. But to escape without him, that will I never do!"

Nothing more was said. The three boys, weary after their long journey, curled themselves up to sleep.

So soundly did young Olaf sleep, that at midnight, when a man's hands unbound the chain about his neck he was not awakened. Very cautiously the man took him up in his strong arms, and carried him away among the dark shadows of the trees to a part of the forest far removed from the campfires. And at last he laid the lad down on a bed of dry reeds and moss at the side of the stream, where the bright moon, shining through an open glade, shed its light upon his fair round face and his short gold hair. There the man stood over him, watching him as he dreamed his childish dreams. Then he knelt down and gently drew aside the lad's cloak and opened the front of his kirtle, so that the moonlight fell upon the white skin of his throat and breast.

Suddenly Olaf awoke and saw the dark figure bending over him.

"Thorgils, Thorgils!" he cried in alarm.

"Be silent!" commanded Sigurd Erikson, gripping the boy's arm. "No harm will come to you."

Olaf struggled to his feet and was about to take to flight, but his master's firm grip held him.

"Silly child!" muttered Sigurd. "Why do you fear me? Have I not already told you that I am your friend?"

"I do not trust your friendship," answered Olaf angrily, remembering Thorgil's warning. "And now I believe that you have brought me here only that you may secretly put me to death."

"I have brought you here for your own good, my child," said Sigurd softly; "and I give you my solemn word that no man, whosoever he be, shall do you any injury while I live to be your protector. Be silent, and listen to me."

Olaf grew calmer.

"Yester eve," said Sigurd, "when you told me that you were the son of King Triggvi Olafson, I could not easily believe your tale. But when you spoke your mother's name and told me that she was from Ofrestead, in the Uplands of Norway, then I knew very well that you were telling me the truth. I looked into your eyes and I saw that they were the eyes of Queen Astrid--the fairest woman in all the Northland. In your very words I thought I could hear the music of Queen Astrid's voice--"

"Can it be that my mother is known to you?" cried Olaf eagerly. "Can it be that you can take me to where she lives?"

"Well do I know her," answered Sigurd. "But, alas! it is many summers since I saw her last, nor had I heard any tidings of her for a long, long while, until you told me that she had taken flight from Norway. Tell me now, what is the name of him whose succour she wished to seek in Gardarike?"

"Her brother's name," said Olaf, "is Sigurd Erikson."

"I am that same brother," smiled Sigurd, taking the boy by the hand; "and it is because I am your uncle that I now take you with me into Holmgard." He drew Olaf nearer to him and put his arm about his neck. "And you shall live with me as my own dear foster son," he added, "and I will take care of you and teach you all that a king's son should know, so that in the time to come you may be well fitted to claim your dead father's realm. But it is not without great risk that I do this thing, for I well know that there are many men in Norway who would gladly hear of your death. Now, if Gunnhild's sons should learn that you are living in Holmgard they would offer a rich reward to the man who should compass your end. You will be wise, therefore, if you breathe no word of your kinship with Triggvi Olafson. Also, you must betray to no man, not even to your foster brother Thorgils, that I am your uncle, or that I know your name and kin; for it is a law held sacred in Gardarike that no one of royal birth shall abide in the land without the sanction of King Valdemar. If it be known that I am wilfully breaking that law, then both you and I will fall into the sorest trouble."

Amazed at hearing all this, and at learning that the man he had taken for a secret enemy was none other than his own uncle, Olaf was speechless. He silently put his hand into Sigurd's great palm, and let himself be led back to the place where Thorgils and Egbert still lay sound asleep.

CHAPTER III: GERDA'S PROPHECY.

On the morrow, when Olaf awoke, he told nothing of this that he had heard concerning his kinship with Sigurd Erikson, and if Thorgils saw that he was very moody and quiet, he no doubt thought that the lad was but sorrowing at being taken away from the sea that he loved so much. And yet Olaf seemed strangely unwilling to favour any plan of escape. Both Thorgils and Egbert were for ever speaking of flight, but Olaf always had some wise reason to offer for yet further delay, and would only shake his head and say that their plans were ill formed. On the second evening of the journey into the south, a halt was made upon the shores of a great inland lake. Thorgils declared that it was a part of the sea, and he urged his two companions to steal away with him under the cover of night so that they might find some fisher's boat and make off with it. But Olaf quickly pointed out that there were no boats to be seen, and that, as the horses and dogs were drinking of the water, it could not be salt like the waters of the great sea. Every day during the long and weary journey Thorgils brought up some new plan. But Olaf was obstinate. So at last the two elder boys, seeing that he was bent upon remaining in bondage, yielded to his stronger will, and agreed to wait in patience and to go with him wheresoever their master had a mind to take them.

The country into which they were taken was in old times called Gardarike. It lay to the southeast of Esthonia, and it was a part of what is now known as the Russian Empire. Many Norsemen lived in that land, and King Valdemar was himself the son of the great Swedish viking, Rurik, who had made conquests and settlements in the countries east of the Baltic Sea. Valdemar held his court at Holmgard--the modern Novgorod. He was a very wise and powerful ruler, and his subjects were prosperous and peaceable, having many useful arts, and carrying on a commerce with the great city of Mikligard. The people were still heathen, worshipping Odin and Thor and the minor gods of the Scandinavians; for the faith of Christendom was as yet but vaguely known to them and little understood.

Sigurd Erikson, who was Valdemar's high steward, lived in the king's palace in great dignity and had many servants. So when he returned with all the treasure that he had gathered as tribute he took Olaf Triggvison into his service. But Thorgils and Egbert were still held as bond slaves and put to hard labour in the king's stables.

The steward was very good to Olaf, and soon grew to love him as his own son, guarding him from all harm, speaking with him whenever chance brought them together, yet never betraying by word or act that the boy was other than a mere thrall, whom he had bought with other chattels during his journey through the king's dominions. Neither did Olaf whisper, even to his foster brother, any word of his close kinship with their new master. Thorgils, who had not forgotten the name of Queen Astrid's brother, might indeed have discovered Olaf's secret. But it so chanced that the king's steward was spoken of only by his title as the Hersir Sigurd, and not as the son of Erik of Ofrestead.

For many months Olaf fulfilled his little duties very meekly, and no one paid great heed to him, for he still bore the traces of his rough work. Sigurd was well satisfied that his secret was safe, and that Valdemar would never discover that his steward was breaking the law. But soon the lad's fair hair grew long and bright, his hands lost their roughness, and his growing beauty of face and limb attracted many eyes. Then Sigurd began to fear, for he knew the penalty he would be forced to pay if it should be discovered that he had wittingly brought a king born youth into the land.

This danger grew greater when it chanced that the Queen Allogia took notice of young Olaf, for the queen was in some sort a spae woman; she was skilled in foretelling the future, and she quickly perceived that the boy's beauty had come to him from some noble ancestor. It seemed that she was bent upon knowing his history, for she besought many persons about the court to tell her whence he had come, and to discover for her the names of his parents. But none could tell.

Now, Allogia was still but two and twenty years of age, and very fair, and the king did not like that she should be seen holding speech with his handsome steward, for fear that Sigurd should win her heart. But one day in the early winter time the queen came upon Sigurd in the great hall, where he was alone with Olaf, teaching the boy to read the runes carved in the black oak behind the king's high seat.

Olaf stood back as she entered, but his eyes rested fearlessly upon her. She wore a blue woven mantle ornamented with lace, and under it a scarlet kirtle with a silver belt. There was a band of gold round her head, and her fine brown hair reached down to her

16

waist on both sides. She approached the steward, and said as he turned to withdraw from the hall:

"I pray you, go on with your lesson, hersir."

"Your pardon, lady," said Sigurd, "I was but teaching the lad the rune of King Rurik, and it is of no account that I should continue."

"Not often have I heard of a mere slave boy learning runes," returned Allogia; "such knowledge is only meant for those who are of high estate." She paused and looked round at Olaf, who stood apart with his hand caressing the head of a great dog that had risen from before the fire. "And yet," added the queen thoughtfully, "I would say that this boy Ole, as you call him, has no serf's blood in him. His fairness is that of a kingly race. What is his parentage, Hersir Sigurd? You who have shown him so much favour, who have dressed him in such fine clothes, and who even go so far as to teach him the reading of runes, surely know him to be of noble birth. Who is he, I say?"

This question, coming so directly and from the queen herself, whom he dared not disobey, brought the guilty blood to Sigurd's brow. But Allogia did not observe his confusion. Her large dark eyes were gazing full upon Olaf, as though in admiration of the boy's silky gold hair and firm, well knit figure.

"I bought the lad in North Esthonia," Sigurd answered after a moment's pause. "I bought him from a bonder in Rathsdale, and the price I paid for him was two silver marks. It may be that he is some viking's son, I cannot tell. He is quick witted and very clever at all games, and that is why it pleases me to teach him many things."

There was a look of doubt in Allogia's eyes, as though she knew that the steward was telling her but a half truth. He saw her doubt and made a sign to Olaf to draw nearer. The boy obeyed, and stood before the queen with bowed head.

"Of what parentage are you, boy?" demanded Sigurd. "Who is your mother, and what is her condition of life?"

Olaf answered promptly, as he looked calmly into his master's face:

"My mother is a poor bondswoman, hersir," he said. "The vikings brought her into Esthonia from west over sea. I have not had tidings of her since I was a little child."

The queen smiled at him pityingly.

"And what of your father?" she asked.

Olaf shook his head, and looked vacantly at the queen's beautiful hands with their many gold rings.

"I never knew my father, lady," he replied, "for he was dead before I came into the world."

"But do you not know his name?" pursued Allogia. Now Olaf feared to tell a deliberate lie, and yet, for his uncle's sake, he dared not answer with the truth. He stammered for an instant, and then, feeling the dog's head against his hand, he caught the animal's ear between his fingers and gave it a hard, firm pinch. The dog howled with the sudden pain and sprang forward angrily. And the queen, startled and alarmed, moved aside and presently walked majestically from the hall.

Not again for many weeks did Allogia seek an answer to her question. Sigurd, still fearing that his secret might be revealed, kept the boy away from the court so that he might not be seen. But for all his care the danger was for ever recurring.

King Valdemar had a mother named Gerda, who was so old and infirm that she always lay abed. She was wonderfully skilled in spaedom, and it was always the custom at yuletide, when the guests assembled in the king's hall, that his mother was borne in thither and placed in the high seat. There she prophesied touching any danger overhanging the country, or similar thing, according to the questions put to her.

17

Now it happened in the first winter of Olaf's being in Holmgard, that at the yule feast, when Gerda had been borne in after this fashion, Valdemar asked her whether any foreign prince or warrior would enter his dominions or turn his arms against his kingdom during the following year.

The old mother ran her bent fingers through the thin locks of her white hair, and gazing with dim eyes into the vast hall, thus spoke her prophecy:

"No token of any disastrous war do I discern," she said, "nor any other misfortune. But one wondrous event I see. In the land of Norway there has lately been born a child who will be bred up here, in Holmgard, until he grows to be a famous prince; one so highly gifted that there has never before been seen his equal. He will do no harm to this kingdom; but he will in every way increase thy fame. He will return to his native land while yet he is in the flower of his age, and he will reign with great glory in this northern part of the world. But not for long, not for long. Now, carry me away."

While these words were being spoken, Queen Allogia's eyes rested upon Olaf Triggvison, who was acting as cup bearer to his uncle Sigurd. She saw the drinking horn tremble in his hand, so that the wine it held dripped over the silver rim, and fell upon the front of his white kirtle; and she divined that it was to him that the prophecy referred. But no sign of this suspicion did she betray, either at that time or in the after days. Yet none the less she watched him always, with her mind fixed upon the thought of his nobility, and the glory that had been promised him. In all that he did she was well pleased, for already she had found that he excelled all others of his age, not only in personal beauty but in skilful handling of all warlike weapons, in the training of dogs and horses, in wrestling and riding, in racing on snowshoes, and in all other exercises. Often she would have spoken with him, but, saving at the time of a great feast, he was never to be seen in the hall.

Throughout the long, cold winter months, Olaf saw nothing of his foster brother or of Egbert the Briton, for they had both been taken across the river to labour on one of the king's farmsteads. There they remained until the early summer, when they brought over their flocks and herds for the sheep meeting. At that time there was held a great fair in Holmgard, with sports and games and manly contests. Many parties of men came into the town from distant parts of the kingdom.

On the second morning of the fair, Sigurd Erikson entered the room in which Olaf slept. The boy was dressing himself in his fine clothes, and girding on his leather belt with its small war axe, which Sigurd had had made for his young kinsman.

"My boy," said Sigurd, "there is little need for you to dress yourself in this holiday attire, for it is my will that you do not attend the games. You must not show yourself amid the crowd."

Now, Olaf had engaged to take part in a great wrestling bout with three young champions from Livonia. Also, he was to have run in a footrace, for which the prize was a silver hilted sword, awarded by the queen. So at hearing his uncle thus forbid him to appear, he became very indignant.

"It is too late for you to try to keep me within doors," he protested. "I have given my word to the wrestlers, and I cannot now withdraw. Do you wish me to be jeered at as a coward? Why do you deny me the honour of taking all the prizes that I may so easily win?"

"It is for your own happiness that I forbid you to show yourself before strangers," returned Sigurd. "But, more than all, I wish you to keep in hiding for this great reason. There has come into Holmgard a man whom I met many months ago. I engaged with him to pit my best horse against his in the horse ring, and the prize was to be--"

"What was the prize?" asked Olaf, seeing that his uncle had paused.

"The prize was to be yourself, my son," said Sigurd gravely. "The man coveted you, and would have bought you from your old master Reas."

"And why did you agree to this, knowing that I am your own kinsman and your sister's son?" asked Olaf.

"I did not then know that you were of my kin," answered Sigurd. "But having given my word, I cannot go back from it. I have seen this man's horse, and I judge it to be a finer animal than mine. Therefore do I fear that I must lose you. But if you will keep within the house, I will tell the man that you are dead, and will offer him the young Englander Egbert in your stead."

"Would you then tell the man a falsehood?" cried Olaf.

"Gladly, if by doing so I still keep you with me, for I would not lose you for all the world."

Olaf, obedient to his uncle's word, began to unbuckle his belt. But his face was very gloomy, and it was easy to see that it was only out of his love for his uncle that he would by any means agree to forego his pleasures. Olaf was already very proud of his own skill. Never yet had he been beaten in any contest, and he had hoped to add to his glory by overcoming all who might come against him on this great day. Moreover, it was a sorry sacrifice for him to make if he was not to be allowed to witness the games.

As Sigurd turned to leave him, the boy suddenly caught his arm.

"I will not promise!" he cried. "I cannot give you my word. I have set my heart upon the wrestling, and in spite of your forbiddance I shall go. Tell me what manner of man this is that you speak of, and I will avoid him. Even though he overcome you in the horse fight he shall not take me from you."

"He is a great viking," answered Sigurd. "Men name him Klerkon Flatface. It is the same who sold you into bondage."

A cloud came upon Olaf's brow, and he sat down upon the side of the trestle bed.

"Klerkon Flatface?" he repeated slowly. Then raising his eyes he looked into his uncle's face and added: "Do not fear, hersir. Klerkon shall not take me from you."

Now, very soon after Sigurd had gone out to attend upon the king, Olaf quitted the house and went by secret ways to the stables, where he found his foster brother at work combing out the mane of Sigurd's fighting steed. A very tall and powerful animal it was, with a glossy brown coat and a long tail that reached nearly to the ground. It was well trained, and many a well won fight had it fought. Sleipner was its name, and it was so called after the eight footed horse of Odin.

Olaf went to Thorgils' side and greeted him with friendly words. Then, when they had spoken for a while together, Olaf bent his head close to Thorgils' ear, and said he:

"I have news, brother."

"Ill news or good?" asked Thorgils.

"Judge for yourself," answered Olaf. "It is that our old enemy Klerkon the Viking has come into Holmgard, with many men and a mighty horse that is to be pitted against Sleipner."

Thorgils drew back with a sudden start.

"Then has our good time come," he cried. "Our vow of vengeance must be fulfilled. No longer are we little boys, weak of arm and failing in courage. Never again shall Klerkon sail the seas."

"And who will hinder him?" asked Olaf, looking the while into the other's brightened eyes.

"He shall be hindered by me," returned Thorgils. "With me alone must the vengeance rest, for it is not well that you, who stand so high in honour with the king and his court, should sully your white hands with blood. It was my father whom Klerkon slew that day upon the ship, and it is my part to avenge him."

Then Olaf shook his head.

"Not so shall it be," said he. "Thoralf was my own good foster father, and I am not afraid to face the man who sent him so cruelly to his death. I and not you shall bring the murderer to his bane."

"Rash that you always are!" cried Thorgils. "Will you never learn to be cautious? Keep your peace. If I should fail, then will it be your turn to avenge my death as our vow of foster brotherhood demands. Now bring me a good weapon, for I have none but an oak cudgel."

"You shall not want for a good weapon," said Olaf, and he drew a small sword from under his blue cloak and handed it to Thorgils. "Here is my new handsax. Take it, and use it to good purpose. But in the matter of Klerkon, it may be that I shall be before you. Odin be with you!"

CHAPTER IV: THE SLAYING OF KLERKON.

It was yet early in the forenoon when the games began. They were held on the great plain beyond the gate, where fences were raised as a girdle round the course. Upon the sunny side was the king's tent, where Valdemar and Allogia sat, attended by many guests and courtiers, among whom was Sigurd Erikson.

For a long while Sigurd, who sat near to the queen, was at his ease in the belief that young Olaf was keeping within doors, and he paid little heed to those who were within the ring. First there were jumping matches. Olaf did not join in these, for he was not yet tall enough to compete with full grown men, and there were no youths of his own height who were skilled enough to match him. Neither, for a like reason, did he take part in the sword feats. But at last it came to a trial of skill with the longbow. The bowmen were at the far end of the course, and their faces could not well be seen from the tent, even had Sigurd searched among them for the face of his wilful nephew. There was one, however, who saw better than he, and this was Queen Allogia.

She waited until it came to the turn of those who were younger than eighteen years, and then she watched with keen eyes. Among them she soon discerned the youth whom she sought; nor did she lose sight of him until his well aimed arrow shot full into the mark, and he was proclaimed the victor. Then, when Olaf came before the tent to make his obeisance, Sigurd saw him, and was very wroth, for he knew that Klerkon the Viking was among the king's guests.

Now, when Olaf was thus near, it seemed to Klerkon that the lad was not wholly a stranger to him. Indeed, had it not been for the long gold hair and the disguise of better clothing, he might have known him to be the same whom he had seen in the last summer playing at the knife feat on the gangplank of the viking ship. But Klerkon only admired the lad's skill with the longbow, and thought what a goodly warrior he would make. So having this in his mind, he watched Olaf closely when again the boy ran past in the footrace, leading his competitors by many yards.

And now, being first in the race, Olaf came once more before the tent, and the queen gave him his well won prize.

As he took the silver hilted sword from Allogia's hand, one of the vikings went to Klerkon's side, and said he:

"Master, this youth is the same who appeared in the last summer as a bond slave at the time when the Hersir Sigurd came on board of us. Was it not this same lad who was to be the prize in our horse fight?"

Then Klerkon fixed his eyes more keenly on the lad, and thought of him as he might be with his fair hair cropped short, and with a slave's white kirtle in place of the fine clothes he now wore.

"It is the same!" he answered. "And now I mind that someone told me it was he whom we captured among others many summers ago off Alland isle. It was we who brought him into Esthonia. Much would I give to have him with us on our longship. And by the hammer of Thor, I swear that if I win him not over the horse fight, then I will take him by force!"

So then Klerkon made his way to the side of Sigurd Erikson, and told him that he had recognized the boy. At which Sigurd grew very pale, and blamed himself in that he had not kept Olaf within doors by main force.

Now, at high noon when the king and queen departed from the tent, Sigurd made his way round to the entrance of the lists, and there searched for Olaf and found him. He spoke to the lad very gravely, and, telling him of the viking's recognition, cautioned him against appearing again within the circle of the course. Olaf, seeing now that it was a serious matter, agreed to abandon the wrestling, and gave his word that he would thereafter be more cautious of showing himself.

"Much do I fear," said Sigurd, "that the mischief is already done. Your future welfare, your happiness, your claiming of your father's kingdom--all depends upon the result of this horse fight. If Klerkon the Viking's horse should overcome Sleipner there is no help for us. You must go with the victor."

Then Olaf smiled almost mockingly.

"Be not afraid, my kinsman," said he. "Should Klerkon come to claim me as his prize he shall not find me. But he will never need to claim me. I have seen this great stallion that he has so much boasted of, and I know full well that it is no match for Sleipner in a fair fight."

"We shall see very soon," returned Sigurd; "meanwhile, if you intend to witness the combat, I beg you to take your stand as far as possible away from the vikings. And when the fight is over--whatever be the result--make your way over the river and keep well hidden in old Grim Ormson's hut. There you will be safe from all discovery until after the vikings have departed."

Now Olaf had no notion of hiding himself thus. He was not personally afraid of Klerkon, neither did he believe that the viking would go to much trouble to secure his prize even if his horse should be successful. Olaf had heard that that horse had been brought from England, and he did not believe that anything good could come from a country so far away. His uncle's horse, on the other hand, was celebrated all through Gardarike, and it had never been beaten either in the race or in the fight. Why, then, should there be any fear for the result of the coming contest?

But Sigurd Erikson was wiser, and knew better that his steed was at last to meet its equal. Never before had he seen an animal so strong and fierce as the stallion that Klerkon the Viking had matched against Sleipner.

Many horses were led forth into the circle, and they were taken in pairs to the middle, where they fought one against the other. Each horse was followed by its owner or the trainer, who supported and urged it on, inciting it with his stick. The crowd of onlookers was very large, for among the Northmen no amusement was more popular than the horse fight, unless it were the combat between men. But at first there was not much excitement, because many of the horses would not fight, and others were too easily beaten. At last Sleipner and the English horse were led forth into the centre. When they were let loose they came together fiercely, and there followed a splendid fight, both severe and long. Little need was there for the men to urge them or to use the sticks. The two horses rose high on their hind legs, biting at each other savagely until their manes and necks and shoulders were torn and bloody. Often the animals were parted, but only to renew the fight with greater fierceness. The combat went on until eleven rounds had passed. Then Klerkon's stallion took hold of the jawbone of Sleipner, and held on until it seemed that he would never yield his hold. Two of the men then rushed forward, each to his own horse, and beat and pushed them asunder, when Sleipner fell down from exhaustion and hard fighting. At which the vikings set up a loud cheer.

King Valdemar was the umpire, and he said now that the fight must cease, for that Klerkon's horse had proved himself the victor in eight rounds, and that it could easily be seen that the steward's horse was no longer fit. Then the king asked Sigurd what prize he had staked, and Sigurd answered:

"The prize was staked many months ago when I met Klerkon over in Esthonia, and it was arranged that if the viking's horse should overcome mine he was to take the young thrall Ole."

"Let the boy be given up to him, then," said the king; "for he has won him very fairly."

"I will take the boy tonight," said Klerkon, who stood near, "for my business in Holmgard is now over, and at sunrise I go back to the coast."

Now Sigurd believed that Olaf had surely taken his advice, and gone at once across the river to hide himself in Grim Ormson's hut, so he was not in any way anxious.

"Take the lad wheresoever you can find him," said he to the viking. "And if you cannot find him before the sunrise, then I will pay you his just value in gold."

"Though you offered me all the gold you are worth," returned Klerkon, "I would not take it in place of the boy. No thrall born lad is he, but of noble descent, and I intend to make a viking of him and take him with me west over sea to England. It is not well that a youth so clever as he should waste his years in an inland town. He was meant by his nature for the sea, and I think that he will some day prove to be a very great warrior."

At this Sigurd Erikson grew sick at heart, for he knew that the viking was a man of very strong will, and that no half measures would serve to turn him from his purpose. Also, he felt that it was now useless to attempt any deception concerning Olaf. The vikings had recognized the boy, and none other could be passed off in his stead.

With a gloomy cloud on his brow, Sigurd left the tent and made his way back to the king's hall in search of his nephew. Olaf was not there. The hours went by, and still there was no sign of him. Neither did Klerkon come to make claim to his prize.

It was in the evening time. Sigurd sat alone in his room at the back of the great hall. He was thinking that Olaf had become strangely restless and unruly of late. Many times the lad had disappointed him and caused him trouble, but never so much as today, when his wilfulness threatened to bring about very serious consequences. Had Olaf taken the advice that had been given him in the morning, the coming of Klerkon might have been a matter of small moment; but the thoughtless boy had boldly shown himself before the tent, and had never striven to hide himself from the quick eyes of the shipmen. He had been recognized--as how would one so distinguished from all other youths fail to be?-- and now Klerkon would not rest until he had safely secured his coveted prize.

Very different now was Olaf from what he had seemed on that day when he stood near the viking ship in the guise of a poor slave. In the year that had passed Sigurd had grown to love the lad with the love of a father, had taught him many useful arts and handicrafts, had given him fine clothes to wear, and had so improved his bodily condition and moulded his mind that no king's son could ever hope to excel him either in physical beauty or in skill of arms, in manly prowess or moral goodness. Never once had Olaf done anything that was mean or unworthy; never once had he told an untruth or gone back from his promise. At any time when Sigurd had told him to do what was not to his liking the boy had simply shaken his golden curls and said, "I will not promise"; but always when he had given his word he held to it firmly and faithfully. He could be trusted in all things. But for all this he had lately become most wilful, and the trouble he was now causing made his uncle very anxious.

Sigurd knew full well that Olaf loved him, and that all the possible glory of being a viking would not lead him away from Holmgard of his own free will. But in the present case he might not be able to help himself, despite his having so positively said that Klerkon should never carry him off alive. So in his heart Sigurd feared that Olaf would take some mischievous and unwise measure of his own to evade the vikings. It might be, indeed, that he had already gone across the river to the security of Grim Ormson's hut; but it was greatly to be feared that he had fallen into the hands of Klerkon Flatface.

Suddenly, as Sigurd sat there in moody thought, the door of the room was flung open, and Olaf rushed in. He was strangely agitated. His hair was rough and his clothing was torn; his large blue eyes flashed in anger, and his breathing was heavy and uneven.

Sigurd sprang up from his seat. He saw that something ill had happened.

"Why are you here?" he cried. "Why are you not in hiding? Have I not warned you enough that you are running into danger by letting yourself be seen? Klerkon has won you from me, and he may be here at any moment to claim you and carry you away!"

Olaf did not reply for a long time. He only bent down and took a handful of rushes up from the floor, and began to quietly clean the blade of his axe that he held under his arm.

"Speak!" cried Sigurd, driven to anger by the boy's silence.

Then at last Olaf said in a steady, boyish voice:

"Klerkon will never claim me from you, my kinsman; for he is dead."

"Dead?" echoed Sigurd in alarm.

"Yes," answered Olaf, "I met him in the gate. He tried to take me. I raised my axe and buried it in his head. Well have you taught me the use of my axe, Hersir Sigurd."

As he spoke there came a loud hum of angry voices from without. They were the voices of the vikings calling aloud for the blood of him who had slain their chief.

Without a word Sigurd Erikson crossed the room, and drew the heavy bar athwart the door. Then he turned upon Olaf.

"Well do I discern," said he, "that you are of King Harald's race. It was ever so with your forefathers; thoughtless, fearless, ruthless! And so all my teaching of you has gone for nothing! Oh, foolish boy! To think that you, who might have lived to be the king of all Norway, have ended in being no more than a common murderer!"

"Murderer?" repeated Olaf. "Not so. It is but justice that I have done. Klerkon was the slayer of my dear foster father. He slew him cruelly and in cold blood, and for no other reason than that poor Thoralf was old and infirm. I have done no murder. I have but taken just and lawful vengeance."

"Just and lawful it may be in our own birthland, Olaf," returned Sigurd gravely; "but in this kingdom wherein we now live the peace is held holy, and it is ordained by law that he who kills another man in anger shall himself lose his life. I cannot save you. You have broken the peace; you have taken the life of one of the king's own guests, and you have insulted the king's hospitality. I fear that you must die."

He broke off, listening to the furious cries of the crowd outside. "Hark!" he went on. "Those wild sea wolves are calling for blood vengeance. Come! come with me quickly. There is but one hope left, and in that hope lies my own despair and my own undoing."

So, while yet the people were clamouring for the young peace breaker's life, Sigurd took Olaf through the back part of the house and by many secret passages into the queen's garth. Here, in a large hall that was most splendidly adorned with carved wood and hung with tapestry, sat Queen Allogia with two of her handmaids working with their needles upon a beautiful robe of embroidered silk.

Sigurd passed the armed sentinel at the door and strode into the apartment, followed closely by the boy. The queen looked up in surprise at the unexpected visitors.

"I crave your help, O queen," cried the steward excitedly.

The queen stood up in alarm. She had heard the turmoil of voices from without.

"What means all this shouting?" she inquired.

Then Sigurd told her how Olaf had killed the viking, and implored her to help the boy out of his trouble.

"Alas!" said she, when she had heard the tale. "Little power have I to meddle in such affairs. The penalty of murder is death, and I cannot hinder the law." She looked at Olaf as she spoke, and saw the pleading in his eyes. "And yet," she added with quick pity, "such a handsome boy must not be slain. I will save him if I can."

She then bade Sigurd call in her bodyguard fully armed to protect the lad, while she went out into the king's chamber and pleaded with Valdemar to prevent the shedding of blood.

Now, by this time, the enraged vikings and many men of the town had gained entrance to the outer court, and they rushed forward to claim the life of the offender according to their custom and laws. Long they waited, hammering noisily at the oaken doors of the hall wherein Olaf was now known to have taken refuge. But at last the door was flung open, and King Valdemar appeared on the threshold, guarded by many armed men. The crowd drew back, leaving only the chief of the vikings to speak for them and ask for justice. He told the king how Klerkon, standing within the gate, had been attacked by young Ole of the golden hair, and how without word or warning the boy had suddenly raised his axe and driven it into Klerkon's head, so that the blade stood right down into the brain of him.

The king then declared that he could not believe a boy so young as Ole could have either the skill or the boldness to attack so powerful a man as Klerkon Flatface. But the viking turned and called upon some of his shipmates to bring forward the dead body of their chief, which they laid down before the king. Valdemar looked upon it and examined the death wound. The skull was cloven with one clean blow from the crown right down to the red bearded chin.

"A wondrous strong blow!" murmured Valdemar. "But I see that it was struck from the front. How came it that Klerkon could not defend himself?"

"Little time had he for that," answered the viking, "for the lad fell upon him with the quickness of an eagle's swoop, and although my master was well armed, yet he could not raise his sword ere he fell dead at our feet, and then Ole turned and fled with such speed that none could follow him."

"Such an act as this," said the king, "cannot have been without some cause. What reason of enmity was there between this boy and Klerkon?"

24

"No reason but wanton mischief," answered the warrior. "It was a causeless murder, and we claim the full and lawful punishment."

"Justice shall be done," returned the king. "But I must first know what the peace breaker may have to say in his own defence. I beg you, therefore, to keep truce until the sunrise, when the penalty shall be adjudged."

At hearing this promise the crowd dispersed in peace. Many grumbled that the customary sentence of death had not been instantly pronounced. But in causing this delay King Valdemar was but yielding to the pleadings of the queen, who had implored him to spare the life of the handsome young murderer, or at the least to save him from the fury of the vikings.

When the crowd had gone from the courtyard Allogia returned to the hall in which the steward and Olaf had been kept under the protection of the guards. Dismissing the men, she turned to Sigurd Erikson.

"You have asked me to save the boy's life, hersir," said she, "but, alas! I cannot do it. All that the king will do is to give a few hours' respite. At sunrise the law is to take its course, and much do I fear that its course will be death."

Olaf heard her words, but did not show any fear of the expected punishment. It seemed, indeed, that he had become suddenly hard of heart and dauntless, as though he thought that the killing of a man was a matter to be proud of. Certainly, in his own mind, he did not look upon the taking of Klerkon's life as an act of guilt deserving punishment. He recalled what he had seen on the viking ship years before. The old man Thoralf had fallen to Klerkon's share in the dividing of booty. Thoralf had held little Olaf by the hand as they stood apart on the ship's deck, and Klerkon had come up to them and roughly separated them, flinging Olaf across to where young Thorgils stood. Then, tearing off Thoralf's cloak, the viking had said: "Little use is there in an old toothless hound, but his flesh may serve as food for the fishes;" and, drawing his sword, he had given the aged man his death blow and tilted him over into the sea. So Olaf and Thorgils had sworn to take vengeance upon this viking, and Olaf had now fulfilled his vow.

The queen came nearer to Olaf, and looked at him tenderly. "It is a great pity," said she, "that one so fair should be doomed to die before he has grown to manhood. It might be that with good training he would become a very famous warrior, and I would gladly see him enlisted in the service of the king."

She broke off and turned to Sigurd. "Hersir Sigurd," she said, looking keenly into the steward's face, "I have noticed many times that you take a more than common interest in this boy. Even now, when he has broken the law of the land, it is you who take it upon yourself to plead his cause. It must surely be that you have powerful reasons for keeping him from harm. Whose son is he? Of what kin is he? It is but right that I should know."

Sigurd demurred, remembering that it was forbidden by the law of the land that any king born person should live in Gardarike, except with the king's permission. He thought that it would go very ill with himself if Olaf's kingly birth should be known.

"Lady, I cannot tell you," he murmured.

"Would you then rather that the boy should die?" she asked with anger in her tone.

"Not so," answered Sigurd, drawing himself up to his full height. "If the boy is to be condemned to death, then I will offer to take the punishment in his stead."

The queen glanced at him quietly.

"If that be so," said she, "then the sacrifice of your own life can only be taken as showing that you count the boy of more value to the world than yourself." She paused for a moment, then added: "I am your queen, Hersir Sigurd, and I command you to tell me what I ask. What is the boy's true name, and what is his parentage?"

She went across to the side of the great fireplace, and, seating herself in one of the large oaken chairs, signed to Sigurd and Olaf to approach her. Then, taking up an end of the silken robe upon which she had before been working, she threaded her needle.

"I am ready," she said.

So Sigurd, seeing that there was no way out of his difficulty and hoping that the telling of his secret might after all be of benefit to Olaf, obeyed the queen's behest, relating the story of the kings of Norway and showing how this boy, Olaf, the slayer of Klerkon, was descended in a direct line from the great King Harald Fairhair.

CHAPTER V: THE STORY OP THE NORSE KINGS.

"On a time very long ago," began Sigurd, as he sat beside Olaf on a bench facing Queen Allogia, "there reigned in the south of Norway a young king named Halfdan the Swarthy. His realm was not large, for the country was at that time divided into many districts, each having its independent king. But, by warfare and by fortunate marriage, Halfdan soon increased the possessions which his father had left to him, so that he became the mightiest king in all the land. The name of his wife was Queen Ragnhild, who was very beautiful, and they had a son whom they named Harald.

"This Harald grew to be a very handsome boy, tall and strong and of great intelligence. He was fond of manly sports, and his skill and beauty brought him the favour and admiration of all men of the northland. Well, when Harald was still a youth of ten winters, his father was one day crossing the ice on the Randsfjord when the ice broke under him and he was drowned, so his kingdom fell to his son. The kings whom Halfdan the Swarthy had conquered then bethought them that they might win back what lands they had lost, and they accordingly made war against the young king. Many battles were fought, but Harald was always victorious. Instead of yielding to his enemies he soon extended his dominions until they stretched as far north as Orkadale. And then he was content."

Sigurd here raised his eyes and looked across at Allogia as she silently plied her busy needle.

"It is a long story, lady," he said; "and it may be that it is not new to you."

"Tell it to the end," returned the queen.

"There lived at that time in Valders a maid named Gyda," continued Sigurd. "She was the daughter of King Erik of Hordaland, and King Harald, hearing that she was exceedingly fair and high minded would fain have her to be his wife. So he sent forth messengers to her, asking her to wed with him. Now the maid was proud as well as beautiful, and when she received this message she answered thus: 'Tell your master,' she said, 'that I will not sacrifice myself to be the wife of a king who has no more realm to rule over than a few counties. Marvellous it seems to me that there is no king who can make all Norway his own and be the sole lord thereof, as King Erik in Sweden, and King Gorm in Denmark. Give this message to King Harald, and tell him that I will only promise to be his wedded wife on this condition, that he will for my sake lay under him all Norway. For only then can he be accounted the king of a people.'

"Now these words of Gyda were taken duly to the king, and they awakened in his mind a thought which had never before occurred to him, and he said, in the presence of many men: 'This oath do I now solemnly make, and swear before that God who made me and rules over all things, that never more will I cut my hair nor comb it until the day when I have conquered all Norway, and have made myself the sole ruler of the Northmen. And if I do not fulfil my vow, I shall die in the attempt.'"

"Spoken like a true king!" interrupted Allogia. "I trust, for the proud maiden's sake, that he did not take long to fulfil his vow."

26

"Ten long years it took him," returned Sigurd. "Northward he sallied with a vast army and conquered Orkadale, Trondelag, and Naumdale, and all the country about Thrandheim, making himself the overlord of all the old kings who thereafter became his earls and vassals. Those who would not be subdued he killed or maimed. He made new laws, took from the peasants their odal estates, and declared all land to be the king's property. Many of the conquered people rebelled against his rule and his strict feudal laws, and some of his provinces had to be conquered twice over. But with every year he came nearer to his goal, and those who opposed him only brought about their own ruin.

"At last the old kings, smarting in their subjection, banded themselves together, resolving to assert their ancient rights in a pitched battle. They assembled a great fleet of warships and met the conqueror in the Hafrsfjord. In the sea fight that followed many of Harald's bravest men were slain; spears and stones fell about them on every side; the air was filled with the flying arrows as with winter hail. But the king's berserks at length took on their fury and won for their master the greatest battle that has ever been fought in Norway. Thus, after a ten years' struggle, did Harald fulfil his vow.

"At a feast which followed this fight his hair was cut and combed. Men had formerly named him Harald Shockhead; but now they marvelled at his new made beauty and called him Harald Fairhair. Then, having done what he set out to do, he married Gyda and lived with her until she died.

"From that day forth," continued Sigurd, "Harald Fairhair ruled with great rigour, and so severely did he tax his people that many of the nobler and prouder sort grew discontented and straightway abandoned Norway to seek new homes across the sea. Many were content to roam upon the waters as vikings; others sailed west to the Faroe Isles, some settled in Shetland and the Orkneys, while others went far north into Iceland-- a country so rich that, as I have heard, every blade of grass drips with butter. But Harald followed these adventurous men who had thus sought to escape his rule, with the result that he reduced all these islands to his sway."

At this point of the steward's narrative the queen moved impatiently and said:

"All this may be very well, Hersir Sigurd. But I fail to see how this history can bear upon the story of the boy Ole."

"You shall see its bearing very soon," returned Sigurd. "But, if you so wish, I will cut it short."

"Nay, tell it in your own way," said the queen, "for my time is of no account."

"You must know, then," pursued Sigurd, "that King Harald Fairhair had many wives, other than Gyda. And as he had many wives, so had he many sons. These sons as they grew up to manhood became to him a serious trouble. They were jealous of each other and for ever quarrelling among themselves. A chief cause of their disagreement was their bitter jealousy of Erik, the son whom Harald favoured above all the rest.

"When Erik was but a mere boy--no older than young Ole, here--his father gave him the command of five great ships of war, and with a picked crew of hardy warriors the boy went a-viking along the coasts, harrying and plundering, fighting and slaughtering wherever he fell in with ships less powerful than his own. He became a terror to all peaceful folk, and for his murderous deeds by sea and land he won the name of Erik Bloodaxe.

"It was through his foolish love of this wild hearted son that Harald Fairhair was led to commit an act whereby he undid all the great work of his life. He had succeeded in uniting all Norway into one nation, and this was good. But now nothing would suit him but that he should once more divide his great realm into many provinces. He therefore

27

created all his sons kings, and gave to each his portion of the country, on condition that after his own death they should all acknowledge Erik Bloodaxe their overlord.

"But no sooner had this unwise course been taken than the sons began to quarrel more wildly than ever. There was but one son among them who was wise enough to enjoy his share in contentment and keep peace. This was Olaf, the son of Queen Swanhild. To him King Harald had given the country of Viken, in the south of Norway. Olaf was the father of Triggvi, and the grandfather of the boy who is now before you.'"

Allogia's eyes were now fixed upon young Olaf, who sat at his ease in front of her with his arm resting on the back of the bench and his fingers playing idly with his long gold curls.

"Truly did I guess," said she, "that the boy had kingly blood in him. Such silken hair, such clear soft skin, and beautiful blue eyes could not possibly have come of lowly birth. And now do I well believe that it was he whom the king's mother meant when, at the yuletide feast, she spoke of the child who was destined to be brought up here in Holmgard, and who was to grow to be a famous prince." She smiled softly on the boy as she said this. "And now, hersir," she added, "we will hear the rest of your saga."

Sigurd rose from the bench and began to pace slowly to and fro with his hands clasped behind his back.

"Of all King Harald's sons," said he, "Erik Bloodaxe was the one who had the most ambition and who fought hardest to win worship from his brothers. In his strivings he did not scruple to act unfairly. He stooped to treachery, and even to murder. He first killed his brother, Ragnvald Rattlebone, because he was said to be a sorcerer. Next he killed his brother Biorn, because he refused to pay him homage and tribute. None of Harald's sons could be safe while Erik was thus allowed to take the law into his own hands; so two other of the brothers attempted to take Erik's life, by setting fire to a farmhouse in which he was feasting. But Erik escaped with four men, secured his father's protection, and for a time there was peace.

"Now King Harald Fairhair had a young son named Hakon, the child of his old age, and this son became in the after years a very great man in the land, and was called Hakon the Good.

"The King of England in those days was named Athelstane the Victorious, and it is told that on a time Athelstane, who was passing jealous of the power of Harald Fairhair, sent a messenger to Norway bearing a precious sword as a gift to King Harald. The sword was done with gold about the hilt and set with dear bought gems, and well tempered in the blade. So the messenger fared to Lade, in Thrandheim, where Harald dwelt, and said he: 'Here is a sword which the King of England sendeth thee, bidding thee take it withal.' So the king took the grip of it. Then said the messenger: 'Thou hast taken the sword even as our king wished, and thou art therefore his sword taker and vassal.'

"Well, Harald was angry at being thus tricked, and he pondered how he might pay back King Athelstane, so the next year he got ship and sent his young son Hakon to England, along with a great berserker, or champion, named Hawk, and thirty warriors. They found the king in London town, and, being fully armed, they entered his feasting hall where he sat. Hawk took the child Hakon and placed him on King Athelstane's knee, saying: 'The King of Norway biddeth thee foster this his child.'

"Athelstane was exceeding wroth, and he caught up his sword that lay beside him and drew it as if he would slay the lad. Then said Hawk: 'Thou hast set the child on thy knee and mayest murder him if thou wilt, but not thus withal wilt thou make an end of all the sons of King Harald Fairhair.'

"Thus did the King of Norway pay back the King of England in his own coin, for men ever account the fosterer less noble than him whose child he fosters. Howbeit, King Athelstane kept the lad and fostered him right well. Thereafter he treated young Hakon with great kindness, taught him good manners and all kinds of prowess, and in the end grew to love him more than any of his own kin. In England, Hakon abandoned his faith in the gods of Scandinavia, and became a worshipper of the White Christ, for in that land all men are Christians, and Thor and Odin have no power.

"Now, while Hakon was away in England, his elder brother, Erik Bloodaxe, went a-warring in his viking ships to many lands--Scotland, Wales, Ireland, and Normandy, and north away in Finland. And in Finland he found a certain woman, the like of whom he had never seen for fairness in all his roamings. She was named Gunnhild, and had learned all kinds of sorcery and witchcraft among the Finns. Erik wedded with this woman, and it afterwards befell that she wrought more evil in Norway than even Erik himself. She was his evil genius, egging him on to deeds of treachery and violence which made him detested of all men.

"Glad was Gunnhild when Harald the Fairhaired, being stricken in years, declared that he felt no longer able to bear the burden of the government. This he did when he was eighty years old. He led his son Erik to his royal high seat and put him there as the king, so that Gunnhild by this became the queen, and could work her evil as she willed.

"Three years afterwards Harald Fairhair died in his bed, having ruled over Norway for seventy-three years."

Sigurd paused in his narrative and sat down beside Olaf. He felt that the queen's interest in his nephew was now secure and that it boded well for Olaf. Allogia set aside her needle and nodded to the steward as if she would tell him to continue his saga. Sigurd leaned back in his seat, crossed his legs, and went on.

"King Erik now held dominion over the larger part of Norway," said he. "But there were two of his brothers who would not yield to him, and who yet peacefully ruled in the realms over which their father had placed them. Olaf--the son of King Harald and Queen Swanhild--was the sovereign king in Viken, and his brother Halfdan in like manner ruled in Thrandheim. Full ill content was Erik that he could not truthfully call himself the lord over all Norway. But, as he could not be king by favour alone, he resolved to become so by other means. Two winters after Erik's enthronement his brother Halfdan died a sudden and painful death at a feast in Thrandheim. It is told that he was cunningly poisoned by Queen Gunnhild. Erik straightway claimed his dead brother's kingdom; but the Thrandheimers would have none of him; they declared against him, and took another brother, Sigrod, for their king. To protect themselves against their overbearing brother, Sigrod and Olaf joined their forces. But Erik attacked them unawares with a great army at Tunsberg and won the day. Both Olaf and Sigrod, champions in the battle, were killed. Olaf's son, Triggvi, escaped, however, and fled away to the Uplands, where he remained as long as Erik Bloodaxe was master in the land. Triggvi was the biggest and strongest of men, and the fairest of face of all that have ever been seen.

"Erik Bloodaxe had now killed four of his brothers and caused the death of a fifth. He had made himself the king of all Norway, even as his father had been. Yet the people misliked him sorely, they were for ever striving to displace him and to set up Triggvi Olafson in his stead. Then Queen Gunnhild swore that, if Erik would not make his rule a certainty, she at least would not rest until she had exterminated all the race of Harald Fairhair outside of her husband's line."

Here Olaf spoke, leaning forward and looking round into Sigurd's face.

"I think," said he, "that if I had been in my father's place I would have rid the earth of so murderous a traitor as Erik Bloodaxe."

"Your father was a peace lover," returned Sigurd, "though, indeed, there was not in all the land at that time a more splendid warrior than he. But there were other reasons. The first was that Triggvi was passing content in the place where he was living, away in the Uplands, for there he had become the friend of a great earl who had most fruitful lands at Ofrestead, and he had won the love of the earl's daughter, Astrid, the most beautiful maid in all Norway. Her he had wedded, and they were very happy together and free from all the cares of state and war. This do I know full well," added Sigurd, addressing Allogia, "for Queen Astrid was my own dear sister, and Earl Erik of Ofrestead was my own father."

"Then," said Queen Allogia, "it must be that Astrid was the mother of this boy whose cause you are now pleading; and in that case you yourself must be our young Ole's uncle?"

"It is even so," replied Sigurd. "And now I must tell the second reason why Triggvi did not try to compass the death of King Erik. It was that Queen Gunnhild had already been seeking to fulfil her vow, and had been attempting through her wicked sorcery to bring about young Triggvi's death. So Triggvi thereupon left Astrid in the care of her father, and went a-warring as a viking. He sailed west over sea to Scotland, and there harried the coasts; and then to the Orkneys, where he had many battles with the vikings of the isles. So that when the people sought for him, wishing to make him their king, he could not be found.

"Well, in the meantime there had appeared another who had rightful claim to the throne. Hakon, Athelstane's foster son, had come back from England on hearing of King Harald's death. He was now a full grown man and a valiant warrior. When he landed in Trondelag the people hailed him with great rejoicing, and declared that old Harald Fairhair had come back once more, gentler and more generous than before, but no less mighty and beautiful. They claimed him as their king, calling him Hakon the Good, and he reigned in Norway for many years, nor did he seek to do any ill to his nephew, Triggvi Olafson, but confirmed him as king in Viken.

"Now when Hakon the Good returned it was an ill day for his elder brother Erik Bloodaxe, for the people had become so wroth against him that he could find no peace. At first he tried to raise an army, but none would serve him, and he was forced to flee from the land with his wife and children and a few weak followers. He thereupon took a ship and roamed about as a viking. He fared westward to the Orkneys, and got many vikings to join him, then he sailed south and harried all about the north parts of England. So greatly did he trouble the English people that at last King Athelstane, to win his peace, offered Erik the dominion over Northumberland, on the condition that he would become the king's vassal and defend that part of the realm against the Danes and other vikings. Erik agreed, allowed himself to be christened, and took the right troth.

"Now Northumbria is accounted the fifth part of England, and the better bargain was on Erik's side. He made his abode in the town of York, and he warded the country well, for full oft did the Danes and Northmen harry there in the earlier time. But very soon, urged, it may be, by Queen Gunnhild, he sought to increase his wealth and to add to his lands; and when Athelstane died and King Edmund became the monarch of England Erik Bloodaxe went far into the land, and forcibly drove the people from their homes. Too greatly did he reckon upon success, for it happened that there was another who, like himself, had been set there by the king for the warding of the country. This other gathered an army and fell upon Erik. There was a great battle, and many of the

English folk were killed; but ere the day was ended Erik lay dead upon the field, and that was the last of him.

"No longer could Queen Gunnhild hope to dwell at peace in England. Her husband's estates were forfeited, and she had no home. So she took her children and sailed east to Denmark. There she was well received by the Danish king, Harald Bluetooth. But in spite of her misfortune her ambitions were not dead, for she had many sons growing up, and she had a mind to make them all kings in Norway. These sons, as you may well suppose, had little goodwill for Hakon the Good, who had dispossessed them of their inheritance. The eldest of them had roved for a while as vikings, and were already skilled in warfare, so Gunnhild contrived to get them ships and followers, and sent them across to Viken, the part of Norway where, as I have said, King Triggvi Olafson reigned. They had many battles with Triggvi, but they could not conquer him. But at last King Hakon came to his nephew's help, and with him pursued the sons of Gunnhild into Denmark.

"This attack upon Danish soil brought about a war between the kings of Denmark and Norway, and in a battle at Sotoness Triggvi Olafson was defeated. He was forced to abandon his ships and save himself by flight. In a later battle Hakon the Good was killed. It is said that Gunnhild had bewitched the arrow that slew him.

"Hakon had never tried very hard to make his people Christians, and he had himself drifted back to the worship of Thor and Odin. One of his friends, when he was dying, offered to take his body over to England, so that he might be buried in Christian soil, but Hakon replied: 'I am not worthy of it. I have lived like a heathen, and therefore it is meet that I should be buried like a heathen.'"

Queen Allogia drew a heavy breath at this point in Sigurd's narrative, as if she thought that the story would have no end.

"Your voice gets tired, hersir," said she, "and it may be that you would wish to keep the rest of the saga for another time!"

"There is but little more to tell," returned Sigurd, looking up with anxious eyes. "And as what is left is the more important part, I beg you to hear it to the end."

The queen assented, and Sigurd took up the thread of his story:

"Little time did the sons of Gunnhild lose," said he, "in claiming the kingdom of their fathers; but it was only the middle part of Norway that they could possess in safety. To gain the whole country they had need to break the power of Triggvi Olafson and Gudrod Biornson, both grandsons of Harald Fairhair, who ruled as independent kings. To do this in open warfare was not easy. Gunnhild, who now forced her sons to action, as she had formerly forced Erik Bloodaxe, found treachery an easier means; so she got one of her sons to feign hostility to his brothers and to make a show of friendship for Triggvi Olafson. King Triggvi was invited by this son to go out on a cruise with him. Triggvi yielded to his false friend's wish, and on reaching the place of meeting he was foully murdered with all his men. His cousin, King Gudrod Biornson, was at about this same time surprised at a feast by Harald Greyfell and slain after a desperate fight.

"Thus did the sons of Gunnhild clear their path. Thus, too, did the wicked queen fulfil the vow that she had sworn many years before, to exterminate the whole race of Harald Fairhair outside her husband's line.

"But," added Sigurd, in a deep and solemn voice, "the flower that is trampled under foot may yet leave its seed behind to come forth in its own season and flourish. The race of King Harald was not yet dead, and Queen Gunnhild presently found that there was a woman in Norway whose true love and faithfulness were better than all the guile and treachery that jealousy could devise. Triggvi Olafson's widow, Queen Astrid, when she heard tidings of his murder, guessed rightly that Gunnhild would pursue her, so she fled from Viken, and journeyed north towards the Uplands, taking with her her two young daughters, Ingibiorg and Astrid, together with such chattels as she might have with her. In her company was her foster father, Thoralf Lusaskegg by name, and his young son Thorgils. Thoralf never left her, but guarded her always most faithfully, while other trusty men of hers went about spying for tidings of her foes.

"Now very soon Astrid heard that Gunnhild's sons were pursuing her with intent to kill her, so she let herself be hidden on a little island in the midst of a certain lake. There on that island her son was born, and she had him sprinkled with water and named Olaf, after his father's father."

Sigurd paused, and laying his hand on Olaf's shoulder, "This," said he, "is that same child, Olaf Triggvison, and he is the one true flower of which King Harald Fairhair was the parent stem. An ill thing would it be for Norway if, for the slaying of Klerkon the Viking, he were now to lose his life. And I beg you, oh, queen! to deal kindly with this king's son so hardly dealt with, and to deal with King Valdemar concerning him that his life may be spared."

Then Queen Allogia answered, looking on the lad, that she would do as Sigurd wished.

"And now," she added, "tell me how it came to pass that the boy was ever brought across the sea to Esthonia."

So Sigurd told how Queen Astrid journeyed farther into the Uplands until she came to her father's manor at Ofrestead; how, dwelling there, she had been at last discovered by Gunnhild's spies, and been forced to take flight that she might save young Olaf from their murderous hands. For Gunnhild had now heard of the birth of this son of King Triggvi, and nothing would content her, but that he should die ere he could grow up to manhood, and so dispute with her own sons the realm that they now usurped.

He told how Queen Astrid, leaving her two daughters at Ofrestead, had fared east away into Sweden, and of what privations she had borne for her son's sake, and of how, still pursued by her enemies, she had at length taken safe refuge with Hakon Gamle, a friend of her father's.

"But even here," continued Sigurd, "Queen Gunnhild's enmity followed her. This time it was not with the sword but with soft words that Gunnhild sought to gain her ends. She sent a message through the King of Sweden, asking that she might have Olaf back in Norway to live in her court, and to be taught and nurtured as behoved one of such exalted birth. But Astrid knew full well that there was falseness underlying this message, and she sent word back to Norway saying that her boy stood in no need of such help, and that she would herself see that he was both well nurtured and fitly taught.

"I have told you," said Sigurd, "that Queen Astrid was my own sister. Now, at the time I speak of I was already in the service of King Valdemar; so Astrid thought that the best means of escaping her enemies and of saving her son was that she should come here with Olaf into Holmgard. The boy was then three winters old and full sturdy. So Hakon Gamle gave her a good company of men, and took her down to the seacoast and gave her into the care of certain traders whose ship was bound eastward.

"But now as they made out to sea vikings fell on them, and took both men and money. Some they slew, and some they shared between them for bondslaves. Then was Olaf parted from his mother, and the captain of the vikings, an Esthonian named Klerkon Flatface, got him along with Thoralf and Thorgils. Klerkon deemed Thoralf over old for a thrall, and, seeing no work in him, slew him and flung him overboard, but he had the lads away with him, and sold them into slavery. Olaf and Thorgils swore foster brotherhood, and they took oath in handshaking that they would bring this viking to his bane. That oath did Olaf fulfil this day, when he drove his axe into Klerkon's head."

Sigurd rose from his seat and stood before the queen.

"And now," said he, "my story is at an end, and you know of what kin this boy has come. Well am I aware, oh, queen! that in fostering a king's son I have broken the law of this land. I seek no pardon for myself. For Olaf alone do I ask your help. And if King Valdemar condemn him to death for his crime, then do I crave that my life, and not the boy's, be taken."

"Go with the boy to your home," returned the queen. "None shall hurt either him or you. Wait in patience until the sun rise, and then you shall know the issue of my pleadings with the king."

And so saying, she signed to them to leave the hall.

CHAPTER VI: THE TRAINING OF OLAF.

Very much of this story that Sigurd had told was strangely new to Olaf, and even the parts that he had before been familiar with came to him with fresh meaning. He had known all along of his descent from King Harald Fairhair, but not until now did he fully and clearly understand that by the death of his father and of all his father's brothers he was himself at this moment the sole heir to the throne of Norway. Now for the first time he realized that during all that past time, when he had been living as a poor and wretched bondslave in Esthonia, he had held this glorious birthright.

As he lay on his bed that night, thinking over all that he had heard, he tried to comprehend all that it must mean to him in the future, and in his own boyish way he made great resolves of how, when the fitting moment should come, he would sail across the sea, and, landing on the shores of Norway, tell his people the story of his royal birth and heritage, so that they might know him and acknowledge him their king, even as they had acknowledged Hakon the Good. But in the midst of his dreaming there came to him the remembrance of the crime that he had just committed, and he began to dread that King Valdemar might hold him guilty, and order him to be slain.

All through the long night this dread haunted him. He had killed Jarl Klerkon, and the sense of his own guilt now preyed upon him like a terrible nightmare. He wondered by what means they would take his life. Would they smite off his head with a sharp sword or shoot an arrow into his heart, or would they slowly torture him to death? Perhaps they would deem him too young to be thus punished by the taking of his life; but if they spared his life he would none the less be punished, for they would throw him into the dark prison that he had once seen under the king's castle, and there they would leave him to languish in chains for many years, so that his strength would go from him, and he would be no longer fit to be called a king.

Not for a moment did Olaf think of allowing his Uncle Sigurd to take the punishment for his crime. He knew that Sigurd had made no idle offer when he had said that he would give up his life for his sake; but Sigurd was guiltless, and it would be a coward's act to allow him to make this sacrifice. With all his newborn hopes burning within him, it was a hard thing for Olaf to think of death. Nevertheless, before the night was half spent he had resolved to take whatever punishment should be meted out to him, and if need be to face even death with a brave heart.

Early on the next morning he was awakened from his sleep by the touch of rough hands upon him. His own hands were seized, and heavy chains were bound upon his wrists and ankles. Then he was taken away and thrust into a dark cell that was cold, and damp, and airless. No food was given to him, and very soon the pangs of hunger made him wild and restless. A sudden dread came upon him that they meant to starve him to death. But not long had he been imprisoned before the heavy door was again thrown open, and he was summoned forth. Two men of the king's bodyguard led him into the great hall, where he was met by a loud clamour of voices. He looked about him fearlessly at the crowd of townsfolk and vikings, who were there, as he now well knew, to bear witness against him and to hear him condemned. As he stood facing them the vikings broke into fierce cries for speedy vengeance, and he felt the hot blood rush to his cheeks and brow. His clear blue eyes flashed in bold challenge as one of the seamen called out aloud:

"Death to him! Death to the slayer of our chief!" Then one of the king's lawmen demanded silence, and Olaf was made to turn with his face to the high seat. There sat King Valdemar in his robes of justice, and with his naked sword lying before him on the oaken table. At his right side sat Queen Allogia, with her eyes fixed gravely upon the young criminal.

Presently, when there was complete silence, Olaf's accuser stepped forward, and making the sign of Thor's hammer, spoke aloud. He was named Rand the Strong, and the vikings had chosen him as their captain in the place of the dead Jarl Klerkon. He told very truthfully how the young prisoner had made his attack upon Klerkon, and showed that it was in no mean and underhand way that he had committed this crime, but with such boldness that none had guessed what was happening until they saw Klerkon fall to the ground with the lad's axe buried deep in his skull.

Then came others, both townsfolk and seafolk, declaring that Rand had spoken truly. And so when all who accused the boy had spoken, Sigurd, the king's steward, was bidden to rise and say what he knew in Olaf's favour.

"The boy is my own servant," said he, "and I bought him as a thrall from a certain yeoman in Esthonia. I know no ill against him, and it was not in his nature to commit any violent act without cause. Rash he certainly was in killing this viking without due warning. But Jarl Klerkon was a man whose skill and prowess have made him well known on all the seas where the vikings are wont to do battle, and I think he might easily have defended himself against this child, who, as you have heard, attacked him face to face in the full daylight. As to the cause of this attack it was this: some seven summers back Jarl Klerkon assailed and captured a certain merchant ship, on board of which were this boy Ole, his mother, and his foster father. Klerkon slew the boy's foster father and sold the mother and her child into bondage. The boy took oath of vengeance, which oath he has now fulfilled. Now," continued Sigurd, raising his voice so that all could hear, "it is not lawful for any Esthonian viking to attack a peaceful trading ship; but Klerkon assuredly did this, and I therefore hold that it was he who was the aggressor. For this reason, and also on account of his youth, I crave that the boy's life be spared."

While Sigurd was speaking, Olaf's eyes rested upon the queen. He saw her lean over and whisper in the king's ear. The king nodded and smiled, waited until there was silence, and then said briefly:

"Little question is there that the offender is guilty. He is guilty, and must suffer the penalty of his crime. But as he is still little more than a child in years the penalty will not be death, but the payment of a heavy fine. He will, therefore, pay to the vikings whom he has injured the sum of two hundred gold marks."

Now Olaf deemed this judgment very hard, for he had not the money wherewith to pay this fine. But his life had been spared, and that was a great matter. It might be that Sigurd Erikson, who was as he knew very wealthy, would help him to meet the weregild.

Meanwhile the vikings had put their heads together in council. They decided that as the young murderer's death would in no way profit them they would accept the fine. But there was yet something that seemed to trouble them, and at last Rand the Strong came forward before the king.

"We are well content with thy judgment, O king," said he, "and we agree that on receiving this money we shall not molest the lad any longer on account of this matter. But we are told that he is only a thrall, and that there is no hope of our getting the gold from him. Therefore we claim that he shall die the death."

Olaf looked towards his uncle as if expecting that he would at once offer to pay this gold. But Sigurd's eyes were fixed upon Queen Allogia, who now slowly rose from her seat and held up her hand to silence the loud murmur of voices that filled the hall.

"As to this money," said she, addressing the vikings in a clear ringing voice, "there is no need that you concern yourselves. The gold shall now be paid to you in full. It is here!" she cried, throwing down a bag of coins upon the table. "Now, loosen the boy's chains! Loosen his chains and set him free."

Then Olaf's warders unbound him, and at a sign from the queen he stepped to the table and took up the bag of gold and carried it to Rand the Strong, who received it from him with willing hands, bidding the boy have no further fear.

On that same day the vikings departed out of Holmgard not ill pleased, for they went away much richer than they had come, and none of them seemed at all sorry at the loss of their chief. Jarl Klerkon had gone to Valhalla, they said, and he was surely happier than they.

Now on the day after the paying of the weregild Olaf had audience with Queen Allogia, and he thanked her well for the great friendship she had shown him.

"Little do I deserve your thanks, Prince Olaf," said she. "What I have done is no more than I would wish any other woman to do for my own son if he were so hardly dealt with in a foreign land. And now," she added, "since I have at length learned of what great kin you are, it is my wish that you shall be received here as becomes your royal birth, and that you shall be educated as behoves a king's son. Too young are you yet to bear arms as a warrior. For the present, therefore, you shall attend upon me as my page, and you will be treated with all kindness."

Not as a servant, but rather as an honoured courtier was Olaf Triggvison received after this time. He was twelve winters old when he came into Holmgard, and he abode in King Valdemar's service other five winters. Little can be told of his life during those years. They were years of preparation for his great work in the after time; and although he learnt very much and acquired a large part of the skill that was to make him famous among men, yet his days were without adventure.

There was one matter which had sorely troubled him for many a long day, and this was the thought of his mother living in bondage. Little did he remember of those early times when she had done so much for his sake; he had been too young then to understand what sacrifices Queen Astrid had made and what privations she had endured. But ever as he grew older he thought more of her, and it pained him very much to know that even now, when he was living in comfort, with good food and rich apparel, she, to whom he owed so much, was perhaps labouring as a bondswoman under some cruel master.

On a certain summer morning he sat in the queen's presence, playing upon a little harp that Allogia had given to him. And as his deft fingers touched the trembling strings he chanted a little song, telling of how the giant Loki, in punishment for all the ills he had done to gods and men, was bound by strong cords against the walls of a cave, with a serpent suspended over him dropping venom into his face drop by drop; and of how

35

Sigyn his wife took pity on him and stood by him for hundreds of years, catching the drops as they fell in a cup which she held.

Suddenly in the midst of his song Olaf stopped. The queen looked round at him and saw that there were tears in his eyes.

"Why do you weep?" she asked. "Are you not happy, Olaf?"

"Happy enough am I for my own sake," he replied. "It was the thought of my mother that brought the tears to my eyes. I was thinking that what Sigyn did for the wicked giant was just such a good act as my mother would do for anyone whom she loved."

"Marvellous it seems to me," said Allogia, "that we can never learn what has become of the good Queen Astrid."

"I think," returned Olaf, "that if ever I were to journey into Esthonia I might get some tidings of her. The last that I heard of her was that she had been sold to a rich fisherman named Hallstein, who made her labour at cleaning the fish for him and mending his nets."

"A sorry occupation for a queen to be at!" Allogia said with a sigh. "But if it be that you have any hope of finding her, then it would be well if you made that journey you speak of. Sigurd Erikson goes north to Esthonia in three days' time, on business for the king. Will you not go with him?"

"Gladly will I go with him," answered Olaf, "if it be that I may."

Well, on the third day Olaf and Sigurd mounted their horses, and with a good company of men-at-arms set off on their journey over the rocky plains. Five days were they riding before they came within sight of the blue sea with its ships and its quiet green islands. That sight brought a restless yearning into Olaf's spirit. It seemed as if nothing would now content him but that he should go out upon the wide ocean and spend all his days in roving. And so much did he speak of the ships and of the viking life that when at last the time came for the return to Holmgard, Sigurd Erikson had hard work to win the boy away with him.

While Sigurd was dealing with the people concerning the king's business, Olaf Triggvison went about from place to place in quest of tidings of Queen Astrid. But nothing certain could he learn, for he dared not say that the woman he sought was the widow of King Triggvi, and when he told of her fairness those whom he questioned only shook their heads. They had seen many bondswomen who were fair, they said, and how could they tell that any one of them was she whom the young hersir was now seeking? At last Olaf found his way to the house of Hallstein the fisher, only to hear that Hallstein had been drowned in the sea full five winters before. But Olaf described his mother to the fisher's widow, who bade him fare to a certain yeoman named Einar Ulfsson, at a farmstead over the hills. So Olaf took horse and rode away to this man and questioned him concerning Astrid. Einar remembered her, for she had been his bondwoman for two summers. He had sold her, he said, to a stranger, who had taken her on board his ship and carried her away across the seas. This was the last trace of his mother that Olaf could discover, and he went back to Sigurd Erikson and told him what he had learned. Sigurd was very sad at this, for he loved his sister, and it pained him to think that she was still in slavery, when, if she could but be found, she might live in comfort and happiness. But he bade Olaf to be hopeful, "for," said he, "I think it may be that some friendly man has bought her and taken her home to Norway. And if that be so, then we shall soon learn the truth. I will send messengers to Ofrestead, and my father, Earl Erik, will surely find her if she is to be found."

36

Now when Olaf returned to Holmgard it was with the resolve that he would not long remain in this foreign land, but would take his first chance to go west over sea to the country of his birth. He had seen the ships passing along the rocky coasts of Esthonia; he had breathed the fresh free air of the sea, and the viking blood in him had been roused. His spirit was filled with the ambition to be the commander of a great warship, and to rove the ocean as his father had done, to visit distant lands and to make himself glorious in battle. But well he knew that to fit himself for the viking life he must increase his strength of body and acquire even greater skill than he now had in the use of all warlike weapons. So he set himself the task of excelling in the games and exercises that were then known and practised.

Already he had been taught by his uncle to read runes, to recite sagas, to play upon the harp, to carve wood, to twist string, to bend a bow, and to shaft an arrow. These and many other arts had come easy to his active mind and his deft fingers. All that a man of peace need know he knew full well. Nor had he neglected to give thought to the religion of his times. Every day he went into the temple to bow down in devout worship of the heathen gods, to take part in the rites and ceremonies of his faith, and even to offer sacrifice to Thor and Odin. The graven image of Odin was to him, as to most of the Norsemen, a sacred and a holy thing. When he took oath it was by the sign of Thor's hammer that he swore; he knew the names and the special powers of all the gods in Asgard, and Valhalla was the heaven to which, after death, he hoped to go.

But these arts and this religion would not alone fit him for fulfilling his ambition. To be such a great viking as he dreamed of becoming he must learn how to use his sword, how to wield his battleaxe, how to throw a spear and to shoot an arrow with greater skill than any other man could boast. He must learn, too, how to defend himself, and how, if wounded, to bear pain without shrinking. He was a king's son, and to be worthy of his father it was well that he should excel even the full grown men who had been well tried in battle and who had never known the meaning of defeat.

To this end Olaf remained three other years in Holmgard, which time he spent in making himself strong. In the neighbouring waters of Lake Ilmen he practised swimming, and with such success that at last he could remain under the surface for many minutes, diving off a ship's prow and coming up again under her steering board. So quickly and strongly could he swim that no man rowing in a boat could keep level with him. He could ride the wildest horse in the king's stable. At running and jumping no man could surpass him. In the use of the sword he was so expert that he could wield the weapon with either hand, and he could throw two spears at once. Never was he known to shoot an arrow without hitting the mark. So long as daylight served him he was always to be found performing some manly feat.

But in these matters it was not his training alone that aided him. Nature had given him a very beautiful and powerful frame, with well proportioned limbs, clear quick eyesight, and wonderful strength to endure all fatigue. Also, through all his life he was never known to be afraid of any danger or to shrink before any enemy. Other men of his race have won undying renown, but Olaf Triggvison has ever been accounted the fairest and tallest and strongest of all the heroes of Scandinavia, and in prowess surpassing all the warriors told of in the sagas.

CHAPTER VII: THE CAPTAIN OF THE HOST.

It befell at a time when Olaf had been in the queen's service some four summers that Sigurd Erikson went out into the far parts of the king's dominions to levy the yearly taxes upon the people, and among those that went with him on his journey were Thorgils Thoralfson and the young Egbert of England. These two had, by Olaf's favour with King

37

Valdemar, been liberated from their bondage and hard labour, and Sigurd had taken them into his service as men-at-arms. Brave and handsome they looked as they sat upon their chargers with their swords hanging at their sides and the sun shining on their burnished bronze helmets and coats of ring mail. Olaf watched them with admiring eyes as they rode away through the town, and wished that he might be of their company. But their journey was one of peace, and it was only their martial array that made him for the moment envious.

Sigurd was expected to be absent for little more than two weeks, but the time went by, the weeks passed into months, and he did not return.

On a certain day Olaf was beyond the gates training a pair of young hounds. As he watched one of the dogs running in pursuit of a hare that had been started he espied afar off a horseman riding swiftly across the plain, almost hidden in a cloud of dust. Nearer and nearer he approached until Olaf at last saw his face, and knew him to be his young friend Egbert. Leaving the dogs in the care of two of the king's servants who were attending him, he set off at a quick run to meet the horseman.

"What brings you back alone, Egbert?" he cried as he came near.

Egbert drew rein. His garments were torn and dusty; he had lost his helmet and sword, and his face was so begrimed and travel stained that he was scarcely to be recognized.

"I have brought ill news," he answered, "and am hastening with it to King Valdemar. It is full five days since I parted company with my fellows. They are all made captive--the Hersir Sigurd, Thorgils Thoralfson, and the rest of them--and I alone have escaped."

Olaf turned, and taking Egbert's stirrup strap in his hand trotted on at the horse's side.

"Seven days ago," Egbert went on, "we crossed in one of the king's ships to an island that lies out to the west of Esthonia. Dago is the name of the island.

"There Sigurd landed, meaning to gather taxes and tribute from the people. But no sooner was he ashore than the people told him that they were no longer the subjects of King Valdemar but of a new king whom they had chosen for themselves. Sigurd disputed their right to elect a new king for themselves, and he asked to see this man and to know the name of him who had dared to set himself up in opposition to Valdemar. Then there was a commotion among the crowd, and one stepped forward and cried out, 'I am the king, and my name is Rand the Strong!' and we all knew him to be the same viking who four summers ago was here in Holmgard in the train of Jan Klerkon. Sigurd grew ill at ease seeing the vast crowd of islanders that had now gathered there, but he spoke boldly, and told them all that they were a pack of rebels, and that King Valdemar would speedily prove to them that he would not brook the interference of this upstart sea rover. At that Rand drew his sword and called to his men to stand by their rights and drive these intruders from their shores. There was a brief fight, in which I know not how many men were slain or wounded, and in the end the islanders got the victory. Sigurd fought bravely until he was disarmed and made prisoner. Thorgils and five others of our men were carried off with him. Our ship, too, was captured. Darkness came on ere the fight was finished, and under the cover of night I crept down to the seashore and waded out into the sea. By the light of the stars I took my bearings and swam out eastward to the mainland. All through the night I swam on and on. The sun rose, and still the land was afar off. But at the midday I came to a firm footing on the beach. At a farmstead I got food and a horse, and for two days I have been travelling without rest."

38

"You have done wondrous well," cried Olaf. "And much do I envy you your adventure."

"There is little cause for envy," returned Egbert. "My limbs are so weary that I can scarcely sit upright upon my horse's back, and he, poor dumb brute, is so wind broken that he can be of little more use in the world. As to adventure, you might now have it in plenty if the king would but agree to your being of those who must go to the rescue of our comrades. You are young, and have had no experience in warfare; but you can, for all that, wield a sword as well as any man in Valdemar's service."

Olaf was silent, and when they entered the gates he did not seek to accompany Egbert into the presence of the king. Instead, he made his way into Queen Allogia's apartments, and there told the news that he had just heard.

Not long had he been in the hall wherein the queen sat when the door opened and King Valdemar entered, looking very grave. Olaf rose from his seat and bowed before him.

"What is your age, my boy?" asked Valdemar.

"Sixteen summers, lord," answered Olaf, wondering at the reason of the question.

The king eyed him from head to foot.

"It is still very young," said he with a smile. "But your strength is greater than your years. Not often have I seen one so young with limbs so sturdy and with figure so nobly upright. I have been thinking that you have lingered long enough about the skirts of our womenfolk. Such skill as yours should be put to more manly uses than fingering the harp and carrying the wine cup, and I have now a mind to see what you can do in active warfare. There is trouble among the people over in the Isle of Dago. I have had news that a rebellion has broken out, and that the islanders have chosen a new king to themselves and refused to acknowledge their rightful sovereign. These rebels must be instantly quelled, and I have therefore resolved to despatch a company of men against them and force them to submit. What say you to your taking the command of the expedition?"

"The command?" repeated Olaf, drawing back in astonishment. "But I am no more than a boy. My heart is willing and bold; but surely I am too young to undertake so grave a trust!"

"Yes," cried the queen, growing white even to the lips at thought of her favourite being thus thrust into a post of danger. "Yes," she cried, "he is assuredly too young for such a charge!"

But King Valdemar shook his head.

"Not so," said he with confidence. "Young though he may be in years, I am well assured that there is no man now living in this kingdom who is better fitted for the leading of an armed host, and I will trust him to the full." Then turning to Olaf he added: "The matter is already settled. It so chances that there are at this present time six of our best warships, with their full number of seamen and warriors, now lying in the haven behind Odinsholm. You will depart hence at daybreak, with such armed horsemen and footmen as you choose to take in your company. Ere you reach the coast the ship captains will have been informed that I have placed you over them as their chief and commander."

Scarcely able to believe in the reality of what he heard, Olaf stood before the king in silent perplexity. He lacked not faith in his own personal prowess, for that had many times been amply proved in the games and exercises that he had daily engaged in, nor did his courage fail him. But to be placed at the head of some hundreds of well tried warriors and told to lead them against an enemy, this was a matter of which he had as yet only vaguely dreamed. For many moments he stood in doubt. But suddenly it seemed that a new light came into his clear blue eyes, and a fuller vigour into his strong young limbs.

"If it be your wish, lord," he said at last, "then I will undertake the trust. My great forefather, King Harald Fairhair, was younger than I now am when he led forth his hosts to battle; and, as I am of King Harald's blood, so will I seek to make myself a worthy man of war."

Thereupon King Valdemar led the boy away, and for a long while they sat together, making their plans of how Olaf's forces were to invade the island and rescue Sigurd Erikson from the hands of the rebel islanders.

On a certain calm summer evening Olaf Triggvison, mounted upon a splendid white horse, and followed by some two score of picked men-at-arms, rode into the little town wherein, four years before, he had lived as a humble thrall. None knew him now for the same wild, wilful boy whom they had been accustomed to see playing barefooted upon the beach or tending his master's sheep upon the hillside. Even Reas the bonder himself, who had many a time flogged him for his disobedience and idleness, and who now watched him riding downward to the ships, did not recognize his former bondslave in the handsome and gaily attired young warrior. The people spoke among themselves of Olaf's beautiful fair hair, of his crested helmet of burnished brass, of his red silk cloak that fluttered in the breeze, and his glittering battleaxe that hung pendant from his saddle. They admired his easy seat upon horseback, and, when he spoke, they marvelled at the full richness of his voice. But none could say that they had ever before set eyes upon him.

Out in the mid bay the king's six longships lay at anchor, with their sails furled and their high gunwales set with shields from prow to stern. The largest vessel had at her prow the towering figure of a winged dragon ornamented with beaten gold. She was the longest ship that Olaf had ever seen, and he counted that she was fitted for twenty pairs of oars. Her hull was painted red and green above the water, and the tent that covered her decks was made of striped red and white cloth. As he stood gazing at her, with wonder and admiration, a small boat came round from her further side, rowed by six seamen and steered by a stalwart, red bearded warrior, whom the young commander had once before seen at the king's court in Holmgard. Jarl Asbiorn was his name. When the boat touched at the wharf Asbiorn greeted Olaf very humbly and bade him step on board. Olaf called Egbert to his side and together they were taken out to the dragon ship and received with great honour by the six captains, who each in turn took vows of submission and obedience to him. Then, while the ships were being got ready for sea, Olaf was shown into a large room under the poop and told that this was to be his private cabin. Here he held counsel with his officers touching the expedition they were now entering upon.

It was a proud moment for Olaf when, just at the sun's setting and at his own word of command, the oars of the six ships were thrust out from the bulwarks and the vessels began to move slowly out of the bay.

The warlike spirit that had been lying quiet within him now filled him with a strange new energy. The fresh sea air and the sense of his own power seemed to have entered every vein in his body, thrilling him with an eager desire for glory, which amounted almost to a madness. As he trod his ship's deck the seamen and fighting men watched him in wondering interest, and declared among themselves that Balder himself could not have been more beautiful. At first they thought that he was too young to be trusted with the sole command of six great vessels of war, but very soon he showed them that he was well able to do all that was expected of him; and there was something in his voice, in the quick glance of his eyes, and in his alertness that made them acknowledge him as one who

40

was born to be a leader of men. So they obeyed him in all things and yielded to his will in such wise that he had no trouble of any sort.

Before this time he had had no experience in the working of a ship; so in the early part of the voyage he gave his mind to the learning of all matters wherein he knew himself to be most ignorant. He watched the setting of the sails and asked many questions concerning them, until he could understand why at any time a certain rope was hauled or loosened, and why when the wind blew strong a reef was taken in. Always he took great interest in the working of the oars. There were in his own ship four score of rowing men--two at each oar--and as he watched them he marvelled how they could endure the hard labour without breaking their backs or tearing out their arms; and to prove to himself what amount of strength the work required he went down into the ship's waist and, taking off his shirt of chain mail, took his turn upon one of the benches, thus winning the praise of all on board. But most of all he loved to take the tiller in his hand and steer the vessel through the dangers of the wind swept sea.

On the evening of the third day the ships came within sight of the island of Dago, and the young commander bade his men get ready their weapons lest the islanders should offer resistance. During the night he brought his fleet to an anchorage under a small holm, whose high cliffs sheltered the ships from the view of the larger island. Then launching a small boat and disguising himself in a rough seaman's cloak, he took Egbert and four of the men with him and they rowed across the channel and made a landing.

Olaf questioned a shepherd whom he met on the upland pastures, and from him learned that Rand the Strong was still recognized among the islanders as their king and that the power of King Valdemar was broken. So Olaf returned to the ships and brought them round into a wide bay, upon whose shores the town was built.

Not long was Rand the Strong in mustering his little army of vikings, for he had seen the six ships approaching; he knew them to be the ships of King Valdemar, and quickly guessed with what intent they had come.

At sight of the islanders massed in battle array upon the beach Olaf bade his rowers draw yet nearer into the shallows. Then the war horns were sounded on both sides, the warriors set their arrows to the bowstring and a fierce fight began. More than once the islanders retreated before the heavy rain of arrows and stones, but again and again they rallied and assailed the ships. Many of the vikings rushed into the water and swam outward to the ships, but before they could climb the bulwarks and set foot upon the decks they were cut down by Olaf's swordsmen or slain, even as they swam, by arrow or spear.

Olaf himself stood at the prow of his dragon ship, surrounded by his berserks, whose shields protected him, and coolly he drew arrow after arrow from his sheath and sent it with unerring aim into the midst of the islanders. Stones and arrows fell about him in a constant rain, crashing upon his helmet and breaking against the close-knit rings of his coat of mail. At last he singled out the tall figure of Rand the Strong, who, rallying his vikings, led them nearer to the water's edge. Olaf chose one of his best arrows and fixed it to his bowstring, then bent his bow with the full strength of his arms, aiming very steadily. The bowstring twanged and the arrow flew whizzing through the air. Olaf watched its quick flight and followed it until it struck its intended mark and stood quivering in the bare part of the viking's throat. Rand staggered and fell. Then the islanders, seeing that their chief was slain, drew back once more to the higher beach, while Olaf brought his ships yet closer into the shallows and ordered his forces to land. With his sword in hand he led his men to the attack. There was a sharp hand to hand fight, in

41

which many were killed on both sides; but at last the islanders gave way before the invaders and Olaf got the victory.

So, when the fight was at an end, Olaf called the chief rebels before him and forced them to acknowledge King Valdemar as their rightful and sole sovereign. When peace was restored he demanded that Sigurd Erikson and those who had been of his following should be set at liberty. Among the first who were freed from the prison in Rand's stronghold was Thorgils Thoralfson. But Sigurd Erikson was found dead in his cell. The islanders declared that he had died of his wounds, but Olaf believed that hunger and hardship were the cause of it.

Greatly did Olaf Triggvison grieve over the loss of his uncle. Sigurd had been as a father to him, had lifted him up out of his sordid life of thraldom and raised him to his present high position in the favour of the court. And now he was dead and there was an end of all his loving kindness.

For the rest of that day Olaf was engaged in the burial of the brave islanders and vikings who had fallen in the battle, and he had a mound built over them and raised stones above them to mark the place. But at night he had Sigurd Erikson's body carried down to the beach with all the other men who had been of King Valdemar's host. One of the smaller ships was then brought in to the beach, and a pyre of tarred wood and dry peat was built upon its upper deck. Olaf placed the dead body of his uncle upon the pyre, with all the armour that Sigurd had worn. The ship was further loaded with the dead men and with weapons. Then, when the tide had risen and the vessel was afloat with her sail hoisted, Olaf went on board alone with a lighted torch and kindled the pyre. The wind blew off shore and the ship sailed slowly out upon the dark sea. There was a loud crackling of dry twigs and the flames rose amid a cloud of black smoke, showing Olaf standing at the stern with the tiller in his hand. Very soon the fire caught the logs of tarred wood, and when the pyre was all aglow and the heat became too great for him to bear, he fixed the steering board with the end of a rope, gave a farewell look at the prostrate body of his uncle, and then stepping to the rail threw himself overboard into the sea and swam back to the land. When he got his feet upon the rocks he climbed up to a grassy knoll and sat there watching the burning ship. The leaping flames lit up the sky and cast a long track of light upon the rippled sea. Presently both sail and mast fell over with a crash, and a cloud of fiery sparks rose high into the black night. Still Olaf sat watching; nor did he move away until at last the ship had burned down to the water's edge, and there was no more to be seen but a tiny gleam of light shining far out upon the dark and silent waves.

On the next morning, having ended this work of quelling the rebel islanders, Olaf led his fleet out of the bay and set forth on his return to the mainland. In three days' time he was once more in Holmgard. There he remained for two other years, enjoying great favour in the court and performing many important services. He sustained a great company of men-at-arms at his own cost from the wealth that he had inherited from his Uncle Sigurd, and from such riches as the king bestowed upon him; and the leading of this host throve so well in his hands that all the younger men of the realm flocked to his side, eager to be enlisted in his service.

Now it befell--as oft it must when outland men win fame and power beyond those of the land--that many folks envied Olaf the great love he had of the king, and of the queen no less. His bravery and his great success in all that he undertook brought him many secret enemies, who whispered all sorts of evil whispers to King Valdemar. They declared that Olaf was but increasing his influence and power so that in the end he might do some hurt to the king and to the realm. They slandered him and spoke all manner of

42

evil against him, representing him as a dangerous rival to Valdemar in the affections of both the queen and the people. So the king, hearing these false charges and believing them, began to look coldly upon young Olaf and to treat him roughly. Olaf then knew that it was time for him to be going, for that confidence once lost could never be wholly restored. So he went to King Valdemar and spoke with him, saying that as he was now grown tall and strong he was minded to travel and to see the land wherein his ancestors had ruled and his own father had been sovereign.

Little sorrow did the jealous Valdemar show at hearing of this resolve. And to hasten Olaf's departure he gave him great gifts of well wrought weapons--a splendid sword inlaid with gold on the blade and set in the hilt with dear bought gems, and a shield of embossed brass. Also he furnished him with a dragonship and four longships, ready manned and equipped for the sea, and bade him go a-roving wheresoever he willed in search of adventure and worldly furtherance.

Queen Allogia, however, was very sad at thought of thus losing her favourite, and it was long ere she would make up her mind to let Olaf leave her. But in the end she saw that it was for his own good and advancement that he should go; so she gave him a beautiful banner of silken embroidery that she had worked with her own hands, told him that he would be accounted a noble and brave man wheresoever he should chance to be, and then bade him a last farewell.

CHAPTER VIII: THE YOUNG VIKINGS.

So Olaf quitted Holmgard and went on shipboard, and stood out with his viking fleet into the Baltic Sea. He now owed no allegiance to any man, but was free to journey where he pleased, a king upon his own decks. At this time he was scarcely eighteen summers old; but his limbs were so well knit and strong, and he was withal so tall and manly, that he seemed already to have attained to man's estate. Yet, feeling that his youth might be against him, he had chosen that all his ship companions should be as near as possible to his own age. He had a score or so of bearded berserks on each of his ships-- men who feared neither fire nor steel, but who gloried in warfare, and loved nothing better than to be in the midst of a great battle. These indeed were full aged men; but for the rest, his crew of seamen and his band of trained men-at-arms was comprised of youths, none of whom were older than Thorgils Thoralfson, or younger than Olaf himself.

Olaf made his foster brother the chief in command under himself, giving him power over both seamen and warriors. He made his friend Egbert the sailing master, while one Kolbiorn Stallare became his master-of-arms.

Kolbiorn was the son of a powerful viking of Sognfiord in Norway. He was of an age with Olaf Triggvison, and so much did the two resemble one the other that, when apart, they were often taken to be brothers. Both had the long fair hair and the blue eyes of the Norseland, both were of nearly equal height; and it was Kolbiorn's habit to strive, by wearing similar clothing, to increase the likeness between himself and his young master. But when the two were side by side the resemblance ceased, for then Olaf was seen to be both the taller and the more muscular; his hair was seen to be more golden and silken, his skin more purely fair; his eyes, too, were brighter and larger than those of Kolbiorn, and his teeth more even and white. So, too, when it came to a test of skill, Olaf had ever the advantage, notwithstanding that Kolbiorn had spent all his young days on shipboard, had been taught by the vikings to perform all manner of feats, and had taken part in many battles on both land and sea.

On a certain calm morning, very soon after Olaf had set out on this his first viking cruise, he stood with Kolbiorn at the ship's rail, looking out over the sunlit sea as his vessel crept along propelled by her forty long, sweeping oars, and followed by his four longships.

"I think," said he, "that we will amuse ourselves today, and try our skill in some new game."

"I am very unfit to try my skill against yours," returned Kolbiorn modestly, "for you have already beaten me at chess, at swimming, at shooting, and at throwing the spear. Nevertheless, it shall be as you wish."

"Choose, then, what feat we are to perform," said Olaf; "I am willing to join in any exercise that you may know, and I do not doubt that there are many in which your skill must be greater than mine."

"There is one," said Kolbiorn, "that I would be glad to see you attempt, although there is danger in it, and I may be doing wrong in suggesting it."

"If it be new to me, then I shall be all the more pleased," said Olaf; "and none the less so though the risk be great."

Kolbiorn drew the young commander across to the shady side of the ship.

"It is that we shall climb over the bulwarks," said he, "and walk outboard along the oars while the men are rowing."

Olaf looked over the side, and for a few moments watched the regular motion of the oars as they dipped into the green water and rose dripping into the air. He measured with his eye the space between each of the twenty blades.

"It seems not so difficult as I had hoped," he said, "but let me see you do it, and then I will follow."

Kolbiorn climbed over the ship's quarter, and worked his way forward to the first rower's bench. Steadying himself for a moment as he hung by one arm from the gunwale, he dropped with his two feet upon the aftermost oar, and stepped out thence from oar to oar until he reached the one nearest to the forecastle. Then, still balancing himself with outstretched arms, he turned and walked aft by the same way to where Olaf and many of the ship's company had stood watching him. All thought it a very wonderful feat.

Olaf praised Kolbiorn's skill, but promptly prepared to follow his example. Throwing off his red silk cloak, lest, by falling into the sea, he should injure it, he climbed overboard, and without hesitation dropped down upon the square shank of the aftermost oar; then going out near to the blade, he ran forward with quick, well measured strides. Once or twice, as the oars were dipped, he faltered and nearly lost his balance, but he reached the foremost one without accident, and returned with greater ease. When he again stepped upon the deck he appealed to Thorgils Thoralfson to decide which had shown the more skill. But Thorgils was unable to determine the matter.

"The game has not yet had sufficient trial," said Olaf; "it must be gone through once more. But this time I will myself take the lead, and let Kolbiorn or any other of our company follow."

Then he asked Thorgils and Kolbiorn to lend him their handsaxes, and taking his own from his belt he again climbed over the side, and walking along the row of moving oars played with the three dirks, throwing them in turn up into the air, so that one was ever aloft and one hilt ever in his hand. Thus he played as he strode forward, without once dropping one of the weapons, and without once missing his sure footing. Climbing over the forecastle deck he then returned along the oars on the other side, and reached the deck with dry shoes.

No one on board could understand how Olaf had done this surprising feat without having practised it many times before, and when he gave back the two dirks to their owners, Kolbiorn stood before him and looked at him in silence.

44

Olaf said: "Why do you stand thus and not try after me?"

"Because I own myself beaten," answered Kolbiorn. "And yet," he added, "I cannot believe that you did this feat by your skill alone and without some secret power. Either you have the favour of Odin to aid you, or else you are descended from some mighty king whose natural skill you have inherited. Marvellous does it seem to me that whatsoever exercise you attempt, in that you are certain to surpass all other men."

Olaf laughed lightly and turned away towards his cabin, while his ship fellows continued to talk among themselves of this new example of his great agility.

Thus, even at the beginning of his free life as a sea rover, he had made upon his companions so deep an impression that they one and all respected him, and openly acknowledged him their superior in all things.

But most of all, they wondered of what kin he had been born that he should so easily and with such little effort excel all men they had known. For although they well knew that he had been a favourite at the court of King Valdemar, yet none even guessed at the truth that he was a blood descendant of the great Harald Fairhair; and less still did any imagine that he was even now heir to the throne of Norway. None but Thorgils Thoralfson knew his true name. At this time, and indeed throughout the whole course of his after adventures in Britain, he was known only as Ole the Esthonian.

Now although Olaf had spoken of his wish to return to the land of his fathers, yet now that he was upon his own dragonship, and free to follow where fortune should lead him, he showed no haste to make a landing in Norway. He bent his course across the Gulf of Finland, and then westward among the many green islands and rocky holms that lie in the mid sea between Finland and Sweden, and for many sunny days and calm starry nights simply enjoyed the idle pleasures of his new life of freedom.

It was the summer season, when all the channels of the sea were clear of ice, and there were many trading ships abroad which might have been an easy prey had Olaf so chosen to fall upon them. But although he was a viking, and had all the viking's lust for war and plunder, he yet remembered the time when his own mother had been taken by Jarl Klerkon and sold into bondage. So he determined to let all peaceful merchant ships alone, and to join battle only with such vessels as were intent upon warfare. In token of this resolve he had the great dragon's head lowered from his prow, so that its wide open jaws and terrible aspect might not strike fear into the hearts of the peaceable traders; and the shields that were ranged along his outer bulwarks were peace shields, painted white, as showing that he meant no harm to those who might chance to meet him on the seas.

His berserks, and many of the young men who had joined his fellowship in the hope of gain, grumbled sometimes when they saw him allow some richly laden ship to go by without attacking her, and they declared that after all he was a viking only in name. Olaf bade them wait in patience, reminding them that there was no lack of good food and well brewed ale on board, and that they had no need to feel discontent so long as their daily life was passed in bodily comfort.

"And as to fighting," he added, "I cannot think that any of you would take pleasure in drawing arms against men who have not been trained in warfare."

Not long did they need to wait ere their instinct for fighting was in part satisfied.

One gloomy forenoon his ships with their sails full set were speeding before a strong wind through the wide channel of sea dividing the two large islands of Gottland and Eyland. Thorgils was at the tiller of the dragon ship--a post which, in the viking times, was always held by the chief man on deck. As he stood there, his eyes swept the wide stretch of the grey sea in search of ships; for Olaf Triggvison had now put his red war shields out on the bulwarks, and the winged dragon reared its great gilded head at the prow, as if in menace. Olaf himself was below in his cabin under the poop, watching a game of chess that Kolbiorn and Egbert were playing.

The chessboard was a very beautiful one, its squares being of inlaid silver and gold, with little pegs in the centre of each space upon which the pieces might be fixed, and so prevented from being upset or from changing place when the vessel rolled. It was accounted a great privilege by Olaf's companions to be allowed to play upon this costly board, and Olaf had made it a condition that all who used it must do so without dispute. For a long time Kolbiorn and Egbert went on peaceably with their game. But while Olaf watched them, he noticed that Egbert became more and more ruffled, as he found himself being constantly baffled by his opponent's better play. So great was Kolbiorn's skill that Egbert at length became desperate, and only made matters worse by his hasty moves. He wanted to move back a knight which he had exposed, but Kolbiorn would not allow it. Olaf advised them to leave the knight where it now stood, and not to quarrel. At this Egbert's anger grew hot, and declaring that he would not take Olaf's advice, he swept his hand over the board, upset the pieces upon the cabin floor, and leaning forward struck Kolbiorn a blow upon the ear, so that blood flowed.

Kolbiorn rose from his seat and quietly turned towards the door. There he was met by one of his shipmates, who called out in an excited voice that there was a large viking ship in sight, and that she was bearing down towards them as though to give battle.

Olaf followed Kolbiorn from the cabin, and together they mounted to the deck. Looking out across the sea they saw the viking ship rowing towards them against the wind. In her wake there was a second vessel, drifting helpless and untended, with her sail flapping wildly in the wind and her oars all inboard. Olaf quickly noticed that there were people on her forward deck, and that she was slowly sinking. It was evident to him that she was a trading ship, which the vikings had but newly attacked and plundered. For a moment he hesitated, wondering whether he should hasten to her rescue or at once enter in battle with the vikings. He saw that his men were already eagerly preparing for a fight. Some, according to their custom before a battle, were busily washing themselves and combing their hair, while others were eating and drinking. There was no need for them to make ready their weapons, for these had been kept well prepared ever since the beginning of the cruise, and there was nothing further to be done than to bring the arrows up on deck and serve them round among the bowmen, twenty arrows to each man's quiver; and as for swords, spears, and armour, every man on board knew well where to put his hand on his own.

Bidding Kolbiorn go forward to the forecastle and marshal his berserks and bowmen, Olaf took down his war horn and blew a loud blast as challenge. At the same moment a red painted shield was hoisted to the yardarm. Then he went aft and took the tiller from Thorgils, and steered his bark as though to meet the approaching foe. But when he got within arrow shot of the stranger he suddenly altered his course, crossing her bows. The vikings, who could not yet have noticed the four consort ships that were still far behind, no doubt thought that he meant to make his escape, and they bore round in pursuit of him. But now Olaf had managed to get his vessel between the two other ships, and, having the wind in his sail and his oars at work, he quickly outdistanced the viking, and sped along at a great rate towards the sinking trading ship. Not too soon was he in getting alongside of her, for the vikings had scuttled her, and she had already settled down with her quarter bulwarks on a level with the water's edge. He rescued a full score of helpless men from her decks, and stood by her until she went down. By this time the viking ship had again come within bow shot of him, and his four longships had appeared in sight from behind the headland of one of the islands.

Olaf had now his sail brailed up to the yard, and his vessel's prow turned towards the oncoming enemy. Having resigned the helm to the charge of one of his seamen, he donned his war armour and went forward to the prow. Here the strongest and most experienced of his men were stationed as stem defenders, armed with swords and spears, and protected by their shields. Among them stood Olaf's standard bearer, round whom they were ranged in battle order. The station abaft that occupied by the stem defenders was manned by the berserks, and behind the mast were the spearmen, archers, and stone slingers.

Olaf and Kolbiorn, who were both armed with their longbows and a large number of picked arrows, as well as their swords, stood side by side by the banner bearer. Olaf again blew his war horn, while Kolbiorn fired an arrow of challenge high over the mast of the viking ship. When the two vessels drew near, Olaf saw that the stranger's forward decks were crowded, with fighting men, whom, by their dark hair and brown skin, he rightly judged to be Danes. The ships crashed together stem to stem, and then grappling hooks were thrown out from either side, and the vessels were bound close together, so that neither might escape until the fighting was at an end.

Thus at close quarters the battle began, and very soon the air was thick with swift flying arrows, and with showers of spears and stones. The chiefs on either side shouted aloud, urging their fellows to the fray, and many a well tried warrior was sent that day to Odin's halls. For a long while it seemed that the Danes were getting the upper hand, for they greatly outnumbered the men on Olaf's dragonship. But as the fight grew fiercer Olaf's berserks worked themselves to a wild fury, and, led by Olaf and Kolbiorn, they made a rush upon the enemy's forecastle, carrying all before them as an autumn wind carries the withered leaves. For three long hours the battle continued, man to man; but at last Olaf got the victory, and took the Dane ship as his prize, with all the treasure and costly armour, all the slaves and stores on board of her. His four longships had not joined in the contest, because it was always considered unfair to oppose an adversary with unequal force. But now they were brought nearer, and when all the wreckage of the fight was cleared away he placed some of his own men on board the prize, divided the spoil among all his fellowship, and once more sailed off, well satisfied with his first success.

Southward he sailed down the Swedish coast, and met with adventures too many to be told. And at length he made for Borgund holm, an island that lies out in the Baltic to the south of Sweden. By this time his stores had run short, so he fell upon the island and harried there. The landsmen came in great force and waged battle against him; but Olaf again won the victory, and got great plunder of horses and cattle.

He lay by Borgund holm for many weeks, with his tents ranged in order along a stretch of the beach, and his ships drawn up to the high water mark. Every day his men held sports, and at night they all sat in their tents drinking and throwing dice, or listening to the sagamen's stories of the great deeds of byegone warriors. Olaf himself joined always in their feasts and revels, and he was ever the merriest and gamesomest in the company.

One day while his ships were still at Borgund holm, his two chief men, Kolbiorn and Thorgils, were boasting of their skill at climbing. They contended as to who could climb the steepest rock, and at last they made a bet. Kolbiorn wagered his gold neck ring against Thorgils' best bronze drinking horn. After this they both climbed the high cliff. Thorgils went so far that he was in danger of falling down, and he returned in fear, saving himself with difficulty. Kolbiorn climbed up to the middle of the precipice; but there he dared go neither forward nor backward, nor even move, for he had no hold upon the rock for either feet or hands. His position was so perilous that he foresaw certain death if

47

he should make the least movement. He shouted in great fear for Olaf or his men to rescue him. Olaf called some brave man to venture the deed and offered a large reward; but not one of his company stirred. Then Olaf threw off his cloak and ran up the face of the rock as though it had been a level plain, took Kolbiorn under his arms, and went farther up with him. He then turned to descend with the man under his arm and laid him unharmed on the ground. All praised this as a great feat, and the fame of it was widely spread. Long afterwards he performed the similar feat of climbing to the topmost peak of the mountain called Smalsarhorn, in Norway, and there suspending his shining shield upon the summit, so that it shone like a sun across the sea.

Many tales are told of his strength and agility--of how he could smite alike with either hand, of how he could shoot with two spears at once. It is said that he could jump higher than his own height both backwards and forwards, and this with his weapons and complete armour on. He was the swiftest and strongest swimmer in all Scandinavia, and at running and climbing no man was his equal.

And yet he was no boaster. His great deeds came of his eagerness in all matters, and not from a desire to belittle his companions. He was kind and lowly hearted, bountiful of gifts, very glorious of attire, and before all men for high heart in battle. It may be that he also was cruel, for it is told that he was stern and wrathful with all who offended him, and that in punishing his enemies he knew no mercy. He, however, sought only to do all things that it was customary for a viking to do. To win fame, to gain wealth, to plunder, and to slay--these were the passions that ruled him. The ocean was his only home. He derided the comforts of a warm fireside and scorned the man who should sleep under a sooty rafter or die on a bed of straw. To give up his last breath amid the clamour of battle was his one unalterable ambition; for only those who died thus, besprinkled with blood, could ever hope to win favour of the pagan gods, or to enter the sacred halls of Valhalla. In the spirit of his times he believed that the viking life was the noblest and most honourable that a man could follow; he believed that the truest title to all property was given by winning it with the sword, and very soon he became as wild and reckless as any sea rover on the Baltic. No danger, howsoever great, had power to daunt him, or to lessen his joy in the fresh freedom of the open sea with its wild hoarse winds and its surging perilous storms.

It was in the autumntide that Olaf encountered the first serious storm. By this time he had added to his fleet many vessels which he had captured in battle, and some that he had had built by his shipwrights; and he bethought him that he would now sail out of the Baltic Sea and make his way round to the coasts of Norway, where, with his great force of men and ships behind him, he might surely hope to win the glory that he coveted. He had kept his favourite companions and his chosen warriors on board his dragonship, so that they might ever be near him in case of need. But Egbert of Britain and Kolbiorn Stallare, after their quarrel over the game of chess, had not been friendly towards each other, so Egbert was placed in command over one of the other vessels of the fleet--a Longship named the *Snake*.

On a certain day the ships were making westward under easy sail when the storm burst suddenly upon them, with a bitter cold wind from the north that quickly whipped the sea into great towering waves. The hail and sleet fell so heavily that the men in the bow of each ship were hidden from those in the stern, and the seas broke over the bulwarks, deluging the decks and cabins, so that the men in the baling room were kept constantly at work with their scoops and buckets. All cried upon Njord, the sea god, and upon Thor and Odin no less, to save them out of their peril; but the raging storm continued throughout the night and the whole of the next day, and all the time Olaf stood

48

at the helm, bravely facing the tempest and keeping his vessel's prow pointing northward to meet the towering waves. Often it seemed that he would be swept overboard by the wild rush of water, but his great strength endured the strain, and though nearly blinded by the pelting hail he still held on.

With the evening of the second day the wind's force abated, and the heavy clouds that had darkened the sky melted away in a glow of sunset gold. Then Olaf looked around upon the wide turbulent sea and counted his ships. Some had lost their masts, and others had been swept far away towards the dim horizon. One of them alone was missing: it was the longship of Egbert of Britain. Olaf had little doubt that she had foundered with all on board, and yet he knew that Egbert was a brave and skilful seaman, and he thought it strange that he should have failed to weather the storm, so, finding no other explanation, he declared that it was because Egbert was a Christian that this disaster had happened. Had he been a true believer in the mighty gods of the northmen, said Olaf, he would surely have surmounted all dangers, and his ship and crew had been saved! And all who heard them regarded the young chief's words as words of wisdom, for they did not know, and neither did Olaf himself at that moment dream, that Egbert and his ship's company were safe and sound in the shelter of the high headland of Borgund holm. Not for many years thereafter did Olaf and Egbert again meet, and when they did so, it was face to face as foemen on the battle plain of Maldon, in far off England.

When the storm had spent its force, and the sea was calm, Olaf brought his ships together, made the needful repairs, and led the way southward to the shores of Wendland. There he got good haven and, faring full peacefully, abode there throughout the winter months.

CHAPTER IX: THE VIKINGS OF JOMSBURG.

Burislaf was the name of the king in Wendland. He was a very wealthy monarch and held in high esteem throughout the countries of the Baltic, and his court was the frequent meeting place of the great men of that time. Now Burislaf had three very beautiful daughters--Geira, Gunnhild, and Astrid--whom many noble and kingly men sought vainly to win in marriage. Geira, the eldest of the three, held rule and dominion in the land, for it was much the wont of mighty kings in those days that they should let the queen, or the eldest daughter, have half the court to sustain it at her own cost out of the revenues that came to her share. So when Geira heard that alien folk were come into Wendland, with a great fleet of viking ships, and that the chief of them was a young man of unusual prowess and noble mien, she sent friendly messengers to the coast and bade the newcomers be her guests that wintertide, for the summer was now far spent, and the weather hard and stormy. And Olaf Triggvison took her bidding, and went with his chosen captains to the court, where he was well received and most hospitably entertained.

It is told that when Geira saw how kingly of aspect Olaf was, and how handsome and courteous withal, she at once yearned for his love and craved that he should wed with her and become a ruler in the land. Many legends which have come down to us from that time even state that she straightway fell a-wooing him, and that in the end they were married, and ruled the realm side by side. But it is not easy to believe that one who was heir to the throne of Norway would be content to remain in Wendland at the bidding of a woman he did not love, and it is to be remembered that Olaf was still little more than a youth, while Geira was already well advanced in years. Moreover, Olaf had at this same time met Thyra, the daughter of the king of Denmark--a princess who was not only more beautiful, but also much nearer his own age than Geira, and who afterwards became his wife and queen. Howsoever it be, Olaf had lived but a few months in Wendland when Geira was stricken with an illness and died.

49

Among the guests of King Burislaf were two men who in the later time had a large share in the shaping of Olaf's destiny, first as his friends, and afterwards as his enemies. Their names were Earl Sigvaldi of Jomsburg and Sweyn of Denmark.

Earl Sigvaldi was the son of Strut-Harald, sometime King of Skaney, and at the time of his meeting with Olaf in Wendland he was lord over the great company of vikings who had their stronghold in Jomsburg. He was a very mighty man, and his wealth and personal prowess were such that Burislaf's daughter Astrid encouraged his wooing of her with the result that they were wedded.

Earl Sweyn was a younger man, the son of Harald Bluetooth, King of Denmark. He had come into Wendland in the company of his friend Sigvaldi, for they had both been a-warring together, and, being beaten in a great sea fight, they had taken refuge in the court of Burislaf. Their warring had been against Sweyn's own father, King Harald. Sweyn had craved dominion in his father's realm, but Harald Bluetooth preferred to retain his throne undivided. Then Sweyn gathered warships together and got the help of the Jomsburg vikings, and stood towards Zealand, where King Harald lay with his fleet ready to fare to the wars against Norway. So Sweyn fell upon his father's ships, and there was a great battle, in which Harald Bluetooth got the victory, but also his death wound. Now the arrow with which King Harald was killed was one bearing marks which showed it to be of his own son's making, and Sweyn fled lest vengeance should overtake him.

Now Sigvaldi, knowing that it would not be long ere the Danes claimed Sweyn as their king, was anxious to assure a peace between Wendland and Denmark, and with this purpose he had brought Sweyn in his company to King Burislaf's court, and it was then arranged that Sweyn should wed Gunnhild, daughter of Burislaf, and that thereafter there should be peace between the two lands. So when the wedding was over, King Sweyn fared home to Denmark with Gunnhild his wife, and they became the parents of Canute the Mighty--the same who in his manhood fought against Edmund Ironsides and reigned as King of England.

In those days the Danes and their neighbours the Wends made great threats of sailing with a host to Norway, and Olaf Triggvison heard much talk of this threatened expedition from Earl Sigvaldi. He learned, too, something of what had been taking place in his native land since the time of the death of King Triggvi.

By their evil work Queen Gunnhild and the sons of Erik Bloodaxe had, as they thought, put an end to the family of Harald Fairhair, for they had lost all trace of Queen Astrid and her boy Olaf, and none remained to dispute the throne of Norway. In the province of Thrandheim, however, there reigned a certain Earl Sigurd, who yet gave them great trouble. To rid themselves of all danger from him they resorted to treachery. They had murdered King Triggvi and his four brothers, and they had little scruple in employing the same means towards Earl Sigurd, so they entrapped him and put him to death. After this deed Harald Greyfell reigned as King of Norway for five troublous and unfruitful years. By the slaying of Earl Sigurd, however, the sons of Erik raised up against themselves an enemy who proved more dangerous to them than any they had yet encountered. This was Earl Hakon, the son of Sigurd, a most powerful and sagacious warrior, whose one desire was to avenge his father's death and drive the whole race of Erik Bloodaxe from the land. Nor was he long in fulfilling his designs. By a daring intrigue, and with help from Denmark, he succeeded not only in bringing King Harald Greyfell to his bane, but also in winning his own way to the throne of Norway. Queen Gunnhild and her two surviving sons then fled over sea to the Orkneys, and that was the end of them.

Now, when Olaf heard these things and understood that Earl Hakon, although not of royal birth or lineage, was still recognized as the king in Norway, he resolved to join issue with the Danes and Wends in their projected expedition, and he spoke with Earl Sigvaldi, offering the support of all his ships and men. Well satisfied was Sigvaldi at hearing this offer made, and he gladly accepted it, for he had quickly discerned that Ole the Esthonian was a young warrior whose help would be most valuable, even apart from the great force of battleships and fighting men that were under his command.

So when the winter had passed by, and the sea was clear of ice, Olaf had his ships refitted, mustered his men, and set sail along the Wendland coast towards the island of Wollin, at the mouth of the river Oder, upon which stood the great stronghold of Jomsburg.

Jomsburg had been founded and built by King Harald Bluetooth of Denmark, who possessed a great earldom in Wendland. He had garrisoned the place with vikings on the condition that they should defend the land, and be always ready to support him in any warlike expedition. There was a very fine harbour or dock made within the Burgh, in which three hundred longships could lie at the same time, all being locked within the strongly built walls of granite with their massive gates of iron. The Jomsburg vikings were a well disciplined company of pirates who made war their exclusive business, living by rapine and plunder. Their firm belief in the heathen gods justified them in following this mode of life, and often they fought for mere fighting's sake. They were bound by very strict laws to obey their chief. No man older than fifty or younger than eighteen winters could be received into the fellowship; they were all to be between these two ages. No man could join the band who was known to have ever yielded in fight to an opponent his match in strength of arms. Every member admitted swore by the hammer of Thor to revenge all the rest as his brother. Slander was forbidden. No woman or child was ever to be molested or carried away as captive, and all the spoil or plunder of war was to be equally divided. One very important law was that no member of the band was ever to utter a word of fear or to flinch from pain, or to attempt to dress his wounds until they had bled for four and twenty hours. Nothing could occur within the Burgh over which the chief should not have full power to rule as he liked. If any broke these rules he was to be punished by instant expulsion from the community.

For two days after the time when Olaf's fleet anchored abreast of the gates of Jomsburg, there was the work of inspecting all his men and ships and arms. Some two score of the men were rejected by Earl Sigvaldi, some because they were at enmity with certain vikings who were already of the band, others because they had killed some near kinsman of one of the members, and yet others who refused to follow or obey any other chief than Olaf Triggvison alone. But the ships and their equipment were all pronounced seaworthy and in good condition; so, after the vows had been made, there was held a great feast, and Olaf was chosen as a captain under Earl Sigvaldi, holding the command of his own division of the Jomsburg fleet.

Now, during the summer months of that same year, Olaf went out upon a viking cruise into the Gulf of Bothnia. On the coast of Jemptland and Helsingialand he encountered many Swedish warships, cleared them, and slew many men, and took all the wealth of them. It was his habit to lie hidden behind some rocky promontory, or at the mouth of some vik, or creek, and thence dart out upon his unsuspecting prey; and he would thus creep along the coast from vik to vik, harrying and plundering wheresoever he went. And in all his battles he never received a wound or lost a ship, but always got the victory. He was accounted the most favoured by the gods among all the vikings of Jomsburg, and his renown spread far and wide.

When Olaf returned at the beginning of the winter to Jomsburg he heard that Earl Sigvaldi's father, Strut-Harald of Skaney, had just died. Now it was the custom in those days that a high born man, before he could take possession of any inheritance left to him by his father, should hold an arvel, or inheritance feast. King Sweyn was at this time preparing to hold such a feast before taking possession of the Danish kingdom, so it was arranged that Sweyn and Sigvaldi should make one arvel serve for them both, and Sweyn sent word to Sigvaldi inviting him with all his captains and chosen warriors to join him in Zealand, and so arrange it that the greatest possible honour should be done to the dead.

Sigvaldi accordingly left Jomsburg with a large host of his vikings and two score of ships. Among his captains were Olaf Triggvison, Kolbiorn Stallare, Bui the Thick of Borgund holm, Thorkel the High, and Vagn Akison. It was winter time, and the seas were rough, but the fleet passed through the Danish islands without disaster, and came to an anchorage in a large bay near which now stands the city of Copenhagen. King Sweyn welcomed Earl Sigvaldi and all his men with great kindness.

The feast was held in a very large hall, specially built for the reception of guests, and ornamented with splendid wood carvings and hung about with peace shields and curtains of beautiful tapestry. King Sweyn was dressed in very fine clothes of purple, with gold rings on his arms and round his neck, and a band of burnished gold, set with gems, upon his head. His beard, which was as yet but short, was trimmed in a peculiar way--divided into two prongs--which won for him the nickname of Sweyn Forkbeard. The tables were loaded with cooked food and white bread; sufficient to serve all the great company for three days. The ale and mead flowed abundantly, and there was much good cheer in the hall. Many high born women were present, and the guests sat in pairs, each man and woman together. Olaf Triggvison had for his partner the Princess Thyra, sister of the king.

In the midst of the feasting Thyra turned to Olaf and asked him his true name.

"Men call me Ole the Esthonian," answered Olaf.

"I had known so much already," returned Thyra. "It is the same name that you bore at the time we first met in Wendland. But when I look at you, and see your silken hair and your fair skin, it seems to me that you must be of kingly birth."

"It is not well always to judge by appearances," Olaf said with a smile. And he drew down the gold ring from the thick part of his bare left arm. Thyra's eyes rested upon his arm for a moment, and she saw imprinted there the seared brand that showed him to have been a slave; and from that moment she ceased to regard him with personal interest.

It was the custom at such feasts as this that the high seat, or throne, of the man whom the guests were met to do honour to, should be left vacant until the memorial toast of the deceased, and of the mightiest of their departed kinsmen, had been proposed. In accordance with this custom King Sweyn stood up and drank the cup of memory to his father. Then he stepped into the high seat, and by this act took possession of his inheritance. The cup was filled and emptied to the last drop by each man in turn.

The Jomsburg vikings drank eagerly on that first evening, and ever as their drinking horns were emptied they were filled again, brimming of the strongest. After it had gone on thus for a while, King Sweyn saw that his guests were nearly all drunk.

"Here is great merriment," said he, rising and holding aloft his silver drinking horn. "And I propose that we shall find a new entertainment which will long hereafter be remembered."

Sigvaldi answered, "We think it most becoming and best for the entertainment, that you, lord, should make the first proposal, for we all have to obey you and follow your example."

52

Then the king laughed and said: "I know it has always been customary at great feasts and meetings that all present should make vows to perform great and valorous deeds, and I am willing to try that now. For, as you, Jomsvikings, are far more famous than all other men in this northern half of the world, so the vows you will make here will be as much more renowned than others, as you are greater than other men. And to set you an example, I will myself begin."

He filled his drinking horn to the brim and held it high, while all waited eagerly and silently to hear what vow he should make.

"This it is," said he in a loud voice which those at the farthest end of the hall could clearly hear. "I vow that I will, before the third winter nights hereafter have passed, have driven King Ethelred of England out of his realm, or else have slain him, and thus have got his kingdom to myself!"

And so saying he quaffed his deep horn.

All wondered at this great vow, for not many had heard even the name of King Ethelred.

"Now it is thy turn, Sigvaldi," cried Sweyn, wiping his wet lips with the back of his hand, "and make no less a vow than mine."

Then the drink bearers bore to the vikings the biggest horns of the strongest drink that was there, and Sigvaldi rose to his feet. He first proposed the memory of his dead father, and before raising the drink to his lips added this oath:

"I swear," said he, "that before three winters are worn away I will sail over to Norway and slay Earl Hakon, or else drive him from the land."

Now, this was the selfsame oath that Olaf Triggvison had resolved to swear when it should come to his turn, and he was annoyed that Earl Sigvaldi had, as it were, snatched it from his lips. He now thought over what other vow he could make in its stead. But it chanced that ere his turn came round all the company were either asleep or so full of strong drink that they could not listen, so in the end he made no vow whatsoever. Yet to the last he was as sober as when he first entered the hall, and he remembered ever afterwards the boastful oaths that had been made. Many of his fellow vikings--as Thorkel the High, Bui the Thick, and Vagn Akison--declared that they would but follow their chief to Norway, while others of Sweyn's following in like manner vowed to accompany the king to England; and once having made these promises, none dared to go back from them.

On the morrow, when the vikings regained their senses, they thought they had spoken big words enough, so they met and took counsel how they should bring about this expedition against Earl Hakon, and the end of it was that they determined to set about it as early as might be. For the rest of that wintertide the men of Jomsburg accordingly bestirred themselves in making preparations for the journey. They fitted out their best warships and loaded them with weapons, and their warriors were mustered to the number of eight thousand well trained men, with eighty chosen battleships.

So, when the snows of that winter had melted in the vales and the seas were clear of ice floes, Sigvaldi led his host north through the Eyr Sound and lay for a time in Lyme Firth. There he divided his forces, leaving twenty of Olaf Triggvison's longships in the firth, so that they might perchance intercept Earl Hakon should he escape the main fleet. This was an ill judged measure, but Sigvaldi was not aware that the forces of Earl Hakon were vastly superior in number to his own. Olaf's ships were left in the charge of Kolbiorn Stallare, while Olaf himself went aboard the dragonship of Vagn Akison.

Earl Sigvaldi then sailed out into the main with sixty ships, and came to Agdir, in the south of Norway. And there he fell to pillaging in the dominion of Earl Hakon.

CHAPTER X: THE BATTLE OF JOMSVIKINGS.

The rumour of the bold vows that the Jomsvikings had made spread quickly throughout the land, and tidings of the great war gathering soon reached Norway. Earl Erik Hakonson heard them in good time at the place where he abode in Raum realm, and he straightway gathered his folk about him and fared to the Uplands, and so north over the fells to Thrandheim to meet Earl Hakon, his father. Now Earl Hakon greatly feared the vikings of Jomsburg, and on hearing this news he sent abroad the war arrow all about the Thrandheim country, and to Mere and Raumsdale, north also into Naumdale and Halogaland; and in answer to this summons there assembled a vast fleet of warships to the number of one hundred and eighty keels, and a force amounting to eleven thousand men. So many vessels and warriors had never before been seen together in the fiords.

Now there was a man named Giermund who was out sailing in a fishing skiff among the Her isles. He fared north to Mere, and there he fell in with Earl Hakon, and told the earl tidings of a host that had come to the land from Denmark.

"How can I know that what you tell is true?" asked the earl. "And what token have you to show?"

Giermund drew forth his right arm with the hand smitten off at the wrist.

"By this token may you know that these ships have come," said he.

Then Earl Hakon questioned the man closely concerning this new come enemy, and Giermund told him that the men were vikings of Jomsburg, and that they had slain many people of the land, and had robbed far and wide.

"Swiftly northward are they coming," said he, "and full eagerly, and no long time will wear by ere they are come upon you."

So thereupon the earl rowed through the firths with his fleet to meet his foes.

The Jomsvikings had sailed northward along the coast, plundering and ravaging wherever they landed. They made great coast raids, and often burned towns and hamlets. They were lying in Ulfasound, off Stad, when they and Hakon Jarl heard of each other. They were in want of food at this time, and Vagn Akison and Olaf Triggvison went on their skiff to the island of Hoed, not knowing that the earl lay in the bay near the island. Vagn and Olaf landed with their men, wishing to make a shore raid if they could, and they happened to meet a shepherd driving three cows and twelve goats.

Vagn cried to his men: "Take the cows and goats and slaughter them for our ships."

The shepherd asked: "Who commands the men on board your ship?"

"Vagn Akison, of Jomsburg," was the answer.

"I think then, that there are not very far from you bigger cattle for slaughter than my poor cows and goats," said the shepherd.

Vagn did not understand his meaning. But Olaf Triggvison looked at the man with quick apprehension, and said:

"If you know anything about the journey of Hakon Jarl, tell us at once. And if you can truthfully tell us where he is, then your cows and goats are safe."

The shepherd did not speak for many moments, but at last he answered calmly: "Jarl Hakon lay yesternight with one or two ships under shelter of the island of Hoed, and you can slay him when you like, for he is still anchored in the bay waiting for his men."

"Then your cattle are safe," rejoined Vagn. "And you shall have a good reward if you will come aboard our ship and show us the way into the bay."

Ulf--for such was the shepherd's name--went on board the skiff early in the day, and Vagn Akison, as quickly as he could, returned to the Jomsburg fleet and told the news, which spread speedily round the ships. Earl Sigvaldi at once weighed anchor and rowed out north of the island, giving word meanwhile to his vikings to make ready for battle.

Greatly did Olaf Triggvison rejoice at this immediate prospect of attacking and vanquishing the proud man who had for sixteen years held sovereign sway in Norway. If, as Ulf the shepherd had reported, Earl Hakon had but one or two ships, then it would be a very easy matter for the Jomsburgers to vanquish him, and who could tell what glorious results might not follow? Despite the fact that he was not himself the leader of this present expedition, Olaf was confident that the expected victory must bring about the furtherance of his own personal plans. It might indeed be that Earl Sigvaldi, on proving himself the easy conqueror, would attempt to place himself in possession of the realm, and to assume the name and dignity of King of Norway. But Olaf, ever hopeful and buoyant, trusted that with very little trouble on his own part, he could readily prove to the people that he, the direct descendant of Harald Fairhair, had claims of which neither Sigvaldi nor even the great Earl Hakon could justly boast.

In his passage with the viking ships up the coast of western Norway, Olaf had looked for the first time upon the wild splendour of the fiords, with their deep blue reaches of the sea penetrating far inland between steep precipices braided with sparkling waterfalls. He had seen the giant mountains rising high into the sky, with their rugged summits capped with snow and their lower slopes covered with vast forests of tall pine trees. Often some fertile valley had opened out before him, with verdant pastures and narrow strips of arable land. This was the country over which King Harald Fairhair had ruled, and now, for the first time, Olaf had realized the greatness of his heritage. He determined to fight boldly and fearlessly in this coming battle, so that he might thus win his way nearer to the possession of his birthright and the goal of his growing ambitions.

He had been placed in command of one of the largest dragonships, and while the fleet was sailing round the island--his own vessel being side by side with that of Vagn Akison--he went below and dressed himself in his strongest armour, and took up his heavy battleaxe and the well tempered sword that King Valdemar had given him. The weather was bright and warm, and he wore no cloak, but only his closely knit coat of chain mail, with his brass helmet, crested with a winged dragon, and his bossed shield. His long fair hair that fell down over his broad shoulders, his finely marked features, his beautiful blue eyes and clear ruddy complexion were on this day more evident than ever before; and his firm muscular limbs and stalwart figure distinguished him as the noblest and handsomest man in all the company of the vikings.

When he returned on deck he went at once to his post at the tiller and looked out over the blue sunlit sea. A lusty cry rose at this instant from the prow of Sigvaldi's dragonship. The fleet was now abreast of a low lying point of land at the inner coast of Hoed Isle, and it was now seen that the wide bay beyond was crowded all over with vessels of war. Ulf the shepherd had betrayed the vikings into the hands of their awaiting foe. When his treachery was discovered he ran to the rail of Vagn Akison's ship and leapt overboard, intending to swim to the shore without waiting for his reward. Vagn threw a spear at him, but missed his aim. Olaf Triggvison, who saw the shepherd swimming astern, caught up a spear with his left hand and flung it at him. It hit him in the middle and killed him.

The Jomsvikings rowed with their sixty ships into the great bay. They were formed into three divisions, and Earl Sigvaldi laid his flagship in the centre of the line of battle. To the north of him he arrayed twenty ships under the command of Bui the Thick and Sigurd Kapa, while Vagn Akison and Olaf Triggvison held the southern wing.

Earl Hakon determined which of his captains should fight against these champions. It was customary in such battles for ship to fight against ship and man against man; but in most cases Hakon, whose forces greatly outnumbered those of his enemies, placed three

55

of his longships against one of the vikings'. He himself was not matched against any one, but had to support the whole line and command it. His son Sweyn held the chief position in the centre of battle, facing the leader of the vikings. Against the division of Bui was placed a great Norwegian warrior named Thorkel Leira. The wing held by Vagn Akison and Olaf Triggvison was opposed by Earl Hakon's eldest son, Erik. Each chief had his own banner in the shield burg at his prow.

War horns were sounded, arrows of challenge were fired over the opposing fleets, the berserks on either side clashed their arms and bit the rims of their shields, working themselves into a wild war fury. Then the fleets closed in upon each other amid a storm of arrows, and the grim battle began.

The ships of the vikings were higher in the hull than those of the Norwegians, and this gave them an advantage, for, when the grapplings were thrown out and the ships were lashed together, the Jomsburgers could fire their arrows and spears down upon the heads of their foes. The onset and attack were faultlessly made, and for a long while it seemed uncertain which side was getting the better hand. But at length Earl Hakon, who was supporting his son Sweyn against Sigvaldi, saw that his northern wing was being forced backward, and he hastened to its aid. Nevertheless, Bui the Thick still pressed the Norwegians back with heavy blows and a ceaseless rain of arrows and spears, and it seemed that at this point the vikings were quickly gaining the victory. On the southern wing, however, the fight was more equal, and Earl Erik thought that he would go to his brother's help. He went thither, accordingly, but could do no more than set the wing in line again. Hakon then returned to fight against Sigvaldi.

Now, by this short absence, Earl Erik had weakened the southern wing, and, when he came back to defend his ships, he found that Vagn Akison and Olaf Triggvison had broken through the line and made great havoc. Erik was a brave warrior, however, and he did not hesitate to make a bold attack upon the ships of these two champions. He encountered them with four of his best longships against their two. The battle at this point now grew furious, and the carnage on both sides was tremendous. Vagn and Olaf, followed by their berserks, jumped on board Erik's ship, and each went along either side of her, clearing his way, so that all fell back before the mighty blows. Erik saw that these two warriors were so fierce and mad that he would not long be able to withstand them, and that Earl Hakon's help must be got as quickly as possible. Yet he goaded his men on, and they made a brave resistance. Olaf was often attacked by three or four berserks at once, but he guarded every blow, and received but little hurt. He fought whiles with his sword and whiles with his battleaxe, and at times even with both weapons, one in either hand, dealing many hard and heavy blows, and slaying many a man. And ever when the decks were cleared there came on board other hosts of men from the neighbouring ships. Olaf wanted to come to a hand to hand combat with Earl Erik, but Erik always avoided him.

In the midst of this conflict one of Erik's men went forward and cut the lashings that bound the ships together, so that Olaf's dragonship drifted apart. Olaf noticed this, and he fought his way across the deck to where Vagn Akison was. At this moment there was a great onrush of Norwegians, and Vagn and Olaf sought the safety of one of their own ships. They jumped on board of her, and had her rowed some distance away, so that they might rest themselves and make ready for a new attack.

There was then a pause in the battle, and it was seen that Earl Hakon's ship had been taken landward, out of reach of the Jomsvikings' arrows. The legend tells that, seeing the battle going against him, he took some men ashore with him, together with his little son Erling--a lad of seven years of age. Entering a forest glade he prayed to the gods, and offered to propitiate them by making human sacrifice. When he thought that his vows and prayers were heard, he took young Erling and put him to death. Then he returned to the battle, and there was a sudden change in the weather. The sky began to darken in the north, and a heavy black cloud glided up from the sea, spreading quickly. A shower of hailstones followed at once, and the Jomsvikings had to fight with their faces against the blinding storm, which was so terrible that some of the men could do no more than stand against it, as they had previously taken off their clothes on account of the heat. They began to shiver, though for the most part they fought bravely enough.

Hakon Jarl now had the advantage, confident that the gods had accepted the sacrifice of his son, and intended to give him the victory. It is said that some saw the maidens of Odin, the Valkyrias, standing at the prow of Hakon's ship, sending forth a deadly hail of unerring arrows.

The vikings fought half blindly, though they were sorely pressed, and their decks were slippery with the slush of blood and melting hail, and in spite of the twilight and the raging storm they still held their own. But at last Earl Sigvaldi began to lose heart.

"It seems to me," he cried, "that it is not men whom we have to fight today, but the worst fiends."

Some one reminded him of the vow he had taken at King Sweyn's inheritance feast.

"I did not vow to fight against fiends!" he answered; and, seeing Earl Hakon making ready for a renewed onslaught, he added: "Now I will flee, and all my men with me, for the battle is worse than when I spoke of it before, and I will stand it no longer."

He turned away his ship, shouting to Vagn and Bui, whose ships were now close to his own, to follow in all haste. But these two champions were braver than their chief. Vagn Akison saw Sigvaldi retreating, and cried out to him in a frenzy of rage:

"Why dost thou flee, thou evil hound, and leave thy men in the lurch? That shame shall cling to thee all the days of thy life!"

Earl Sigvaldi made no reply, and it was well for him that he did not; for at the same instant a spear was hurled from Vagn's hand at the man who was at the helm, in the post usually occupied by the chief. But Sigvaldi, being cold, had taken one of the oars to warm himself, so that the man at the rudder was killed instead.

Confusion now spread throughout the fleet of the vikings. The line was broken, and five and twenty of their ships followed in the wake of Earl Sigvaldi. At last only Vagn Akison and Bui the Thick were left. And now Earl Hakon pulled up alongside the ship of Bui, and a combat ensued, which has scarcely had its equal in all the battles of the Northmen. Two great berserks of Jomsburg--Havard the Hewer and Aslak Rockskull-- vaulted over the gunwale of Hakon's ship and made tremendous havoc, until an Icelander seized an anvil that lay on the deck and dashed it against Aslak's head. Havard had both his feet cut off, but fought on furiously, standing on his knees. The spears and arrows whizzed about the head of Earl Hakon, and his coat of mail was so rent and cut that it fell off from him. It seemed now that the few Jomsvikings who were left would have the glory of victory all to themselves. But in the thick of the fight Earl Erik Hakonson, with a throng of men, boarded the galley of Bui the Thick, and in the first onslaught Bui received a sword cut across his lips and chin. He did not flinch, but tried to pass off his injury with a jest.

"The pretty women in Borgund holm will not now be so fond of kissing me," said he.

Then the Norwegians pressed in a great throng against him, and he saw that further resistance was useless. He took up two chests of gold, one in either arm, and mounting the gunwale of his ship, cried out: "Overboard all folk of Bui!" and sprang into the sea.

57

Thereupon many of his men followed his example, while the rest were slain. So was Bui's ship cleared from stem to stern.

Vagn Akison and Olaf Triggvison were now the only two champions remaining out of all the vikings of Jomsburg, and they had no more than fifty men to support them. Earl Erik now boarded their dragonship, and there was a fierce fight. But the Norwegians had the larger company, and when all but thirty of the vikings were slain, Vagn Akison surrendered and called upon Olaf to follow his example.

"Never shall it be said that I surrendered to any man!" cried Olaf proudly. "Rather would I die fighting."

And, gripping his battleaxe, he prepared to resist all who should come near him. But strong and valiant though he was, he could not hold his own against the crowd of warriors then gathered about him. He was seized from behind, disarmed, and bound hand and foot with strong ropes. In like manner were Vagn Akison and all the other captives bound.

At nightfall they were taken to the shore where Earl Hakon had landed and pitched his tents.

Now, it was a question with Earl Hakon what he should do with these thirty captives. He did not doubt that, because they were all that remained of the Jomsburgers, they were therefore the bravest and stoutest of all the vikings who had engaged in the great battle, and he feared that if they were allowed to live they would surely bring some great trouble upon him. So he ordered them to be slain. This order, added to the fact of his having sacrificed his own son for the sake of victory, was remembered against him by the Norwegians in the after time, and it went far towards gaining for him the hatred of his people.

Early in the morning Vagn and Olaf, with their thirty comrades, were led out in front of the tents for execution. They were made to sit in a row on the trunk of a fallen tree. Their feet were bound with ropes, but their hands were left free. The man who was to act as executioner was one Thorkel Leira, a stalwart warrior, who had done great deeds in the battle. Now, this same Thorkel was an old enemy of Vagn Akison, and at the arvel of King Sweyn, Vagn had taken a solemn oath that he would be the death of him. It seemed that, like all the other vikings who had spoken so boldly at that feast, Vagn was to be cheated of his vow, yet he resolved to meet his death bravely.

When all was ready Thorkel appeared before the captives, carrying a great axe. He put Vagn Akison at the end of the log, intending to keep him to the last in order to increase his agony. But Vagn sat chatting and joking with his companions, and there was much laughter. Earl Hakon wanted to know if these men were as hardy, and if their disregard of death were as firm, as report told, and each of them, when his turn came to be dealt with by the executioner, was asked some question, as--"How likest thou to die?" and each answered in his own fashion.

"I should not be a worthy Jomsviking if I were afraid of death," said one; and then Thorkel dealt him the blow. Another said: "It is a great satisfaction to die by the hand of a brave warrior, although I would like better if I were allowed a chance of first striking a blow at him." And a third: "I shall at least die in good company; but first, let me tighten my belt." One of them said: "I like very well to die, but strike me quickly; I have my cloak clasp in my hand, and I will thrust it into the earth if I wot of anything after my head is off." So the head was smitten from him, and down fell the clasp from his nerveless hand.

Eighteen of the vikings had been slain when it came to the turn of Olaf Triggvison, and at this moment Earl Erik came upon the scene. Olaf bared his neck, and swept up his long golden hair in a coil over his head.

"Let none of the blood fall upon my hair!" said he. So Thorkel told one of the bystanders to hold the coil of hair while he struck off Olaf's head. The man took the beautiful hair in his two hands and held it fast, while Olaf stretched forth his neck. Thorkel hove up his axe. Then Olaf snatched back his head sharply, and so it happened that the blow hit the man who had hold of his hair, and the axe took off both his hands.

"Who is this goodly young man?" asked Earl Erik, stepping forward in front of Olaf.

"The lads call me Ole the Esthonian," Olaf replied.

"You are no Esthonian born," returned Erik. "Of what land are you, then?"

"What matters it, so long as I am from Jomsburg?" asked Olaf.

"I had thought you were of Norway," Erik said, "and if that be so it were not well that you should die. What is your age?"

Olaf answered: "If I live this winter I shall be three and twenty winters old."

Erik said, "You shall live this winter if I have my will, for I do not like to see one so handsome and strong put to such a death as this. Will you have peace?"

"That depends upon who it is that offers me life," said Olaf.

"He offers it who has the power--Earl Erik himself," answered the earl.

"Then I gladly accept," said Olaf. And Earl Erik ordered his men to set Olaf free from his tether.

At this Thorkel Leira grew wrothful, fearing that since the earl was in a forgiving mood he himself would perhaps be thwarted in his vengeance on Vagn Akison.

"Though you, Earl Erik, give peace to all these men," he cried, "yet never shall Vagn Akison depart hence alive." And brandishing his axe he rushed towards his enemy. One of the men on the log, however, seeing his chief's danger, flung himself forward so that Thorkel stumbled and fell, dropping his axe. Instantly Vagn Akison sprang to his feet, seized the axe, and dealt Thorkel Leira his death blow.

Thus Vagn Akison was the only one of the Jomsvikings who accomplished what he had vowed to do.

Earl Erik, full of admiration of this feat, then said to Vagn:

"Will you have peace, Vagn Akison?"

"I will take peace gladly if it be that all my comrades have it also," answered the viking.

"Let them all be set free," ordered the earl. And so it was done. Eighteen of the captives had already been executed, but fourteen had peace.

These remaining fourteen, as the price of their liberty, were expected to take service under Earl Hakon. Even Olaf made a pretence of agreeing to this condition, and he helped the Norwegians to clear the devastation of battle and to take possession of the various viking ships that had been either deserted by their crews or whose fighting men had all been slain. But he had no intention to abide by his compact. In the general confusion he contrived to get on board his own disabled dragonship. There he exchanged his tattered armour for a good suit of seaman's clothes, with a large cloak, a sword, and a bag of gold. He remained on board until nightfall, and then, dropping into a small sailing boat that he had been careful to provide himself with, he stole out of the bay and was soon far away among the skerries, safe from all pursuit.

The disappearance of Olaf Triggvison was scarcely remarked by the Norwegians, who were at that time holding high revel in celebration of their victory. But had Earl Hakon of Lade been able to look into the future, and see the disasters that awaited him at the hands of this fair haired young viking, he would surely have swept every fiord and channel in Norway in the endeavour to drag the runaway back and bring him to the doom that he had so easily escaped.

CHAPTER XI: WEST-OVER-SEA.

Now when Earl Sigvaldi, finding that the chances of war were going so directly against him, fled from the battle, many of the vikings followed him in the belief that he was but intending to make a new rally and to presently return to the fray. That the chief of Jomsburg could be guilty of mean cowardice surpassed their understanding; moreover, they were bound by their oaths to obey him in all things. Some twenty of his ships followed him out of the bay, and the captains watched him, ready to turn back with him at his first signal. But Sigvaldi made no signal whatsoever, and only showed, by his extreme haste, that he was indeed bent upon making an unworthy and cowardly retreat.

Justin and Guthmund, two of the viking captains who were sailing in the chief's wake, turned their ships and cried aloud to their neighbours to go back with them to the battle and to the rescue of the brave men who had been so heedlessly deserted; and many put about their prows. But already it was too late: not only were the fortunes of the fight now entirely in the hands of the Norwegians, but the storm of hail and wind, which was growing every moment more severe, made it impossible for the ships to make headway against its fury. All who followed Sigvaldi were therefore ever afterwards accused of cowardice, notwithstanding that the larger number of them were both willing and anxious to return.

Southward before the wind sailed Sigvaldi in all haste, until he entered one of the wider channels; and then the storm ceased as suddenly as it had begun. In the evening the ships took shelter under the lee of one of the islands, and there they were anchored, so that the decks might be cleared and put in good order. That night, unknown to the chief, a council was held, and the captains, headed by Guthmund, decided that they would no longer serve or obey a leader who had so far forgotten the strict laws of the vikings as to show fear in the face of an enemy.

In the early morning, therefore, when Earl Sigvaldi hoisted his standard and made out for the open sea, none followed him. He quickly guessed the reason, and, instead of attempting to win over his former friends, he had his sail set to the wind and sped out westward across the sea.

Guthmund was then elected commander of the twenty longships, and when Sigvaldi's vessel had passed out of sight the anchors were weighed and the little fleet moved southward among the isles. Here, where the channels were narrow, and dangerous with hidden rocks, sails were of little use, and the men, wearied with fighting and smarting from their wounds, had little strength left for labouring at the oars, so that progress was slow.

The ships were still but a few miles to the south of Ulfasound very early on the third morning, when they fell in with a small sailing boat far out beyond the sight of land. The boat had only one man in it, and he sat at the stern, holding the sheet in one hand and the tiller in the other. His head was bowed, and his chin rested on his chest. He was sound asleep.

Guthmund, whose ship was nearest, called aloud to him, asking if he had caught any fish that night. But the boatman still slept. Then Guthmund took up an arrow and fired it so that it struck the boat's mast. In an instant the man started to his feet, threw off his cloak, and stood up. The morning sunlight shone on his head of tangled gold hair and on part of his coat of chain mail. He looked very noble and beautiful, and all the shipmen stared at him in amazement.

"By the ravens of Odin! It is young Ole the Esthonian!" cried Guthmund. And he called to Olaf to come aboard.

Olaf at first refused, saying that although he had been without food for two days and was also sick and weak from loss of blood and the want of rest, yet he would never demean himself by taking the hospitality of men who had deserted their comrades in the heat of battle.

"Where is Earl Sigvaldi?" he cried. "Let me see him that I may tell him to his face that he is a coward!"

"We have broken off from him, and are no longer his men," answered Guthmund. "He has sailed west over the sea towards the Orkneys. We are now without a chief, and would be very well satisfied if you, who are a well proved champion, would take the command over us; and we will one and all take oath to serve you and follow you wheresoever you may choose to lead us."

"If that be so, and if there are none but brave men among you," said Olaf, "then I will do as you suggest."

And he brought his boat to the quarter and climbed on board.

When he had taken drink and food and had washed himself and combed his hair, he told of how the battle had ended and of how he had escaped.

Now the vikings were well pleased to have such a chief as Olaf Triggvison, for not only had they the fullest confidence in his prowess, in his skill as a leader of men, and in his unfailing bravery, but they also remembered that he was the owner of the squadron of battleships which had been left in Jutland in charge of Kolbiorn Stallare; and they rightly guessed that Olaf, with these combined fleets, would not rest long ere he should start on some new and warlike expedition.

During the southward voyage nothing was said by Olaf concerning his plans. But when he joined his other fleet in Lyme Firth, he went straightway on board his dragonship and held council with Kolbiorn. Glad was Kolbiorn to see his master once again, and they greeted each other as brothers.

"It seems to me," said Kolbiorn, when Olaf had told him of the defeat of the Jomsvikings, "that now with these forty ships that are ours we might very well fare to Norway, and take vengeance upon Earl Hakon. If we could take him unawares our chance of defeating him would be great, and who can tell but you would succeed where Sigvaldi failed, and so make yourself the King of Norway?"

But Olaf shook his head.

"Not so," said he; "Earl Hakon is a much greater man than you think, Kolbiorn. His power is well established in the land, and his people are well content and prosperous under his rule. I am not afraid to meet him in battle. But our forces are very small compared with the great host of men and ships that Hakon could muster at any moment, and to attempt this journey you propose would only mean disaster. A better plan have I been nursing in my mind these three days past."

"What plan is that?" Kolbiorn asked.

Olaf answered: "When we were at King Sweyn's inheritance feast the oath that Sweyn made was, that he meant to fare across the seas to England and drive King Ethelred from his realm. Now it appears to me that England offers a far easier conquest than Norway, or Sweyn Forkbeard would never have resolved to make such an attempt. I have heard that King Ethelred is but a youth--five years younger than myself--that he is not a fighting man, but a weak fool. Certain it is that he has very few ships to defend his coasts. Moreover, the people of England are Christians, and it seems to me that we should be doing a great service to Odin and Thor, and all others of our own gods, if we were to sweep away all the Christian temples and restore the worship of the gods of Asgard. Whereas, if we make war in Norway we fight against those who worship as we ourselves worship, we slay men who speak the same tongue as we speak, whose blood is our own blood, and whose homes are the homes of our own birthland. Many Norsemen have reaped great plunder in England and have made great settlements on the English coasts. Why should not we follow their example?--nay, why should we not conquer the whole kingdom?"

Kolbiorn strode to and fro in the cabin without at first expressing any opinion on this bold scheme.

"We have now between seven and eight thousand men," continued Olaf.

"A small enough force with which to invade a great nation such as England," said Kolbiorn. "I think there would be a far greater chance of success if we joined with Sweyn Forkbeard."

"My experience with Earl Sigvaldi has already taught me that I can manage with better success when I am my own master," said Olaf. "Moreover, King Sweyn is at present at enmity with the Danish people, and it would not be easy for him to go a-warring in foreign lands without the risk of losing his own throne. The glory or the failure of this expedition must be ours alone, and so soon as we can make ready our ships I intend to set sail."

Now it was at about this time that Olaf Triggvison's followers gave him the name of king. It was a title which the sea rovers of the north often gave to the man whom they had chosen as their chief, and it implied that he was a leader who ruled over warriors and who had acquired a large number of warships. Not often did such a king possess lands. His realm was the sea--"Ran's land"--and his estates were his ships. In the English chronicles and histories of this period, Olaf is referred to as King of the Norwegians; but he was not yet a king in the sense that Sweyn Forkbeard was King of Denmark or Ethelred King of England. The fact that he was of royal birth was held a secret until long after his invasion of England and his subsequent friendship with King Ethelred. Nevertheless, his companions called him King Ole, and the name clung to him throughout all his wanderings.

There were many wounded men on board the ships, and, while Olaf was still lying in Lyme Firth, some of them died; others, whose limbs were lamed and who were no longer able to work at the oars or to engage in battle, were left behind in Jutland. Only those who were in every way fit and strong were allowed to remain in the fleet. When all was ready Olaf hoisted his standard and arrayed his war shields and set out to sea.

To Saxland first he sailed. There he harried along the coasts and got a good store of cattle and corn, and won many men and two other ships to his following. Then about Friesland and the parts that are now covered by the Zuyder Zee, and so right away south to the land of the Flemings. By this time the autumn was far advanced, and Olaf thought that he would seek out some creek or river in Flanders where he might lie up for the winter.

On a certain sunny evening he was out upon the deeper sea in one of his fast sailing skiffs. He chanced to look across the water in the direction of the setting sun, and far away on the line of the horizon he espied a ridge of white cliffs. Thorgils Thoralfson was at his side, and the foster brothers spoke together concerning this land that they saw. They presently determined that it could be no other country than England. So they put about their skiff and returned to the fleet.

At noon on the following day the forty-two ships were within a few miles of the North Foreland of Kent. The cliffs stood out white as snow against the gray autumn sky, and where the line of the headland dipped the grassy slopes of a fertile valley could be seen dotted over with browsing sheep.

Olaf Triggvison steered his dragonship down the coast, until at length he saw a film of blue smoke that rose in the calm air above the little seaport of Sandwich. The town stood at the mouth of a wide creek whose banks sloped backward into sandy dunes and heather covered knolls. The river lost itself in a forest of beech trees that still held their trembling leaves that the summer sun had turned to a rich russet brown. Across one of the meadows a herd of cattle was being driven home to the safety of one of the farmsteads. Olaf turned his ship's head landward and blew a loud blast of his war horn. The shrill notes were echoed from the far off woods. His fleet closed in about his wake, and he led the way inward to the creek, rowing right up to the walls that encircled the town. A few arrows were fired. But already the folk had fled from their homes alarmed at the sight of so large a force, and the invaders landed without the shedding of a drop of blood.

When the ships had been safely moored in the harbour, with their masts lowered and their figureheads taken down, Olaf had his tents sent ashore, and he made an encampment along the margin of the river and in the shelter of the beech woods. His armourers built their forges and his horsemen their stables. A small temple was formed of heavy stones and dedicated to Odin; and so the northmen made ready their winter quarters and prepared to follow their daily lives in accordance with old time customs. There was pure water to be got in abundance from the higher parts of the river, while fish could be got near hand from out the sea. When corn and meat fell short, it was an easy matter to make a foraging raid upon some inland farm or monastery. At such times Olaf would send forth one of his captains, or himself set out, with a company of horsemen, and they would ride away through Kent, or even into Surrey, pillaging and harrying without hindrance, and returning to the camp after many days driving before them the cattle and swine that they had taken, each bullock and horse being loaded with bags of corn or meal.

These journeys were undertaken only for the sake of providing food for the vikings and not with the thought of conquest. And, indeed, Olaf would often give ample payment to the folk who were discreet enough to show him no resistance, for he had a great store of gold and richly wrought cloth upon his ships, and his heart was always generous. But at the monasteries and holy places he made no such return, for he was a great enemy of Christianity.

All through that winter he remained unmolested, in peaceful possession of the two towns of Sandwich and Richborough.

Now the monks of Canterbury and Rochester were greatly annoyed by the near presence of the heathen pirates, and they sent messengers to their king, telling him that the Norsemen had made this settlement upon his coasts and imploring his protection. It was no great news to King Ethelred, however. The Danes and Norwegians had so often made descents upon the English shores that it seemed to him useless to oppose them; so he sent word back to the monks that if their monasteries and churches were in danger it would be well to build them stronger, but that, for his own part, he had quite enough to trouble him without raising armies to fight against a pack of wolves. As well, he said, fight against the sea birds that eat the worms upon our fields.

This calm indifference of the English king only gave greater boldness to Olaf Triggvison, who very naturally considered that the monarch who would thus allow an alien foe to settle upon his shores must be a very child in weakness--a man with no more spirit than a shrew mouse.

Not without cause was King Ethelred nicknamed The Unready. The name stands not as meaning that he was unprepared, but that he was without counsel, or "redeless". His advisers were few and, for the most part, traitorous and unworthy; they swayed him and directed him just as it suited their own ends, and he had not the manly strength of will that would enable him to act for himself. Of energy he had more than enough, but it was always misplaced. In personal character he was one of the weakest of all the kings of England, and his reign was the worst and most shameful in English history. In the golden days of his father, Edgar the Peaceable, all things had gone exceeding well in the land. There was a strong and well disciplined navy to protect the coasts, and all intending invaders were held in defiance. Edgar did much for the good order and prosperity of his kingdom, and he personally saw to the administration of justice and the forming of good laws; trade and husbandry were encouraged by him, and commerce with foreign lands was increased. Archbishop Dunstan was his friend and counsellor. After the death of Edgar came the short reign of Edward the Martyr, whose murder at Corfe Castle brought about the fall of Dunstan and the enthronement of Ethelred.

Ethelred was but ten years old on his coronation at Kingston. Little is told of the early years of his reign, and nothing to the young king's credit. Already the great fleet raised by Edgar had disappeared, and the vikings of the north had begun once more to pillage the coasts. There were other troubles, too. London was burnt to the ground, a great murrain of cattle happened for the first time in the English nation, and a terrible plague carried off many thousands of the people. For some unknown reason Ethelred laid siege to Rochester, and, failing to take the town, ravaged the lands of the bishopric. And now, with the coming of Olaf Triggvison, a new danger was threatening.

Olaf was the first of the vikings to attempt anything like a planned invasion on a large scale, and his partial success was the signal for a yet greater descent of the northmen, which had for its object the conquest of the whole kingdom. It was Olaf Triggvison who, if he failed in his own attempt, at least pointed out the way by which King Sweyn of Denmark and his greater son Canute at length gained possession of the throne of England and infused the nation with the blood which now flows in the veins of every true born Briton. The ocean loving vikings of the north were the ancestors of the English speaking people of today. Our love of the sea and of ships, the roving spirit that has led us to make great colonies in distant lands, our skill in battle, our love of manly sports, even perhaps our physical strength and endurance--all these traits have come to us from our forefathers of Scandinavia. Nor must it be forgotten that the Normans, who conquered England just five and seventy years after the landing of Olaf, were themselves the sons of the vikings. Rolf the Ganger was a famous warrior in the service of King Harald Fairhair. Exiled by Harald from Norway, he made a settlement in northern France, whither many of his countrymen followed him. That part of France was thereafter named Normannia, or Normandy--the land of the Norsemen. Rolf was there made a duke. His son William was the father of Richard the Fearless, who was the grandfather of the great William the Conqueror.

Now, when that same wintertide had passed, and when the new buds were showing on the trees, Olaf Triggvison arrayed his ships ready for the sea. Leaving some of his older men in occupation of Sandwich, he stood out northward past Thanet and across the mouth of the Thames towards East Anglia, where, as he understood, the bravest of the English people dwelt. His four best dragonships were commanded by himself, Kolbiorn, Guthmund, and Justin. His foster brother Thorgils had command of one of the longships. The fleet numbered forty sail, and each ship was manned by some two hundred warriors and seamen. When the men were landed to fight, one third of the company remained behind to guard the ships. Thus the forces that Olaf usually took ashore with him numbered between five and six thousand warriors.

The first place at which the vikings landed was at the mouth of a wide vik, leading far inland. A man named Harald Biornson was the first to leap ashore. Olaf named the place Harald's vik, but it is in these days spelled Harwich. Olaf followed the banks of the river for many miles, pillaging some steads, and carrying off much treasure from a certain monastery. The monks and friars fought well against him, but were soon defeated, and their houses and barns were left in flames. Farther inland the northmen went until they came to a made road, which crossed the river by a stone bridge. Olaf thought that this road must lead to some large town, so he took his forces over it northward into Suffolk, and at length he came within sight of Ipswich, and he resolved to attack the place. But he was not then prepared to enter battle, as many of his men had come ashore without their body armour and shields, deeming these too heavy to carry in sunny weather. So they returned to the ships and approached the town by way of the sea. They sailed up the Orwell river, and fell upon the town first with arrow and spear and then with sword and axe. The men of Ipswich met their foes in the middle of the town, and there was a great fight. But ere the sun went down Olaf had got the victory. He pillaged the houses and churches, and having emptied them of all that was worth taking he carried off the booty to his ships. He found that this was a good place to harbour his fleet in for a time, so he remained in Ipswich until the blossom had fallen from the trees.

CHAPTER XII: THE BATTLE OF MALDON.

Now this sacking of the town of Ipswich brought terror into the hearts of the men of East Anglia, who well knew how useless it would be for them to appeal for help to King Ethelred. There were brave men in that part of the country, however, who, at the first alarm of the landing of the Norsemen, made themselves ready to defend their homes and the homes of their neighbours. Chief among these was a certain holy and valiant man named Brihtnoth. He was at this time Earldorman of East Anglia. He had already done great work in spreading the Christian faith among the poor and ignorant people over whom he stood in authority, and his beneficent gifts to the monasteries of Ely and Ramsey had won for him the reputation almost of a saint. The monks regarded him as a man of quiet and thoughtful life, absorbed in acts of charity; but he proved that he could be a man of action also, for he was soon to become the hero of one of the most famous and disastrous battles ever fought on English soil.

When Brihtnoth heard that the vikings had taken possession of Ipswich he put aside his books, and, taking down his sword, rode about the country side gathering men about him. He assembled a goodly army of soldiers, both archers and swordmen, and marched towards the coast. It is told that during this march he came to a certain monastery and asked for food for his army. The abbot declared that he would willingly entertain the Earldorman and such well born men as were with him, but would not undertake to feed the whole host. Brihtnoth answered that he would take nothing in which all his soldiers could not share, so he marched on to the next monastery, where he fared with more success.

Now it speedily came to the ears of Olaf Triggvison that this army was being assembled against him, and he sent out spies, who in time came back with the news that Brihtnoth was encamped upon a hillside near the town of Maldon, in Essex.

Olaf at once weighed anchor, and took his fleet southward past the Naze until he came to the mouth of the river Panta (now called the Blackwater). He led his ships inward on the top of the tide. Two hours' rowing brought him within sight of the houses of Maldon. The town stood upon a hill overlooking the river, which at this point branched

65

off in two separate streams, one stream passing by the foot of the hill, the other flowing at a little distance to the north and passing under a strong stone built bridge. Olaf brought his ships into the branch nearest to the town, and his men, on landing, gathered in a confused crowd in occupation of the space between the two streams.

Brihtnoth had already taken up a position of vantage to the north of the bridge, having both streams between his army and the town. He had arrayed his troops in a compact mass in the form of a wedge or triangle, whose narrower point was opposite to the roadway of the bridge. The men occupying the outer lines stood with their large shields locked together so closely that they made a strong rampart or shield fortress, behind which the archers and spearmen might remain in safety while assailing their advancing foes. It was considered very important in the early part of a battle that the shield fortress should not be broken or opened, nor could such a breach be easily effected except by overpowering strength or stratagem. Mounted on a sturdy little white horse, the Earldorman rode backward and forward in front of the lines to see that his men stood firm in their ranks. When all was ready he alighted, sent his horse to the rear, and took his place among his troops, determined to share every danger of his lowlier comrades. From where he stood he could see the fair haired vikings making a landing. Their great numbers appalled him, but he spoke no word of fear. Presently he noticed two men whom, by their glittering gold helmets and beautiful shields, he took to be chiefs. They walked some distance apart from the host of shipmen, and took their stand on a grassy knoll overlooking the opposing armies.

"Not wrong were the reports we heard concerning these sea wolves," said he to a young man at his side. "Look but at those two chiefs standing apart! Giants they are in sooth. The younger one--he with the flowing yellow hair, and with the belt of gold about his thick arm--is surely a head and shoulders taller than any East Anglian I have seen. It will be a tough encounter if we come hand to hand with that man. But let us all be brave, for we have our homes to defend, and God will not desert us in our hour of danger. And we have many good chances on our side. Very often the more numerous host does not gain the victory, if there are bold and fearless men against them."

The yellow haired chief was Olaf Triggvison, and Guthmund was his companion. They had climbed the higher ground, so that they might better calculate upon the chances of the coming battle, and great was their surprise to see how skilfully Brihtnoth had arrayed his men. That triangle form in which the English stood was called by the Scandinavians the "swine array", and it was believed to have been introduced by Odin himself. Olaf well knew how strong that formation always proved to be against the assaults of an enemy, and how almost impossible it was for human force to break through it.

"The man who has marshalled that little army is no unworthy foe," said he; "and I think we shall do well to carefully consider our plans before making an advance. Well has he foreseen that we should land upon this spot, and he has so placed his host at the farther side of the river that we shall not reach him without great difficulty. The water is deep, and the rising tide flows quick and strong."

"But there is the bridge by which we may cross," returned Guthmund.

Olaf smiled and shook his head.

"The bridge is very narrow," he said, "and the old chief has wisely placed three of his champions there to defend it and bar our passage."

"Though he had placed there three score of champions, I see no danger in our crossing," said Guthmund.

66

"Nevertheless, the bridge would still be secure to those who hold it," answered Olaf. "Indeed, I would myself engage to hold such a position with my own hand against a far greater force than ours. It is but a matter of endurance, and one good sword, well wielded, is as good as the strongest gate ever made."

As he spoke he noticed the figure of Earldorman Brihtnoth, who now left his place in the ranks, and advanced towards the three champions at the bridge. The old man stood there awhile giving some directions to the bridge defenders. He was about to return when he saw that Olaf was sending Guthmund down to him with some message, and he waited.

When Guthmund stepped upon the bridge he laid down his sword upon the ground. Brihtnoth went forward to meet him.

"What is your will?" asked the Earldorman.

"I have come with a message from my king," answered the viking.

"What says your king?"

"He says that since it appears to be the common practice in this country for kings and earls to buy off an unwelcome foe with offers of gold, he will engage to withdraw and go back to his ships on your paying him a sum of money that he will name."

Brihtnoth drew back in anger at such an offer, not guessing that King Olaf was but testing his bravery.

"And who is it that has told your chief that such is the habit of our English kings?" he demanded.

"Little need was there for anyone to tell the tale," answered Guthmund, "for it is well known throughout the countries of the vikings that King Ethelred has not so many brave warriors at his call that he can afford to lose them for the sake of a few bags of gold. Not once but many times has he thus sought to buy off the Norsemen."

"Go back to your chief," cried Brihtnoth, with an indignant sweep of his arm; "go back and tell him that steel, and not gold, is the only metal that can now judge between him and me!"

"It is the metal that King Olaf has ever favoured," returned Guthmund; "and right glad will he be to hear that there is at least one man among the English who is brave enough to be of that same opinion."

So, when Olaf's messenger returned, there arose a loud cry from the deep throats of the vikings. The cry had scarcely died away ere the air was filled with arrows, that fell in a heavy shower among the English. Then Brihtnoth's archers answered the challenge, and the battle began in good earnest. For a long time the two armies stood facing each other, with the river running between, and arrows alone were the weapons used. But at last one of Olaf's captains--Justin it was--ran forward, sword in hand and shield on arm, towards the bridge. He was closely followed by a large number of the vikings.

Bravely did the three champions stand at their post. With their feet firmly set, and their shields before them, they met the onrush of their foes, wielding their long swords with such precision and strength that Justin and five of his fellows fell dead without striking a single blow. Onward the vikings pressed, leaping over the bodies of their fallen companions, but only to be themselves driven back again under the terrible blows that met them. Very soon the roadway of the bridge was so crowded with the slain that many of the men fell over the parapet into the deep water of the river. A party of Olaf's bowmen stood by the nearer end of the bridge, assailing the three dauntless defenders with their arrows. Again the northmen charged. This time they were led by Kolbiorn Stallare, who advanced slowly, and not with a heedless rush as the others had done. He carried his heavy battleaxe; but before he could raise his weapon to strike, the nearest of the defenders stepped unexpectedly forward and dealt him a tremendous blow which made him stagger backward. The blow was met by his strong shield, and he received no hurt; but in stepping back he tripped upon the arm of one of his fallen comrades, and was borne down under the weight of the men who, following close behind him, rushed headlong to the death that he had escaped. There Kolbiorn lay for a long while, and Olaf Triggvison, who had seen him fall, believed him to be dead.

Now it was Guthmund and not Olaf who had given the command to the Norsemen to attempt the taking of the bridge, and Olaf was very angry at seeing so many of his best men sacrificed. He had seen that the tide in the creek was ebbing, and that very soon the bridge would cease to be an important post. Accordingly he ordered that those who were still endeavouring to cross should be withdrawn.

The three champions who had thus succeeded in keeping the bridge were named Wulfstan, Elfhere, and Maccus. Wulfstan was the man who had struck Kolbiorn Stallare, and he knew that the blow could not have killed him. So when the vikings had left the bridge he rescued Kolbiorn from under the weight of slain men who had fallen over him, and Kolbiorn limped back to the rear of the Norse archers who, all this time, had kept up a constant firing of arrows upon the Englishmen.

When at last the tide had fallen, and the ford could be passed, the bridge defenders retreated, and Brihtnoth allowed the northmen to cross over unhindered. Olaf led his chosen men across by the road, while the larger number of his warriors waded through the stream. And now the fight began in desperate earnest.

Separating his forces into three divisions, Olaf advanced to the attack. He directed his left wing, under the command of Guthmund, upon Brihtnoth's right flank; his right wing, under Harald Biornson, wheeled round to the attack of Brithnoth's left. He reserved for himself the position which was considered the most difficult to deal with--the point where the English chief himself stood, surrounded by his strongest and most experienced soldiers. This was the narrowest part of the formation, and Olaf knew that if he could but break through the wall of shields at this point the whole mass of men, now so compact and impregnable, would quickly be thrown into confusion.

Kolbiorn fought at Olaf's right hand, and Thorgils Thoralfson at his left. Behind and about them were a thousand of the most valiant vikings and berserks.

The attack began on all sides with the hurling of javelins, but very soon the northmen approached closer to their enemies, and carried on a closer combat with their swords, and at first the vikings got the worst of it.

Olaf and his fellows had already caught sight of the white bearded Brihtnoth, and they were making their way towards him when Thorgils Thoralfson fell forward, pierced to the heart with a spear. Now, the spear was one which Olaf himself had before thrown into the midst of the English ranks, and it had now been returned in such a manner that Olaf at once knew it had been hurled by some man trained as the vikings were in the use of the weapon. Advancing yet nearer, he searched with quick eye among the faces of the men before him. As he did so another spear was flung; this time it was aimed at Kolbiorn, who caught it on his uplifted shield.

Kolbiorn had seen the face of the man who had thus picked him out, and throwing his shield aside he gripped his battleaxe, and flinging himself with all his great strength against the wall of men he burst through the ranks. Olaf saw him fighting his way into the midst of the soldiers, who fell back before the weighty axe. At last Kolbiorn reached the man he sought, and engaged with him hand to hand, while Olaf and the vikings followed into the breach. In a very few moments Olaf was at Kolbiorn's side, and then he too saw the face of the man who had killed Thorgils. It was the face of his own fellow-slave in far off Esthonia, his companion in Holmgard, his shipmate Egbert, whom he had believed to be drowned.

The duel between Kolbiorn and Egbert lasted for several minutes, but it was evident that Kolbiorn was but playing with his adversary, for he gave him many chances.

"Less skilful are you than when we last met," he said with a laugh, "and your wrist is not so strong. Gladly would I have given you a few more lessons had opportunity served; but instead I must now repay the blow you gave me over our game of chess."

Egbert then fell, and Kolbiorn turned to the help of Olaf, who was now engaged with the English chief and three of his special comrades.

Brihtnoth wanted to fight Olaf sword to sword, but Olaf respected his bravery and his grey hairs, and chose rather to encounter a very broad chested Englishman, who had already slain three of the vikings. As Kolbiorn entered the fray he saw Brihtnoth turn away from Olaf and cross swords with one of the berserks. The berserk fell, with a great cut across his head. His place was taken by one of his shipmates, whom the old chief also overcame. The Earldorman was wounded, but he went on bravely fighting until at last he was cut down by a viking named Harek the Hawk.

The spot where the English chief had fallen became now the centre of the battle. Here, in defence of their dead leader's body, the bravest among the English fought and fell. Wulfstan, Maccus, and Elfhere--the three who had held the bridge--again fought shoulder to shoulder at this place. Wulfstan was vanquished by Olaf, and his two companions fell to Kolbiorn's blade. The names of some of the other English warriors are Alfwine, a lord of the Mercians, Eseferth, Brihtwold, Edward the Long, Leofsuna, and Dunnere; all of whom fell in defending the body of Brihtnoth. One of the vikings, thinking that Olaf meant to gain possession of it, carried off the body of the dead hero; but Olaf would not allow his men to do dishonour to so brave a foe, and he afterwards delivered the body to Brihtnoth's friends, who gave it a worthy resting place in Ely cathedral.

Meanwhile the battle had fared ill with the East Anglians on the other parts of the field. The breaking of the fortress of shields had thrown the ranks into confusion. The vikings, under Guthmund and Harek, followed up their advantage and fought with fierce onslaught. The English were but ill armed; many of them had bills and swords, others had spears and arrows, but some had no better weapons than such as they had themselves contrived out of their farm implements.

When it was seen that the northmen were gaining the victory on all hands many of the English began to lose courage, and one, a caitiff named Godric, mounted the horse on which Brihtnoth had ridden to the field, so that many thought that it was the Earldorman himself who had fled. After this there was a general retreat, and so the battle of Maldon ended.

Olaf Triggvison made no assault upon the town, but pitched his tents on the high ground between the two streams where he had landed. He allowed the East Anglians to carry off their dead and give them Christian burial. His own dead numbered over four hundred, and he had them laid in a mound with all their armour and weapons, and built a cairn over them according to the heathen custom.

He lay with his ships off Maldon during the rest of the summer, and raided in Essex and Suffolk without hindrance.

Now it might be thought that King Ethelred, hearing, as he soon heard, of the taking of Ipswich and of the defeat of the East Anglians at Maldon, would lose no time in gathering an army to expel the invaders.

The spirit of the nation was ready for a vigorous resistance of the northmen, and with a few such men as Brihtnoth to lead them the English might without much difficulty have driven every viking out of the land. But Ethelred was a man of quite another stamp from the valiant Earldorman of East Anglia, and he adopted the fatal system of looking to gold to do the work of steel.

Olaf Triggvison and a party of his captains returned to the camp one day, after a great boar hunt, and they found that in their absence certain messengers had arrived from Andover, where the king held his court. Olaf directed that the men should be brought to him in his tent, and there he held speech with them. On entering the tent the messengers set down before the viking chief two heavy bags containing the sum of ten thousand pounds in gold, This money, the men said, had been sent by King Ethelred as a gift to the leader of the Norsemen.

"And for what reason should King Ethelred send such a gift to me who have done him no good service, but have only been despoiling his lands and disturbing his peaceful subjects?"

"It is because the king wishes you to cease your ravaging in East Anglia and take away your ships and men," returned the spokesman. "That is the condition he imposes on your accepting the gold."

"And how if I refuse the gold and say that it does not suit my purpose to remove my ships?" asked Olaf. "Will your king then march with his armies against the vikings, and give us the exercise of another good battle?"

The messenger shrugged his shoulders.

"King Ethelred does not doubt that you will take the gold," said he. "And as to his marching against you, of that matter he has said no word."

"In that case you may leave the money in my keeping," said Olaf. "And I charge you to thank King Ethelred for his generosity. It so happens that this part of the country is already becoming somewhat bare of food and we are wearying for new scenes. I think, therefore, that before the winter days are far advanced we shall weigh anchor and set sail. But our going shall not be one day earlier on account of Ethelred's desire to be rid of us."

The messengers wanted a more definite promise from Olaf that he would not only sail away at this present time but also that he would not again invade the English coasts. But to this Olaf would not agree. Either the king must be satisfied that the vikings intended to quit the shores of East Anglia in a few weeks' time, or he might take back his gold and suffer his kingdom to be invaded and ravaged at whatever point the Norsemen chose to make a landing.

It seemed for a long time that they could come to no agreement; but finally the matter was so arranged that the gold was delivered into Olaf's hands and the messengers departed, with a mere half promise of peace and the assurance that Olaf would remove his ships within twenty days. Olaf did not hold himself bound to keep these conditions; nevertheless he resolved to abide by them. He had already discovered that his forces were too small to attempt, with any certainty of success, a deliberate conquest of England; and, indeed, even before the arrival of Ethelred's messengers, he had determined to presently withdraw his fleet until such times as he had gathered about him a host large enough and strong enough to lay siege to London. His departure from Maldon was therefore of his own choosing and not the result of any threats upon the part of the English king.

Meanwhile Olaf did not lose sight of the fact that the foolish policy of King Ethelred, instead of having the effect of securing the kingdom against invasion, only set forth a very strong encouragement to the vikings to repeat their incursions as often as they were in want of money. Ethelred and his advisers seem never to have learned this

70

lesson, and for many years after the battle of Maldon the sea rovers, both Danish and Norwegian, continued to harry the English coasts, with the invariable result that, so soon as they had plundered a few monasteries and reduced a few villages to ashes, they were sure to receive the offer of a very handsome bribe as an inducement to put to sea again.

CHAPTER XIII: THE HERMIT OF THE SCILLYS.

On a certain day in the late winter of the next year Olaf Triggvison led his fleet across the turbulent waters of the Pentland Firth, and steered his course for the islands of Orkney. On his way northward along the coasts of England he had many times made a landing to plunder some seaside village and to replenish his stores of food and water. He had harried wide on both shores of the Humber and in Northumberland, had stormed King Ida's fortress of Bamborough, and made a raid upon Berwick. In Scotland, also, he had ravaged and plundered. But of these adventures there remains no record. Before the time of his crossing to the Orkneys he had lost five of his ships and a large number of his men, and from this it may be judged that he had either encountered very stormy weather or suffered some reverse at the hands of his enemies.

The snow still lay deep upon the islands when he entered the wide channel named Scapa Flow, and anchored his fleet under shelter of the high island of Hoy. Many of his vessels were by this time in need of repair, so he crossed the sound and beached them near to where the port of Stromness now lies, and at this place he took up his quarters until the coming of the summer.

The Orkney Islands were then, and for many generations afterwards, peopled by Scandinavian vikings and their families, who paid tax and tribute to Norway. Olaf therefore found himself among men who spoke his own tongue, and who were glad enough to make friends with a chief, of whom it could be said that he had done great and valiant deeds in battle. One thing which more than all else won these people to him was their knowledge that he was the same Ole the Esthonian who, with Vagn Akison, had stood out to the end in the great sea fight against Hakon of Lade. Earl Hakon was now the ruler over the Orkney islanders, but he was beginning to be so bitterly hated by them that they looked upon all his enemies as their own particular friends. For a little time they had centred their hopes in Earl Sigvaldi of Jomsburg, who had lately taken refuge in the Orkneys. But Sigvaldi had now gone back to his stronghold on the Baltic, in the hope of restoring his scattered company of vikings. The coming of Olaf was therefore regarded with great favour by the Orcadian vikings, who thought it possible that he would join them in an attempt to drive Earl Hakon from the Norwegian throne.

In order to delay Olaf's departure from the islands the people got him to help them in building a great temple on the shores of one of their lakes, and, when the temple was finished and duly dedicated to Odin, they proposed to Olaf that he should lead an expedition across to Norway. Olaf replied that he did not consider the time ripe for such an attempt, and that for the present he had other plans in hand; but he bade them, in the meantime, busy themselves with the building of ships.

Now while Olaf was still in Orkney there came one day into Scapa Flow one of the ships of King Sweyn Forkbeard of Denmark. Olaf learned from her captain that the Dane folk had rebelled against Sweyn, for the reason that, having accepted Christianity and compelled his people to follow his example, he had now thrown off the true belief and turned back to the worship of the heathen gods, demanding that his subjects should again acknowledge Odin and Thor to be greater than the God of the Christians. Rather than do this, the Danes had resolved to drive their unbelieving king into exile; and Sweyn Forkbeard, having lost his throne, had taken to vikingry.

71

On hearing this, Olaf Triggvison gave the ship captain a message to take back to his master, bidding Sweyn remember the vow he had sworn at his inheritance feast, and saying that if he had a mind to fulfil that vow he might now make the attempt, for that he--Ole the Esthonian--was now preparing his forces for a great invasion of England, and would be well pleased if Sweyn would join him in the expedition. The place of the gathering of the forces was to be Ipswich, in East Anglia, and the time of meeting was to be the middle of the harvest month in the next summer.

Olaf did not wait in the Orkneys for an answer to this message. His vikings were already growing weary of idleness and eager to be again upon the sea. So the ships were put in readiness, and when a fair wind offered, the anchors were weighed and the sails set, and the fleet sped westward through Roy Sound towards Cape Wrath. Thence they sailed down among the Hebrides--or the Southern Isles, as the Norsemen always called them. Here Olaf had many battles and won many ships from the descendants of Harald Fairhair's rebel subjects, who had made settlements in the Isles. Here, too, he gained some hundreds of men to his following. He harried also in the north parts of Ireland, and had certain battles in the Island of Man. By this time the summer was far spent, so he sailed east away to Cumberland and there rested throughout the winter.

His men thought that this part of England, with its mountains and lakes, was so much like their own birthland in distant Norway, that they showed great unwillingness to leave it. Many did, indeed, remain, and the settlements they made in the lake country have left traces which even to the present day may be recognized, not only in the remains of heathen temples and tombs, but also in the names of places and in certain Norse words that occur in the common speech of the Cumbrian folk.

From Cumberland Olaf sailed south to Wales. There again he harried wide about, and also in Cornwall, and at length he came to the Scilly Isles. King Athelstane had conquered these islands half a century before, and had established a monastery there, the ruins of which may still be seen.

Now when Olaf Triggvison lay at Scilly, sheltering from a storm that had driven him out of his intended course, he heard that in the isle of Tresco there was a certain soothsayer who was said to be well skilled in the foretelling of things which had not yet come to pass. Olaf fell a-longing to test the spaeing of this man.

"I will try him by means of a trick," Olaf said one day to Kolbiorn; "and in this wise: You shall go to him instead of me, and say that you are King Ole the Esthonion; and if he believes you, then is he no soothsayer."

Now Olaf was already famed in all lands for being fairer and nobler than all other men, and he chose Kolbiorn as his messenger because he was the fairest and biggest of his men and most resembled himself, and he sent him ashore, arrayed in the most beautiful clothing.

Kolbiorn searched long among the trees and rocks before he found the little cave in which the lonely hermit dwelt; and when he entered he saw a gray bearded old man, deep in meditation before a crucifix, and wearing the habit of a Christian priest.

The hermit looked up at the tall figure of his visitor, and waited for him to speak. Kolbiorn answered as Olaf had bidden him, saying that his name was King Ole. But the hermit shook his head.

"King thou art not," said he gravely; "but my counsel to thee is, that thou be true to thy King."

No other word did he speak, and Kolbiorn turned away and fared back to Olaf, who, on hearing of the answer that had been given, longed all the more to meet this hermit, whom he now believed to be verily a soothsayer.

So on the next day, while the wind was high and the waves broke with a heavy roar upon the rocks, Olaf dressed himself very simply, without any body armour, and went ashore, attended by two shieldmen. When he entered the hermit's cell he found the old man sitting at an oaken table with a roll of parchment before him, upon which he was inscribing some holy legend. He greeted Olaf most kindly, and when they had spoken together for a while, Olaf asked him what he could say as to how he should speed coming by his rightful inheritance or any other good fortune.

Then the hermit answered:

"In the time that is to come, thou shalt be a very glorious king and do glorious deeds. Many men shalt thou bring to the right troth and to christening, helping thereby both thyself and thy fellow men."

"As to the first part of your prophecy--that I shall become a great king, that I can well believe," returned Olaf; "but that I shall ever help men to christening, I cannot believe, for I am now, and always shall be, a faithful worshipper of the gods of Asgard and an enemy to all believers in Christ."

"Nevertheless," answered the hermit, "the second part of what I have said is even more certain to come true than the first; and, to the end that my words may be trusted, take this as a token: Hard by thy ship thou shall presently fall into a snare of a host of men, and battle will spring thence, and thou wilt be sorely hurt, and of this wound thou shalt look to die and be borne to ship on shield; yet thou shalt be whole of thy hurt within seven nights and be speedily christened thereafter."

Olaf laughed at the good man, and presently went his way. But as he passed downward towards the boat that awaited him among the rocks, he was met by a party of unpeaceful men who fell suddenly upon him with their swords. Olaf called upon his two guards, who had lagged behind, but ere they came to his help he, being without any arms, received a great sword thrust in his chest. His assailants fled when they saw the two guards approaching from among the trees, and Olaf was left bleeding where he fell. His two men lifted him upon one of their shields, and carried him down to the boat and bore him wounded upon his ship. For six days he lay unconscious, and, as all thought, upon the point of death. But on the seventh night the danger was passed, and thereafter he speedily grew well.

Then Olaf deemed that in having foretold this matter so exactly the old hermit had proved himself to be indeed a very wise soothsayer. So he went ashore a second time, and the two talked much and long together.

It seemed that Cerdic was the hermit's name. He had once been a bondslave among Norsemen, and had known Olaf's father, King Triggvi, whom Olaf personally resembled. He could speak very well in the Norse tongue, and his soft and gentle voice was very soothing to all who heard it. At first he spoke of the ways of heathen men, of their revengeful spirit and their cruelty in warfare, and he condemned their offering of blood sacrifices and their worship of graven images. Such gods as Odin and Thor, Njord and Frey, were, he said, but the creations of men's poetic fancy, and had no real existence. Odin was at one time but an earthly man, with all man's faults and sins. The earthquake and the thunder had nothing to do with the rolling of Thor's chariot or the throwing of Thor's hammer. The waves of the ocean would rise in anger or fall into calm peace though the name of Njord had never been spoken; and the seasons would change in their order, fields and pastures would grow, without the favour of Frey.

So spoke the hermit, and then he told the story of the Creation and of Adam's Fall, and showed how Christ had come to preach peace on earth and to save the world. It was a principle of the Christian faith; said Cerdic, that men should remember the Sabbath day

73

and keep it holy, that they should not bow down to graven images, that they should not steal, nor be covetous, nor do murder, nor bear false witness; that they should love their enemies and bless those who cursed them.

Olaf listened in patience to all these things, asking many questions concerning them. At last Cerdic appealed to him and besought him most earnestly to come to repentance and to make himself a faithful follower of Christ, so that he might at the close of his earthly life be worthy to enter into the kingdom of heaven.

Now Olaf Triggvison had until this time lived always in the firm hope that when he died he would be admitted into the shining hall of Valhalla, where he might expect to meet all the great heroes of past times. He believed that Odin would receive him there, and reward him well for all the glorious deeds that he had done. So he was not at all willing to abandon this Norseman's faith in a future life which, as men promised, should be full of warfare by day and of merry carousing by night.

Yet it was evident that Cerdic had not spoken without good effect; for Olaf agreed-- as many of the Scandinavians did in these times--that he would at once be christened, on the one condition that, while calling himself a follower of Christ, he should not be expected to abandon either his belief in Odin or his hopes of Valhalla. The holy man of Scilly well knew that this divided faith would not last long, but he was also assured that in the contest the victory would certainly rest with Christ.

Accordingly Olaf was christened, with all his warriors and shipmen. He lay among the Scilly Isles for many days thereafter, and learned the true faith so well that it remained his guiding light throughout the rest of his life, and made him, as shall presently be seen, one of the most zealous Christians of his time.

Now, as the summer days passed by and it drew near to the harvest time, Olaf bethought him of his tryst with King Sweyn Forkbeard, so he raised his anchors and sped out into the open main and round by the forelands, and so north to Ipswich. It was three years since he had first besieged the East Anglian town, and in the interval the folk had returned to their devastated dwellings and built them anew. Olaf now took forcible possession of the town for a second time. He was not yet so entirely a Christian that he had any scruples in attacking Christian folk and turning them out of their homes.

He lay with his ships in the Orwell for three weeks, and at the end of that time King Sweyn and his fleet arrived from the Baltic. Olaf had already gathered about him some fifty-five vessels of war, fully manned and equipped; and with those which Sweyn added to the number, he had now a force of ninety-four ships of all sizes, from small skiffs of ten banks of oars and a crew of a hundred men, up to great dragonships with thirty pairs of oars, two towering masts, and a complete company of about four hundred seamen and warriors. The whole force of ninety-four ships carried with them some thirty thousand men.

This was not to be one of the old plundering raids of a body of adventurers seeking merely to better their fortunes by winning themselves new homes at the point of the sword. It was an expedition greater than any that Brihtnoth had ever met with steel or Ethelred with gold, and its purpose was one of deliberately planned invasion and conquest.

At first when Olaf and Sweyn met and joined their fleets and armies there was a disagreement between them as to which chief was to assume the higher command. Sweyn declared that the leading position was his by the right that he was a king, and should be accorded the more power in all things over Olaf, who (as Sweyn supposed) was lowly born. But Olaf stoutly maintained that as it was he who had proposed the expedition, and as he had the larger number of men and ships, the sole command should be his own,

Sweyn taking the second place. In the end it was agreed that this should be so, and that, in the event of their success, they were to divide the kingdom of England between them-- Sweyn taking the Northern half, including Northumbria and the upper part of Mercia, and Olaf the Southern half, including East Anglia and the whole of Wessex.

The first point of attack was to be London--a city which, although not yet the capital of the kingdom, was a chief bulwark of the land and daily becoming one of the most important centres of trade in Western Europe. Alfred the Great, who had himself rescued the city from the Danes, had built a strong fortress for her defence, and her citizens had always been regarded as among the most valiant and patriotic in all England. Olaf Triggvison was well aware that if he should succeed in taking London, his conquest of the rest of Ethelred's realm would be a comparatively easy matter. Unfortunately for his plans, he did not foresee the obstacles which were to meet him.

He led his procession of battleships up the Thames. Never before had such a splendid array been seen upon those waters. The early morning sun shone upon the gilded birds and dragons on the tops of the masts. At the prow of each vessel there was reared the tall figure of some strange and terrible animal, formed of carved and gilded wood or of wrought brass, silver, or even amber. Many of the ships had sails made of the finest silk, woven in beautiful designs. The decks were crowded with men whose glittering spears and burnished helmets gave them a very warlike aspect, and struck terror into the hearts of the people who saw them from the river's banks.

The alarm spread quickly from point to point, and before the invaders had come well within sight of the city the gates were securely closed and barricaded, and the valiant burghers were fully prepared to make a stout resistance.

As the ships came abreast of the Tower they were assailed by volleys of well aimed arrows, fired from the battlements. Heedless of Olaf's plans, King Sweyn drew his division yet nearer under the walls, with the intention of making an assault upon the citadel. But the attempt was useless. The defenders were hidden behind the ramparts and beyond reach of all missiles, while Sweyn's forces were fully exposed to the ceaseless hail of arrows and stones which seemed to issue out of the very walls. So many of his men fell that Sweyn was forced to retire.

The garrison could frustrate an assault upon the fortress, but they could not prevent so vast a number of ships from passing higher up the river and making an attack upon the old Roman rampart. While King Sweyn crossed to the opposite side of the stream and led an attack upon Southwark, Olaf effected a landing near Billing's Gate and directed all his strength upon the wall. He lost many men in the attempt, but at last a breach was made, and at the head of many hundreds of desperate warriors he entered the city. He had depended upon Sweyn following him; and had the Danish king been content to obey, London might indeed have been taken by sheer strength. As it was, however, Olaf quickly found that he had made a fatal mistake. Vast crowds of armed citizens met him at the end of each narrow street and dealt the invaders such lusty blows, with their bills and swords and volleys of heavy stones, that those who were not maimed or killed outright were forced back by overpowering strength, their ranks being driven into hopeless confusion. At one moment Olaf Triggvison found himself, with some six or seven of his men, surrounded by several scores of the defenders. He fought his way through them back to the city wall, where, through the breach that had been made, his hosts were escaping on board the ships. The besiegers were utterly defeated. Once again had the men of London rescued their city from its foes.

Sweyn Forkbeard had fared no better than Olaf had done. He had made a bold attempt to burn the town, but, like Olaf, he had been driven back to his ships with great slaughter.

On that same day the two defeated chiefs sailed away in wrath and sorrow, and with the loss of seven ships and two thousand men.

Now, under Alfred or Athelstane such a reverse as the invaders had met with before London would surely have been followed up by some crushing victory. But under the wretched Ethelred there was no attempt made to prevent the more fearful desolation of other parts of the kingdom. Olaf and Sweyn were calmly allowed to avenge their defeat by ravaging the coast at pleasure, and to pillage, burn and murder without meeting the slightest resistance. At the mouth of the Thames the two chiefs had divided their forces, Sweyn sailing northward towards the Humber, while Olaf took his course southward, and ravaged far and wide in the old kingdoms of Kent and Sussex.

Late in the summer, Olaf crossed into Hampshire, and now at last King Ethelred was roused, for the invaders threatened not only the royal city of Andover but also the royal person. The king had no army of sufficient strength to encounter his Norse enemy, and his navy was of still less consequence. The only course he seems to have thought of, therefore, was the old cowardly policy of again buying peace with gold. Olaf was allowed to anchor his fleet for the winter at Southampton, and in order to avert any raiding into the surrounding country, Ethelred levied a special tax upon the people of Wessex to supply the crews with food and pay. He also levied a general tax upon all England to raise the sum of sixteen thousand pounds as a bribe to the invaders to quit the kingdom.

This large sum of money was conveyed to Olaf Triggvison by the king's ambassadors, among whom was a certain Bishop Elfheah--a zealous Christian, who, in addition to gaining Olaf's solemn promise that he would keep the peace, took upon himself the task of converting the young chief to the Christian faith. Olaf had already been baptized by the good hermit of the Scillys; but he had not yet received the rite of confirmation. He now declared that he was willing to become entirely a Christian, and to set aside his belief in the old gods of Scandinavia. The bishop then led Olaf to the court at Andover, where Ethelred received him with every honour and enriched him with royal gifts. At the confirmation of Olaf, which took place with great pomp, King Ethelred himself was present, and even stood sponsor.

Olaf lived for many weeks at Andover, as King Ethelred's friendly guest, and before he left to join his ships he signed a treaty in which he engaged never again to invade England. This promise he faithfully kept, and for a time there was peace in the land. Ethelred believed that he had now rid his kingdom of all danger from the vikings. But he did not reckon with King Sweyn Forkbeard. Tempted by the great sums of money that had been extorted from the English, Sweyn returned again and again, and at last succeeded in expelling Ethelred from the land. For many years Sweyn was the virtual ruler of England, and he thus prepared the way for his son, Canute the Mighty, who was afterwards the chosen king of the English people.

Now, while Olaf Triggvison was still the guest of King Ethelred, there also lived at the court a certain princess named Gyda. She was the sister of the King of Dublin, in Ireland, and she was considered very beautiful. A great many wooers sought to wed with her, and among others a man named Alfwin, a renowned champion and man slayer. A day was fixed on which Gyda had promised to choose a husband, and many high born men had come together, hoping to be chosen. All were splendidly attired.

Olaf Triggvison, clad in a coarse, wet weather cloak with a fur hood, stood apart with a few of his comrades, merely to look on.

Gyda went here and there among her wooers, but seemed to find none that pleased her. But at length she came to where Olaf stood, with his head half hidden under his fur hood. She went nearer to him, lifted up his hood and looked long and earnestly into his eyes.

"A taller and handsomer man I have never seen," said she. "Who art thou, and whence came you?"

"I am an outland man here," he answered; "and I am named Ole the Esthonian."

Gyda said, "Wilt thou have me? Then will I choose thee for my husband."

Olaf replied that he was not unwilling to take her at her word. So they talked the matter over and, being of one mind, they were forthwith betrothed.

Alfwin was ill content at this, and in great wrath he challenged Olaf to fight. It was the custom of those days in England that if any two men contended about a matter they should each bring twelve men and dispute their rights in a pitched battle. So when these two rivals met, Olaf gave the word to his men to do as he did. He had a great axe, and when Alfwin attacked him with his sword, he quickly overpowered him, and then bound him fast with ropes. In like wise were all Alfwin's men defeated; and Olaf forced them to depart from the land and never come back. Alfwin was a very wealthy man, and his wealth was forfeited to Olaf. Then Olaf wedded Princess Gyda, and went with her to Ireland, and lived in great happiness for many days.

CHAPTER XIV: THORIR KLAKKA.

During all this time of Olaf Triggvison's wanderings Earl Hakon of Lade continued to hold the sovereign rule in Norway, and there was great peace in the land, with fruitful harvests and good fishing. In his early years he was very popular for his kindliness and generosity, his fearless courage and his great strength in battle. But it seems that the greater power which he afterwards acquired disturbed the fine balance of his mind, and he became deceitful, even to his nearest friends, and cruel to a degree which presently won for him the hatred of his people, who murmured against him in secret while fearing to break out into open rebellion.

Earl Hakon knew nothing of the strong feelings that were rising against him, nor did he doubt that he should enjoy his power unmolested to the end of his days. One thought alone disturbed his sense of security. It chanced that rumours had reached him concerning a certain viking who called himself Ole, and who was said to have won great renown in the realm of King Ethelred. Now Hakon was told that this same Ole had spent his younger days in Gardarike, and he deemed that the lad must be of the blood of the Norse kings, for it was no secret that King Triggvi Olafson had had a son who had fared east into Gardarike, and been nourished there at the court of King Valdemar, and that he was called Olaf.

Earl Hakon had sought far and wide for Olaf Triggvison, but in vain. Some men had, indeed, said that in the battle of the Jomsvikings they had seen a young champion, named Ole the Esthonian, whose aspect was that of the race of Harald Fairhair, and it was said that this same champion was one of those who had been made prisoners and put to death. But, in spite of this story, Hakon still believed in the later rumours. He believed that the adventurous Ole the Viking was none other than Olaf Triggvison, nor could he doubt that this daring young rover would sooner or later lay claim to the kingdom of Norway.

As his own popularity grew less and less, Hakon looked forward with increasing uneasiness to the inevitable conflict. He well understood the devotion of the Norse people to the family of Harald Fairhair, and he now considered that his own safety could only be secured by the death of this possible rival.

Earl Hakon had a great friend named Thorir Klakka, a man who had been many years at viking work, and had often gone on trading voyages to England and Ireland and other lands bordering on the Western Sea. The earl spoke with Thorir and confided to him his plan, bidding him go on a trading voyage to Dublin, where Ole the Esthonian was then supposed to be living, and if it was found that this man Ole was indeed the son of King Triggvi, or any other offspring of the kingly stem of the north, then Thorir was either to kill him or to entice him over to Norway where Hakon himself would deal with him.

So without delay, Thorir went forth upon his mission, and sailed west into Ireland. It was in the early springtime when he reached Dublin, and he was not long in learning that Ole was then living at the court of King Kuaran, his brother-in-law.

On a certain day Thorir was in the marketplace, buying some Irish horses that were for sale. There was a beautiful white pony that he greatly coveted, and he offered a high price for it. But there was another who offered yet more--a tall young man, with long fair hair and very clear blue eyes, who wore a very beautiful cloak of crimson silk bordered with gold lace. Thorir at once knew him to be a Norseman, and he also guessed that this was the man of whom he was in search. Now the pony at last fell to Thorir's bidding. Then Thorir took the animal by its halter and went and stood by the side of the handsome Norseman.

"I beg you will take the pony as a gift from me," said he, speaking in the English tongue; "for I see that you are a great lord in this land, and such a beautiful animal is better suited to such as you than to a mere seafarer who has little use for it."

"And why should I take such a gift from a stranger, who owes me nothing in the world?" returned Olaf Triggvison. "The pony is yours, my man, for you have bought it and paid for it in fair market. If it indeed be that you have no wish to keep the animal, then I will gladly buy it from you at the price you paid. But I cannot take it as a free gift."

Olaf paid him his price in gold of Ethelred's coinage, and sent the pony away in charge of one of his servants. But even when the business was over, Thorir did not seem willing to leave, but stood near to Olaf looking searchingly into his face.

"Why do you linger?" asked Olaf. "Is there something so very unusual about me that you stare at me so?"

"There is much that is unusual about you, lord," answered Thorir; "and little marvel is there that I should look upon you with interest. Nowhere, save in my own birthland of Norway, have I ever seen a man so tall and strong and fair."

"Certainly, there are many such men in Norway," said Olaf; "but also there are many in these western lands; as to which witness those who are about us here in this marketplace."

He glanced across to where his friend Kolbiorn Stallare was standing.

"There is one at your back who seems not less strong than I."

Thorir looked round at Kolbiorn, then back at Olaf. "You are well nigh a head and shoulders taller than that one," said he; "and there is that about you which seems to tell me you have spent the larger part of your life in Norway."

Olaf said: "Since I was a babe in arms, I have been but once in that land; and then only during two changes of the moon or so. Nevertheless, I will not deny that there is indeed a vein of the Norse blood in me, and for that reason I should be well enough pleased to hear from you some news of what has been happening in Norway these few summers past."

"Little is there to tell," returned Thorir; "for, since the rascally sons of Erik Bloodaxe were driven from the land, there have been no great wars. True it is, that Earl

78

Sigvaldi of Jomsburg did lately make an attempt to win dominion in Norway. He led his host of vikings, with I know not how many battleships, against Earl Hakon; but he was defeated with great slaughter and took to flight."

"Of that famous fight I have already had tidings," said Olaf. "I have heard that many well known vikings were vanquished on that day, and that Vagn Akison was the only chief who stood his ground to the end."

Thorir looked with quick eyes into Olaf's face, and said: "Yes, Vagn proved himself a valiant warrior in that encounter. But there was one who was quite as brave and mighty as he--one who named himself Ole the Esthonian. Men say that this same Ole has since won great renown in England."

Olaf smiled, but was silent for some moments. Then at last he began to ask many questions concerning the Upland kings, and who of them were yet alive, and what dominion they had. Of Earl Hakon also he asked, and how well beloved he might be in the land.

Thorir answered: "The earl is so mighty a man that he now has the whole of Norway in his power, and none dares to speak a word but in his praise. And yet," he added, remembering the terms of his mission, "Earl Hakon is not all that a peaceful people would wish. Many would prefer some other monarch if they but knew where to find one better to their taste. A pity it is that there is no man of the blood of King Harald Fairhair living, whom the Norsemen could put upon the throne. None such have we to turn to; and for this cause it would little avail any man not kingly born to contend with Earl Hakon."

Now, when Olaf Triggvison heard these things, there came upon him a certain impatient desire to fare across to Norway and proclaim himself a direct descendant of Harald the Fairhaired and the rightful heir to the throne. So on the next day he again sought out the man Thorir, and when they had spoken together for a little while, Olaf said:

"A long time ago, as I have heard, there was a young son of King Triggvi Olafson who escaped with his mother, Queen Astrid, into Sweden. Has no one heard whether that lad lived or died? Why do none of the Norse folk seek him out and set him to reign over them in place of this Hakon, who is neither kingly born nor kingly mannered?"

Thorir answered: "It was not for lack of trying that Queen Gunnhild did not bring the child to his death. She pursued him far and wide; but the gods protected him and he escaped. It is said by many men that he fell into bondage; others say that he took refuge in Holmgard, where King Valdemar reigns; and I have even heard it hinted that the viking naming himself Ole the Esthonian, who has lately been warring in England, is none other than Olaf Triggvison. Howbeit, there now lives in Viken a woman who is said to be the widow of King Triggvi--Astrid is her name--and she has declared that her son Olaf is surely dead, else would he have come back to Norway of his own accord to claim his great inheritance."

As he spoke these last words Thorir saw for the first time that a change had come into Olaf's face, and he deemed that here truly was the man whom Earl Hakon had sent him to entrap. Yet he held his own counsel for a while, believing that if this were indeed Olaf Triggvison the fact would speedily be brought to light, and that he would soon have some chance of either putting him to death or of beguiling him into the hands of Earl Hakon.

For many moments Olaf strode to and fro in silence. There was a new light in his eyes, and his cheeks were flushed, and when he spoke there was a tremor in his voice that showed how deeply this news of his long lost mother had affected him.

"How long time is it since this woman, this Queen Astrid, came back into Norway?" he asked.

"Many years," answered Thorir.

"Then it may be that she is already dead?" said Olaf.

But Thorir shook his head.

"That is not likely," said he, "for I saw her with my own eyes at Yuletide past, and she was then living very happily with her husband in Viken."

"Her husband?" echoed Olaf. "And what manner of man is he? A king surely, for none but a king is worthy of such a wife."

"He is no king, but a wealthy man and of good kin," returned Thorir. "His name is Lodin, and he went oft on trading voyages aboard a ship which he owned himself. On a certain summer he made east for Esthonia and there did much business. Now, in the marketplace of one of the Esthonian seaports many thralls were brought for sale, and, among other thralls who were to be sold, Lodin saw a certain woman. As he looked upon her he knew by the beauty of her eyes that she was Astrid, Erik's daughter, who had been wedded to King Triggvi Olafson. And yet she was very unlike what she had been in her earlier days, being pale now, and lean, and ill clad. So Lodin went up to her and asked her how it fared with her, and how she came to be in such a place, and so far away from Norway. She said: 'It is a heavy tale to tell. I am sold at thrall markets and am brought hither now for sale,' and therewith she, knowing Lodin, prayed him to buy her and take her back with him to her kindred in Norway. 'I will give you a choice over that,' said he. 'I will take you back to Norway if you will wed me.' Then Astrid promised him so much, and he bought her and took her to Norway, and wedded her with her kindred's goodwill."

Then Olaf said, "This is indeed the gladdest news that I have heard for many a long year!" But the words had scarcely fallen from his lips when he realized that he had unwittingly betrayed his long kept secret, for why else should he look upon this as such glad news if he were not himself the lost son of this same Queen Astrid? And it seemed that Thorir had already guessed everything, for he said:

"Glad news must it always be when a son hears that his mother, whom he thought dead, is still alive."

"I did not tell you that Queen Astrid was my mother," Olaf cried in assumed surprise.

"There was no need to tell me," returned Thorir. "For even before I had spoken a word with you I had guessed both your name and kin. You are the son of King Triggvi Olafson. It was you who, in your infancy, were pursued through the land by Queen Gunnhild's spies. It was you who, escaping from Sweden with your mother, were captured by Esthonian vikings and sold into slavery. Then, by some chance which I know not of, you were received at the court of King Valdemar the Sunny. Afterwards you joined the vikings of Jomsburg and passed by the name of Ole the Esthonian. It was you who, in the sea fight against Earl Hakon, rivalled in skill and prowess the most famous vikings of all Scandinavia. A pity it is that instead of going a-warring in England you did not again direct your force against Earl Hakon and drive him from the throne which you, and you alone of all living men, should occupy. It is you, and not Earl Hakon, who are the rightful king of all Norway. The realm is yours by the right of your royal descent from King Harald Fairhair, and I make no doubt that were you to sail into Thrandheim fiord, you would at once be hailed by the people as their deliverer and accepted as their sovereign king."

Thus with guileful speech and subtle flattery did Thorir Klakka seek to entice Olaf over to Norway, to the end that Earl Hakon might secretly waylay him and bring him to his death, and so clear his own path of a rival whom he feared. And Olaf, listening, received it all as the very truth, nor doubted for an instant that the people were waiting ready to welcome him back to the land of his fathers.

There were many reasons urging him to this journey. In the first place, his beautiful young wife, the Princess Gyda, had died very suddenly only a few weeks after their coming to Dublin. She had been taken off by a fever, and her death gave Olaf so much sorrow that he found no more happiness in the home to which she had brought him. There was all her wealth for Olaf to enjoy if he had so wished, and he might even have become the king in Dublin. But he had wealth of his own and in plenty, and had no great desire to wait for the death of his brother-in-law before being raised to the Irish kingship. There was also the thought of again joining Queen Astrid, his mother, who had done so much for him in his infancy, and who now, doubtless, believed him to be dead. For her sake alone, if for no other, he wanted more earnestly than ever before to go back to Norway. Moreover, he had heard from Thorir that the people of Norway were still strong believers in the old gods, and in blood sacrifice and the worship of wooden images; he had heard that Earl Hakon was a bitter enemy of the Christians, that he forebade his people to give hospitality to any christened man or woman; and this knowledge had put a new ambition into Olaf's mind--the ambition to establish the Christian faith throughout the length and breadth of Norway.

So not many days had passed by ere he got ready five of his ships and set sail. He took with him several Christian priests who had followed him from England, and Thorir was in company with him. He sailed first to the South Isles, and thence up north into the Pentland Firth. Here he encountered a terrible storm. His seamen were afraid, but he called upon them to put their trust in God, and they took new courage. Yet the storm did not abate, so Olaf made for the Orkneys, and there had shelter in a quiet haven.

Right glad were the Orkney folk to see him among them once again, for now they deemed that he had come to fulfil his former promise and deliver them from the oppressive rule of Earl Hakon.

Now Thorir had charged Olaf not to reveal his true name to any man until he should be safe in Norway and sure of his success. Accordingly the islanders regarded him as a brave viking and nothing more. Nevertheless, they gathered round him, saying that they were ready and willing to follow him across the sea and to help him to drive Earl Hakon to his deserved doom. To test their fidelity Olaf summoned a great meeting of the folk and called one of their jarls before him. Few words were spoken before Olaf, to the surprise of all present, declared that the jarl must let himself be christened or that there and then he should die.

"If you and your people refuse to be baptized," Olaf said, "then I will fare through the isles with fire and sword, and I will lay waste the whole land!"

Thorir Klakka laughed to himself at hearing this bold threat, and he thought how ill it would go with any man who should attempt such a thing in Norway.

But there was something in Olaf Triggvison's nature which compelled obedience. The Orkney jarl saw well that the threat was made in serious earnest, and he chose to be christened.

Now this meeting of the islanders was held on the margin of one of the lakes, where stood the heathen temple which Olaf himself had helped to build. And now he had his men pull down this temple to the ground, so that not a stone of it remained standing in its place. Having thus made a semblance of banishing the old faith in Odin and Thor, he set about teaching the greater faith in Christ. He had in his company a certain priest named Thangbrand, a mighty man who could wield the sword as well as any viking, and whose voice was as the sound of thunder. Thangbrand stood up to his knees in the lake, and as the people came out to him, one by one, he sprinkled them with water and made upon them the sign of the cross. Thus were all the islanders, men, women, and children, made Christians. So when these ceremonies were over, Olaf weighed anchor and sailed out eastward for Norway.

Ill content was Thorir Klakka at seeing with what ease Olaf Triggvison had gained influence over these people, and how ready all men were to follow and obey him. If his power were so strong over men who owed him no allegiance, and who did not even know of his royal birth, how much greater must it be over the people of Norway, whose adherence to the family of Harald Fairhair would give them a double reason for obeying him? If Olaf should ever set foot in Norway and proclaim his real name then it might go far more ill with Hakon of Lade than the earl had supposed, when he sent his friend Thorir across to Ireland. As the ships sailed eastward across the sea Thorir thought this matter over, and it came into his mind that it would be better for Hakon's safety that Olaf Triggvison should never be allowed to reach his intended destination.

On a certain night Olaf stood alone at the forward rail of his ship, looking dreamily out upon the sea. The oars were inboard, and there were but few men about the decks, for a good wind that was blowing from the southwest filled the silken sails and sent the vessel onward with a rush of snowy foam along her deep sides, and there was no work to be done save by the man who stood at the tiller. To the south the sea and sky were dark, but in the northern heavens there was an arch of crimson, flickering light, from which long trembling shafts of a fainter red shot forth into the zenith, casting their ruddy reflections upon the waves. The gaunt, gilded dragon at the prow stood as though bathed in fire, and the burnished gold of Olaf's crested helmet, the rings on his bare arms, the hilt of his sword, and the knitted chains of his coat of mail gleamed and glanced in the red light as though they were studded with gems.

This red light, flashing in the midnight sky, was believed by the Norsemen to be the shining of Thor's beard. But as Olaf Triggvison now looked upon it from his ship's bow, he understood it to be a message of hope sent from Heaven, beckoning him onward to his native land in the north, there to avenge his father's death, to reconquer his realm, and to reign as the first truly Christian King of Norway. And yet as his vessel sailed on, plunging through the dashing foam, with her prow rising and falling within the wide span of that great rosy arch, strange doubts came over him, the old beliefs still lingered in his mind, and he began to think that perhaps his new learning was false, that Thor might after all be supreme in the world, and that this red light in the sky was an evidence of his continued power, a visible defiance of Christ.

Olaf was thinking these thoughts when, above the wailing of the wind and the swishing of the waves, he heard, or fancied he heard, someone walking behind him across the deck. He turned quickly. No one could be seen; but his eyes rested upon the shadow cast by the hilt of his sword upon the boards of the deck. The shadow was in the form of the cross. The sign was prophetic, and in an instant all his doubts vanished.

"Christ is triumphant!" he cried.

The words were still on his lips when he heard the creaking of a bowstring. An arrow flashed before him, struck against the peak of his helmet and fell at his feet upon the deck. Then he saw the cloaked figure of a man steal quickly away into the shadow of the sails.

Olaf picked up the arrow and examined it. By a mark upon its shaft and the trimming of its feathers he knew it to be an arrow taken from his own cabin. He also knew that its point was poisoned.

"Never did I suspect that I had a traitor in my following," he said as he went aft towards his cabin. "Some man has attempted to take my life. But whosoever he be, I shall surely find him and punish him!"

He searched among the shadows of the bulwarks and down among the rowers' benches, but saw no trace of his secret enemy. When he entered his cabin he found only Thorir Klakka, lying, as it seemed, asleep upon the floor with an empty drinking horn beside him and breathing heavily. Olaf thought that the man had been taking over much mead, so left him there and went out upon the deck to tell his friend Kolbiorn of this attempt upon his life. But as soon as Olaf was out of the cabin Thorir rose, wakeful enough now that he was alone, and took from under him a longbow which he placed in the rack.

"The man bears a charmed life!" muttered Thorir, "or else he has eyes in the back of his head. Ill luck is mine! Had I but aimed a finger's breadth lower he would now have been dead, and Earl Hakon might have been saved the trouble of laying traps for him!"

Throughout that night Olaf was engaged searching for his unknown enemy; but without avail. He questioned every man on board, but all swore by the sign of the cross that they had seen nothing. For a time Olaf was forced to suspect Thorir Klakka; but he soon dismissed the thought. Thorir's conduct towards him had been from the time of their first meeting so full of goodwill and seeming friendliness that it was impossible to fix suspicion on him, and indeed there was no man among all the ship's company who showed more concern over this matter than did Thorir, or who made greater efforts to discover the miscreant who had dared to attempt the life of the well beloved chief.

CHAPTER XV: THE EVIL EARL.

Early on the next morning the ships were within sight of the high lying coast of Norway. By Thorir's treacherous advice, Olaf had steered his course for a part of the country where Earl Hakon's power was greatest, and where it was expected that Hakon himself might at that time be staying. Steering in among the skerries Olaf made a landing on the island of Moster, in the shire of Hordaland. Here he raised his land tent and planted in front of it the cross, together with his own standard; and when all the men were ashore he had his priests celebrate the mass. He met with no opposition, for the people of the place were then busy on their fields, and there was nothing unusual in the sight of a few peaceful ships anchoring off their shores.

Thorir had advised a landing on this particular island because, as it had been arranged, he knew that here he would gain private news of Earl Hakon, and learn how he might best betray King Olaf into Hakon's clutches. When Thorir heard, therefore, that the earl was at Trondelag, he told Olaf that there was nothing for him to do but to keep it well hidden who he was, and to sail northward with all diligence, so that he might attack Earl Hakon unawares and slay him. At the same time he sent secret word to Hakon, bidding him prepare his plans for the slaying of Olaf Triggvison.

Believing every word that Thorir told him, and trusting in the man's seeming honesty, Olaf accepted the advice, and fared northward day and night until he came to Agdaness, at the mouth of the Thrandheim fiord, and here he made a landing.

Now a great surprise was in store for Thorir Klakka. All this time, since his setting out west to Ireland in search of Olaf, he had rested assured that the power of Earl Hakon was unassailable, and that the bonders, or landholders, were not only well disposed towards him, but also ready to stand firmly by him through all dangers. He had intentionally deceived Olaf Triggvison by representing that the earl might easily be overthrown and his subjects as easily won over to the side of a new king. To his great dismay he now discovered that, while telling a wilful untruth, he had all the time been unwittingly representing the actual condition of the country. During the absence of Thorir from Norway, Hakon had committed certain acts which had gained for him the hatred and contempt of the whole nation. The peasants of Thrandheim were united in open rebellion against him; they had sent a war summons through the countryside, and had gathered in great numbers, intending to fall upon the Evil Earl and slay him.

Olaf Triggvison could not, therefore, have chosen a more promising moment for his arrival in the land. He had only to make himself known in order to secure the immediate allegiance and homage of the people.

When Olaf entered the mouth of the fiord with his five longships and anchored off Agdaness, he heard that Earl Hakon was lying with his ships farther up the firth, and also that he was at strife with the bonders. So Olaf made no delay, but weighed anchor again and rowed east into the sunlit fiord. He had not gone very far when, from behind a rocky headland, three vessels of war appeared upon the blue water, rowing out to meet him, with their red battle shields displayed. But suddenly, as they drew nearer to him, they turned about towards the land and fled in all haste. Olaf made no doubt that they were Hakon's ships, so he put extra men to the oars and bade them give chase.

Now the retreating ships were commanded, not by Earl Hakon, but by his favourite son Erland, who had come into the fiord to his father's help against the bonders. When Erland found that he was being pursued a great fear came upon him lest he should be driven farther into the fiord and into the clutches of the bonders, whom he knew to be waiting to give him battle, so when he saw that Olaf was coming close upon him he ran his ships aground, leapt overboard, and straightway made for the shore.

Then Olaf brought his five ships close in upon him and assailed him with arrows, killing many of his men as they swam to land. Olaf saw a man swimming past who was exceedingly fair; so he caught up the tiller, and, taking good aim, flung it at him, striking him on the head. This man was Erland himself, and so he lost his life.

Olaf and his folk took many of the men prisoners and made them take the peace. From them he heard the tidings that Earl Hakon had taken flight and that all his warriors had deserted him.

Now, when this little battle was over, and Erland's ships had been captured, Olaf Triggvison rowed yet farther into the fiord to Trondelag, where all the chieftains and peasants were assembled. Here he went ashore and, dressed in his finest body armour, with his towering gold helmet and his cloak of crimson silk, walked up into the midst of the people, attended only by his friend Kolbiorn Stallare and two guards.

The peasants stared at him amazed, wondering what manner of great man this was who had so suddenly appeared before them. And two of their chieftains went forward to meet him, uncovering their heads. One asked him his name and the reason of his coming.

"Your questions are soon answered," said he; and the clear ring of his voice was heard even by those who stood far apart. "I am come to offer myself to the people of this land, to defend them against all wrong, and to uphold their laws and rights. My name is Olaf. I am the son of King Triggvi Olafson, who was the grandson of King Harald Fairhair."

At hearing these words the whole crowd of people arose with one accord and rent the air with their joyous greetings, for it needed no great proof for them to be assured that he was indeed of the race of the old kings of Norway. Some of the elder men, seeing him, declared that he was surely King Hakon the Good come back to earth again, younger and fairer and nobler than he had been of yore. The young warriors who stood near were lost in admiration of his tall and handsome figure, of his giant strength, his large clear eyes and long golden hair, and they envied him the splendour of his costly armour and beautiful clothing. To follow such a man into battle, they thought, would be worth all the glories of Valhalla.

"All hail to King Olaf!" they cried. And the cry was echoed upon every side.

Many of those present wanted Olaf to be at once formally proclaimed king of all Norway, but others of the more sober sort objected.

"King he shall surely be," they said. "But let him be made so without undue haste. Let him first prove his worthiness by some act of prowess."

"I am ready to prove it in whatsoever way you wish," said Olaf. "What would you have me do?"

One of the chieftains then stepped in front of him and said:

"There is one thing, lord, that we would have you do; and by the doing of it you would gain the gratitude of every man and woman in Thrandheim."

"And what thing is that?" asked Olaf.

"It is that you shall follow in pursuit of Earl Hakon and bring him to his bane."

"Gladly will I pursue him," returned Olaf, "if I may know what direction he has taken, or in what part of the land I may most surely find him."

Then the chieftain called one of the young warriors to him and questioned him closely concerning Hakon.

The young man explained that the earl had escaped from out of Gauldale, where he had been in hiding, and that he had gone off attended only by a certain thrall named Kark. Men had given chase to him, and at the edge of a deep morass they had found the footprints of the earl's horse. Following the footprints they had come into the middle of the morass, and there they found the horse itself struggling in the mire, with Hakon's cloak lying near, seeming to show that the morass had been his death.

"Earl Hakon is wily enough to have put both horse and cloak in the morass with intent to deceive his pursuers," said one of the bystanders. "For my own part I would stake my hopes of Valhalla upon it that he might even now be found at the farmstead of Thora of Rimul; for Thora is his dearest friend of all the dale folk."

Thora of Rimul sat spinning at the doorway of her home in a sheltered dale among the hills. The birch trees were breaking out into fresh buds, the young lambs gambolled on the flowery knolls, and the air was musical with the songs of birds. Thora was considered the fairest woman in all Thrandheim. Her hair was as fair as the flax upon her spindle, and her eyes were as blue as the clear sky above her head. Her heart was lightsome, too; for she had won the love of the great Earl Hakon--Hakon, the conqueror of the vikings of Jomsburg, the proud ruler of all Norway. It was he who had given her the gold ring that was now upon her white finger, and he had promised her that he would make her his queen. She did not believe that what people said of him was true--that he was black of heart, and cruel and base. His hollow words had not sounded hollow to her ears nor had she seen anything of deceitfulness in his eyes.

He had praised her beauty and declared that he loved her, and so she loved him in return.

As she sat there spinning, there was a sudden commotion among the ewes and lambs. She looked up and beheld two men standing in the shadow of the trees. One of them presently left the other and came towards her. He was a low browed, evil looking man, with a bushy black beard and long tangled hair. She rose and went to meet him, knowing him for Kark, Earl Hakon's thrall. He bade her go in among the trees, where the earl was waiting. So she went on into the wood, wondering why Hakon had not come forth and greeted her in the open as was his custom.

Now, so soon as she saw him she knew that some great ill had happened, for his hands trembled and his legs shook under him. His eyes that she had thought so beautiful were bleared and bloodshot, and there were deep lines about his face which she had never before seen. It seemed to her that he had suddenly become a decrepit old man.

"Why do you tremble so?" she asked as she took his hand.

He looked about him in fear.

"Hide me!" he cried. "Hide me! I am in danger. Shame and death are overtaking me. The young King Olaf is in the land, and he is hunting me down!"

"And who is the young King Olaf that he has power to fill the heart of the great Earl Hakon with terror?" asked Thora. "You who have vanquished the vikings of Jomsburg can surely withstand the enmity of one weak man."

"Not so," answered Hakon in a trembling voice. "King Olaf is mightier far than I. And he has the whole of Norway at his back, while I--I have but this one faithful servant. Saving him alone every man in the land is against me."

He looked round in renewed fear. Even the rustling of the tree branches struck terror to his heart.

"Hide me! hide me!" he cried again.

"Little use is there in hiding you in this place," returned Thora. "King Olaf will be seeking you here before very long, for many men know that I would fain help you, and they will surely lead him here and search for you in my household both within and without. Yet, for the love I bear you, Earl Hakon, I will indeed hide you so that neither shame nor death shall come near you."

She led him through among the trees to the back of the steadings. "There is but one place where I deem that King Olaf will not think of seeking for such a man as you," she said; "and that is in the ditch under the pig sty."

"The place is not one that I would have chosen," said Hakon. "But we must take heed to our lives first of all."

Then they went to the sty, which was built with its back against a large boulder stone. Kark took a spade and cleared away the mire, and dug deep until by removing many stones and logs he opened up a sort of cave. When the rubbish had been borne away Thora brought food and candles and warm rugs. Earl Hakon and the thrall hid themselves in the hole and then Thora covered them over with boards and mould, and the pigs were driven over it.

Now, when evening was falling there came along the strath certain horsemen, and the leader of them was King Olaf Triggvison. Thora of Rimul saw them coming, with the light of the setting sun glittering on their armour, and when they halted at her door she greeted them in good friendship.

King Olaf dismounted and asked her if she knew ought of Earl Hakon of Lade. At sight of the handsome young king she for a moment hesitated, thinking to betray the earl. But when Olaf asked her again she shook her head and said that she was not Earl Hakon's keeper, nor knew where he might be.

Nevertheless, King Olaf doubted her, and he bade his followers make a search within and without the farmstead. This they did, but none could find trace of the man they sought. So Olaf called all his men about him to speak to them, and he stood up on the same boulder stone that was at the back of the swine sty. He declared in a loud voice that he would give a great reward and speedy furtherance to the man who should find Earl Hakon and bring him to his death.

Now, this speech was plainly heard by both Earl Hakon himself and his thrall as they crouched together in the cave, and by the light of the candle that stood on the ground between them each eagerly watched the other's face.

"Why are you so pale, and now again as black as earth?" asked Earl Hakon. "Is it not that, tempted by this offer of reward, you intend to betray me?"

"Nay," answered Kark. "For all King Olaf's gold I will not betray you."

"On one and the same night were we both born," said the earl, "and we shall not be far apart in our deaths."

For a long time they sat in trembling silence, mistrustful of each other, and neither daring to sleep. But as the night wore on Kark's weariness got the better of him, but he tossed about and muttered in his sleep. The earl waked him and asked what it was that he had been dreaming.

Kark answered, rubbing his eyes: "I dreamt that we were both on board the same ship, and that I stood at the helm as her captain."

"That must surely mean that you rule over your own destiny as well as mine," said Earl Hakon. "Be faithful to me, therefore, and when better days come you shall be well rewarded."

Again Kark curled himself up to sleep, and again, as it seemed, he was disturbed by dreams; so Hakon roused him once more and asked him to tell his dream.

"I thought I was at Lade," answered the thrall, "and there I saw King Olaf Triggvison. He spoke to me, and I thought that he laid a gold necklace about my neck."

"The meaning of that must be that Olaf Triggvison will put a blood red ring about your neck whensoever ye meet," said the earl. "Therefore beware of him, Kark, and be faithful to me. Then you will enjoy good things from me always, as you have done before; so betray me not."

Thereafter they both sat wakeful, staring at each other with the flickering candlelight between them. Neither dared to close his eyes. But towards morning Earl Hakon leaned back against the rock, with his head thrown back. Sleep overwhelmed him, yet he was troubled, for he started and rolled uneasily as though in a nightmare, and at times he moaned and muttered as if in anguish, so that Kark could not look upon him but with horror. At last, when the earl was quiet, Kark sprang up, gripped a big knife from out of his belt and thrust it into his master's throat.

That was the bane of Earl Hakon.

On the next day Olaf Triggvison was in Lade, and there came to him a man naming himself Kark, bringing with him the severed head of Earl Hakon, which he offered to the king. When Olaf had received proof that the head was indeed that of the earl, he asked Kark how he had come by it, and the thrall told all that had befallen and claimed his reward.

Now King Olaf hated a traitor beyond all men, so he had Kark led away, and ordered one of his berserks to smite the head off him, thus fulfilling the murdered earl's prophecy, for a ring not of gold but of blood was put about the traitor's neck.

King Olaf then fared with many of the bonders out to Nid holm. This island, at the mouth of the river Nid, was kept in those days for the slaying of thieves and evil men, and a gallows stood there upon which the head of Earl Hakon was now hung, side by side with that of his thrall. The bonders crowded round the foot of the gallows, throwing stones and clods of earth at the heads, and crying out that there they fared meetly together, rascal by rascal.

And now that Earl Hakon was dead the people did not shrink from speaking their minds concerning him, and giving free vent to their hatred of his low cunning and his

87

faithlessness, his cruelty and his profligacy. Even his zeal for blood offering and his strong belief in the pagan gods were now regarded with wide disfavour, for it could not be forgotten that he had sacrificed his own son to propitiate the god of war, and this act, added to the evil deeds that he had more recently committed had brought upon him such contempt that the whole of Norway rejoiced at his death.

Olaf Triggvison's claim to the throne of Norway was not for a moment disputed. In the first place his manly beauty and his resemblance to King Hakon the Good gained him immediate favour, and his personal strength and prowess might have been in itself sufficient to warrant his being chosen as a successor to Earl Hakon. But in addition to this there was the undoubted fact that he was a direct descendant of Harald Fairhair, and had therefore the greatest of all claims to the kingdom in which his fathers had reigned. So, very soon after the death of Hakon, a general Thing, or gathering of the people, was held in Trondelag, and Olaf was formally proclaimed the king of all Norway, and the rule given to him according to ancient laws.

The district of Thrandheim was at that time the most populous and important in the land, and the Thranders had exercised the right (a right which they reserve to this day) of proclaiming a new monarch in the name of the whole nation. Nevertheless it was necessary for King Olaf to travel throughout the country to lay personal claim to his dominion, and to receive the allegiance of his subjects remote and near. The news of his coming into Norway was not long in reaching the farthest extremities of the realm. Everywhere it was told how, having by help of his mother's bravery escaped the wrath of the wicked Queen Gunnhild, he had lived as a slave in Esthonia, how he had been rescued by Sigurd Erikson and educated at the court of King Valdemar, how he had roved as a viking on the Baltic, and, after invading England, had at last come back to his native land to claim his own. So that wherever he journeyed he found that his fame had gone before him to prepare the way. He was greeted everywhere with enthusiastic homage. His natural kindliness, his manly bearing, and his winning manners attracted everyone with whom he came in contact, and he was recognized as a king of whom the nation might well be proud. In token of the glory that he had won in foreign lands the people gave him the name of Olaf the Glorious.

CHAPTER XVI: THE CHRISTENING OF NORWAY.

King Olaf's first thought on ascending the throne of Norway was that he would make it his mission to convert the country to Christianity. This had been once before attempted by his own uncle, King Hakon the Good, the foster son of Athelstane of England; but Hakon the Good was a weak man, who, instead of winning his people to the true faith, had allowed himself to drift back into paganism. Olaf was by nature better fitted for the task, being zealous in the faith and strong in the conviction of the sanctity of his cause. He resolved to stand firm against all opposition, and if gentle persuasion should not avail he would have no scruple in employing physical force. To abolish the custom of blood sacrifice, to destroy all heathen temples, and to supplant the worship of the pagan gods by preaching the gospel of Christ--this was to be his life work.

He was, however, wise enough to recognize that in order to succeed in his mission it was necessary for him first to make his own position as monarch perfectly secure and unassailable. So rapidly did he establish himself in the hearts of the people that even at the end of the first summer he found that he might with safety begin his task. His one possible rival and natural enemy, Earl Erik Hakonson, with some few others of the kin of the late earl, had fled in fear from the land, leaving him in absolute possession; and the lords of Viken and other districts of the south, who had hitherto held their lands of the King of Denmark, now became King Olaf's men, and paid him homage and tribute.

At this time Olaf could only depend upon his priest Thangbrand for practical help. Thangbrand was a Saxon who had formerly been attached to the see of Canterbury. He was a man of very violent temper, and his readiness to enter a quarrel and to draw his sword must have made him a very singular exponent of the gospel of peace. Olaf saw very soon that he would require further help than this pugnacious priest could give; so he sent Thangbrand over to England, bidding him fare to Canterbury and bring back with him as many holy men as might be willing to serve him as missionaries.

Meanwhile King Olaf, with some of his chosen companions, journeyed south into Viken, where his mother lived with her husband Lodin--the same who had bought her out of her bondage. There he abode throughout the winter among his own kindred as well as many who had been great friends with his father. They welcomed him with very great love.

And now, while the king was living with his friends in quiet comfort and homeliness, he laid his plans most earnestly before them, craving that they should help him with all their might. He said that he intended to have the Christian faith set forth throughout all his realm, and that he would bring about the christening of Norway or else die in the endeavour. Accordingly he began by going about in Viken, bidding the peasants take baptism, so it came to pass that the district which his father, Triggvi, had formerly ruled over was the first part of Norway to receive the true faith.

He was still in Viken when at the end of the winter Thangbrand returned from England with a company of priests. Among them was a certain Bishop Sigurd, a man of grave and gentle spirit, most learned and eloquent, who stood at Olaf's right hand during the whole five years of his reign.

Now Bishop Sine, of Canterbury, had presented Thangbrand with a very costly and curiously wrought shield. It was made of burnished bronze, inlaid with gold and precious stones, and it bore the image of the crucified Christ. Olaf admired this shield and desired to buy it. Thangbrand loved money more than ornament, and he sold the shield to the king for a very large sum. Finding himself suddenly rich, the priest went off to enjoy himself. He fell into a drunken brawl with a certain viking, who challenged him to fight. A desperate duel was fought and the viking was killed. Great ill feeling was aroused against Thangbrand by this unpriestly incident, and he went back full of penitence to King Olaf.

Olaf foresaw that he would have trouble with this man, and he would no longer bear to have him about his house; so, to get rid of him, he sent him on a mission to Iceland, to convert the heathen there. Thangbrand was absent in Iceland for three winters, and although he had great success and brought the country to the true faith, yet he was not well liked, and the people vexed him by making songs about him. Here, as in Norway, he was boisterous and boastful and over fond of the drinking horn. It is told that in a quarrel with the islanders he slew three men. Howbeit, he was obliged to return to Norway with his mission only half fulfilled.

King Olaf met with no opposition in his endeavour to convert the people of Viken and Agder. In the district of Ringarike he christened a certain little boy, the son of Harald Groenske, who was of the race of Harald Fairhair. The king named the boy Olaf, and in giving him his blessing said that he would one day be a very great man. This same Olaf Haraldson afterwards became the King of Norway and a very great evangelist. He is known in history by the title of Olaf the Saint, and he is to this day regarded as the patron saint of Norway. He fought many battles in England, and, for this reason perhaps, he is often wrongly confused with his godfather, Olaf Triggvison.

To tell of all the good and ill happenings that King Olaf met with in his progress through the land would make a long story. In many districts he had but to announce his mission, and the people at once yielded. In other places the people were very slow to understand that there could be any advantage in changing their religion; but Olaf never left them before every man and woman had been christened. Often, however, he was met by bands of armed men who declared that they would sooner die than consent to give up their old faith in Odin and Thor, and then the king enforced his doctrines at the point of the sword, or even by torture. When moved to anger he was guilty of committing cruelties which in his calmer moments he sorely regretted, but it is to be supposed that he never took to violent measures unless when very severely provoked. For the most part he generally found that wise words were a better argument than either the sword or fire.

Always when he came to a place where the people were still pagan it was his custom to summon a great meeting, and then he would tell of how the folk of another district had accepted Christianity and torn down their sacrificing houses, and now believed in the true God, who shaped heaven and earth and knew all things. Then perhaps he would fall into argument with one of the leading men of the place and show how the God of christened men was almighty, and how Thor and Odin must therefore be rejected.

On one such occasion a chief named Gudbrand answered him thus:

"We do not know about whom you are talking, O king. Do you call him God whom neither you nor any other man can see? We have a god whom we may see every day, but he is not out today because the weather is so wet. He will look terrible and great to you, and fear will creep into your breast if he comes to the gathering of our people."

The king then asked how their god was made, and Gudbrand answered that he was made in the image of Thor, that he had a hammer in his hand, was of large size and hollow inside, and that there was a platform made under him on which he stood when outside the temple.

Olaf said, "I would very much like to see that god. But for my own part I have made up my mind never to believe in logs and stones, though they be in the shape of fiend or man, whose power I do not understand; and although I have been told that they have great power, yet it seems to me very unlikely, for I find that those images which are called gods are in every way uglier and less powerful than myself. How much less powerful are they therefore than the great God who rules over the whole universe, who makes the rain to fall and the sun shine!"

"If, as you say, your God is so powerful, then let him send sunshine tomorrow and not rain as we have today," said Gudbrand.

On the next day, as it chanced, there was no rain, and when the people were all gathered together in the early dawn Bishop Sigurd rose in his gown, with a mitre on his head and a crozier in his hand, and preached to the peasants and told them many tokens which God had shown. And presently King Olaf saw a crowd of men approaching, carrying a large image, ornamented all over with gold and silver. The people all stood up and bowed to the monster, which was placed in the middle of the meeting place.

"Where is your God now, O king?" cried Gudbrand, rising and addressing Olaf. "It seems to me that your boasting, and that of the horned man, whom you call your bishop, is far less than yesterday. It is because our god, who rules all, has come, and looks on you with keen eyes. And I see that you are full of terror at sight of him! Now throw off this new superstition of yours--this belief in a God who cannot be seen--and acknowledge the greatness of Thor!"

King Olaf whispered to Kolbiorn, who was at his side: "If during my speech it happens that the people look away from this idol of theirs," said he, "then go you forward and strike the thing a lusty blow with your club."

And aloud he said: "The god with whom you have threatened us is blind and deaf and can help neither himself nor others; nor can he move anywhere from his place unless he be carried. Of what use is such a god? Now look into the east!" he added, pointing to the rising sun. "Behold! There comes the messenger of our God, bringing light and warmth into the world!"

The people all turned with their faces to the sun. At the same moment Kolbiorn raised his club and struck their god so that the image fell to pieces; and it is said that vipers and rats and mice ran out of it and that the peasants were afraid.

"You see what has become of your god!" cried King Olaf. "What folly it is to believe in such things! One blow has shattered your Thor into fragments. Now I demand that you shall never again make images of wood or stone, nor worship any but the one true God. And I offer you two choices. Either you accept Christianity here on this spot, or you fight a battle with me today."

So the people, unwilling to take to arms and seeing that the king had a great host of warriors at his back, agreed to listen to the teachings of the bishop, and finally to have themselves baptized. Olaf left a priest among them to keep them steadfast in the faith, and to keep them from lapsing into paganism.

King Olaf stood north along the land, christening all folk wheresoever he came. But in the wintertime he went back into Trondelag. He built a town on the bank of the river Nid, and a great hall for himself up above Ship Creek. He called the town Nidaros, and it is to this day the capital of Norway, although its name has been changed to Trondhjem, or Drontheim.

Now on a certain winter's night the king had been feasting in his hall. His guests had been drinking deeply, and the gray haired scalds had been singing and reciting until a late hour. But at last Olaf was left alone beside the fire, with the doors locked. He sat in his oaken chair gazing into the glowing wood upon the hearth. Suddenly the door swung wide open, and a blast of cold night air came in. He looked round and saw upon the threshold a very old man whose cloak was sprinkled with snow. Olaf saw that the stranger had but one eye.

"Oh, pale and shivering graybeard!" cried the king. "Come, warm your vitals with this cup of spiced ale. Be not afraid. Sit here at my side in the light of the flames."

The aged guest obeyed, quaffed the foaming draught, and then stretched out his withered hands before the fire. Then he began to speak to the king and to tell him of things that had happened many hundreds of years before and of many lands whose very names were strange to the king. And it seemed that he would never bring his tale to an end.

At last Bishop Sigurd entered and reminded Olaf that the night was far spent and that it was time for him to go to sleep. But still the guest spoke on, and the king listened enthralled until sleep came over him and his head fell back. Yet even in his sleep he fancied that he still heard the old graybeard's voice telling him of the gods of Asgard and the glories of Valhalla.

When King Olaf awoke he was alone before the black hearth, and it was full morning. He asked after the guest and bade his men call him; but nowhere could the guest be found, nor had any man seen him. They found the doors securely locked, the watchdog was asleep in the yard, and the snow bore no trace of footprints. All declared that no such stranger had ever entered the hall, and that the king had but been dreaming.

Then Olaf called the bishop to his side and, crossing himself, said:

91

"It is no dream that I have had. I know that my guest will never return, and yet I know that he was here. The triumph of our faith is sure. Odin the Great is dead, for the one eyed stranger was his ghost!"

So certain was King Olaf that the power of Odin was broken that after this time he was less eager to follow up his mission, for he believed that he had already established the Christian faith. He said to his bishop that all the old gods were no more and that Christ alone was supreme.

"Not yet is it so," answered the bishop, "for Thor still reigns among the sea rovers of the far north. I have heard that there lives a great viking in Salten fiord who is skilled in sorcery. A wizard he is, for he has power over the wind and the sea, and he and his great horde of heathens still worship Odin and Thor and offer them blood sacrifice. Rand is his name, and he is chief over all the Godoe Isles."

Roused from his apathy, Olaf declared that he would conquer this bold viking and bring him to christening or himself be conquered. So he got together his ships and sailed into the north.

At the mouth of Salten fiord he encountered foul weather, and was forced to lie there storm stayed for many days. So long did the storm continue that at length he questioned the bishop, asking if he knew any remedy.

Bishop Sigurd answered that it was surely Rand the Wizard who, by his sorcery, had caused the winds to blow, and he ascended to the ship's forecastle and raised a large crucifix, lighting tapers around it and sprinkling holy water about the decks. It is told that the storm abated near to the ships while it still roared wildly some distance away from them. The lashed waves stood like a wall on either side, leaving a track of calm water, through which the vessels sailed.

When at last King Olaf came abreast of Rand's stronghold he saw the viking's dragonship lying at anchor in the bay. It was the largest and most splendid ship that he had ever seen. The king landed with his priests and fighting men, and went straightway up to the wizard's homestead and broke open the door. Rand was taken prisoner and bound hand and foot, as were also a great many of his men.

King Olaf had the viking brought before him, and bade him take christening.

"I will not take your possessions and your riches from you," said the king, "but will be your friend if you will be worthy thereof, and accept the true faith."

But Rand cried out at him, saying that nothing would induce him to believe in Christ. He blasphemed so much that Olaf became wrothful and said that Rand should die the worst of deaths. This threat had no effect upon the blasphemer. So, according to the legend, he was taken and tied to a tree. A gag was set between his teeth to open his mouth, and a live adder was forced down his throat. The adder cut its way through his side, killing him with its poison.

This cruel act has always been regarded as a blot upon the fame of Olaf Triggvison, but Olaf's fanaticism led him to believe that praise rather than blame was due to him for thus punishing the enemies of God. Moreover, this man Rand had been the terror of all peaceful men. He had laid waste many villages, and made human sacrifices to the pagan gods. In bringing him to his death Olaf was, in his own way, but giving just punishment to a criminal.

King Olaf took very great wealth from Rand's stronghold, and all the men who had been in the viking's service were allowed to go free on condition that they would first be christened. The dragonship which Rand had commanded now became King Olaf's property, for it was the most beautiful vessel in all Norway, and very much larger than the *Crane*, which Olaf had had built for himself. Forward at the prow there was a very tall dragon's head, overlaid with thick gold, and at the stern was a long dragon's tail, also of gold. When the sails were aloft they took the form of dragon's wings. The king named the ship the *Serpent.*

While Olaf was in Halogaland he deemed it well to sail yet farther north; so he fared out to the Lafoden Isles, and thence along the coasts of Finmark as far even as the North Cape. He baptized all those regions and destroyed many heathen temples and established Christianity far and wide.

In that same summer King Olaf was back again in the Thrandheim country, and had his fleet anchored off Nidaros. Now it was in this part of Norway that Earl Hakon's power had always been greatest, and so zealous had Hakon been in the keeping up of pagan customs that many of the chief men of those parts withstood all King Olaf's efforts to win them over to Christianity, and during his absence in Halogaland these men did all they could to undo the good work that he had done in the earliest days of his reign.

Not many days had Olaf been back in Nidaros when he heard that the Thranders had re-established their temples, restored their idols, and offered blood sacrifice to their gods. The young king was so disturbed in mind over this that he resolved to put a speedy stop to it. He therefore sent his messengers through all the lands bordering on Thrandheim fiord summoning a great meeting of the bonders at a place named Frosta.

Now the bonders quickly guessed the meaning of this summons. They knew that the king would have them abandon their old customs and accept the new faith. But they considered that he had no right to dictate to them; so they turned this summons into one of war, and drew together, both thane and thrall, from all parts of Thrandheim.

When King Olaf came to the meeting, thither also had come the hosts of the bonders, all fully armed, ready to confront him.

When the Thing was established the king rose and spoke before his lieges, first concerning matters of peace and law, and finally he bade them take christening again.

There was one among the bonders named Skeggi Ironbeard, a very rich farmer who cared little for king or earls, but loved only the freedom of his farm, his ale at night, and the warmth of his fireside. He was a huge and cumbersome man with an iron gray beard, and as he stood by the side of his horse his feet were seen to be covered with the mud of his ploughed fields. Near him there was a beautiful girl with very black hair and dark brown eyes. She was his daughter Gudrun.

Well, when King Olaf began to rebuke the people for having gone back from Christian worship, many men looked round at Ironbeard with wise glances.

"Now hold your peace, O king!" cried he, addressing Olaf. "Say not another word of this Christian faith of yours, or, by the hammer of Thor and by the ravens of Odin, we will fall upon you and drive you away out of the land. Thus did we with King Hakon the Good, nor do we account you of a whit more worth than him."

So when King Olaf saw with what fierce minds the bonders confronted him, and how great a force of armed men there were, he felt that he was not prepared to withstand them, and he so turned his speech that it appeared he was at one accord with them.

"It is my wish," said he, "that we make peace and good fellowship together, even as we have hitherto done. I am willing, therefore, to be present at your worship at any time, and to witness your greatest ceremony of blood offering. We may then take counsel together and consider which form of worship shall prevail."

Then the bonders thought that the king might easily be persuaded to adopt their old time customs, and their indignation against him was appeased. Thereafter all the talk went peacefully, and at the last it was determined that a great midsummer feast of offering should be held at Mere, and thither should come all the lords of the land and chiefs of the bonders. King Olaf promised also to be present.

When it wore towards the time appointed for the sacrifice, Olaf gave a great feast at Lade, to which were invited all the chieftains and most powerful land owners of the country side. The guests were royally entertained, and when the feast was over the king ordered his priests to celebrate the mass. A crowd of armed men from Olaf's ships attended the service. The guests saw that they were powerless to resist, so they joined in the worship and awaited the course of events.

When the service was at an end the king rose and addressed his guests. He said:

"When we held Thing the last time, at Frosta, you will remember that I demanded of the peasants that they should accept baptism; and they, on the other hand, demanded that I should join them in sacrifice and make blood offering, even as my kinsman King Hakon the Good had done. I made no objection to this, but promised to be present at the sacrificial feast at Mere. Now I wish to tell you that if I am to make human sacrifice, then I will make the greatest offering of blood that has ever been made in Norway. I will offer human sacrifice to Odin and Frey for good crops and fine weather. But, mind you, it will not be thralls and evildoers that I shall offer to your gods. I will sacrifice the most high born men among you." He then pointed to several of his guests in turn, saying, "You, Ligra of Middlehouse, shall be offered as a sacrifice; and you, Kar of Griting; and you, Haldor of Skerding."

Eight other of the nobles he named, and bade them prepare themselves for death. They all stood back aghast. King Olaf laughed at their craven fears.

"Plainly do I see that you do not relish this proposal," he said. "But if I am to be king in this land I will be obeyed. I have commanded that Norway shall be a Christian land, and I shall have it so, even if I lose my own life in bringing it about. Here is my bishop, ready to baptize you. Take christening, therefore, and you shall still live. Refuse, and you shall surely be sacrificed in the manner I have said."

Not long did they meditate before choosing the easier alternative. They agreed to be christened there and then, and Bishop Sigurd at once baptized them, and all the bonders who were present. Before they were allowed to depart King Olaf demanded that they should give him their sons or brothers as hostages. Thus by a peaceful stratagem he gained his ends.

Now, when the time arrived for the midsummer sacrifice at Mere, Olaf went thither with a great host of followers. But such of the peasants and land owners who had still resisted Christianity, gathered once more, armed to the teeth and defiant as ever. Skeggi Ironbeard was the ringleader of the pagans, and he was everywhere active in the forefront of the opposition.

The king attempted to speak, but the tumult was so great that no one could hear him. At last, when he got a hearing, he repeated his commands that all present should accept baptism and believe in Christ the White.

Ironbeard stepped forward, sword in hand, and, confronting the king, said:

"Now, as before, O king, we protest against your interference with our liberty, and we are here to prevent your breaking our laws and ancient customs. It is held as a sacred custom among us that we shall make sacrifices to our gods, and we now hold that, although you are our king, you have no power to decide which gods we are to believe in, or in what manner we shall worship. It is our intention, therefore, that you shall make blood offering here as other kings have done before you."

King Olaf listened patiently to this speech and declared himself ready to keep his promise. So, accompanied by many of his men, he entered the temple.

It was a very large and splendid building. The door was of beautifully carved oak, and the handle was in the form of a large gold ring which Earl Hakon had had put there. In the inside there were two great rooms, the first or outer one being the chamber in which feasts of sacrifice were held; the inner one was the more sacred, for here the images of the heathen gods stood on their various altars. The walls were hung with tapestries and adorned with costly metals and precious stones. Even the roof was covered with gold plates.

All who entered were unarmed, for no one was allowed to go through the door bearing a sword or other weapon. But the king carried a stout stick with a heavy gold head. He watched the bonders preparing the pyre for the sacrifice, but before it was lighted he went into the inner chamber and inspected the images of the gods. There sat the figure of Thor, chief among all, with his hammer in his hand and gold and silver rings about him. He was in a chariot of gold, into which were harnessed a pair of goats made of wood and silver.

"What god is this one?" asked Olaf of the bonders who stood near him.

"It is our god Thor," answered one of the chieftains. "He is the most celebrated of all gods, saving only Odin. His eyes flash in the lightning, the wheels of his carriage rumble in the thunder, and the blows of his hammer ring loud in the earthquake. The most powerful of all gods is he."

"And yet," said Olaf; "it seems to me that he is made of nothing more strong than wood. You call him powerful; but I think even I am more powerful than he."

As he spoke these words he hove up his gold headed stick, and while all were looking, he smote Thor a great blow, so that he fell down from his seat and tumbled to fragments upon the stone floor. At the same instant Olaf's men struck down the other idols, while at the temple door Ironbeard was assailed and slain.

Olaf took possession of many of the treasures of the temple, and then razed the building to the ground. And none of the bonders dared to oppose him. After the death of Ironbeard they had no leader bold enough to encounter the king and his men. So the end of it was that they all forsook their heathenish customs and yielded to the king's demands that they should take christening.

After this time King Olaf had no more trouble in Thrandheim, and in the whole of Norway no man dared to speak a word against the faith of Christ. In all places where the temples had been destroyed, the king had Christian churches built. He instituted monasteries throughout the land, governed by bishops and abbots brought over from Rome and Canterbury. From these monasteries many missionaries were sent out into the remoter parts of the country to preach the gospel and to hold the people firmly to the faith. Never again, so long as King Olaf lived, did the Norwegians attempt to return to paganism, and after his death his good work was taken up by his godson and namesake, Olaf the Saint.

CHAPTER XVII: SIGRID THE HAUGHTY.

Now, although the peasants of Thrandheim yielded to King Olaf in the matter of their faith and the forms of their religious ceremonies, yet they were none the less enraged against him on account of the destruction of their beautiful temple and the slaying of Iron Skeggi. This man had been a great chief among them, much honoured for his bodily strength, for his wealth, and for his spirit of independence. Some of his nearer kin had even looked upon the possibility of his being a successor to the great Earl Hakon, and accordingly they regarded Olaf Triggvison as an interloper, who had come to spoil all their hopes of worldly advancement. When their favourite was slain they therefore cast about to find some pretext for either picking a quarrel with King Olaf or of forcing him to make some atonement for the wrong that he was supposed to have done them. And then they thought of Ironbeard's daughter, Gudrun, and of what a good thing it would be for them if the king could be made to wed her. So on a certain day they took Gudrun to where King Olaf was and made their proposals to him.

King Olaf looked at the girl and thought her very fair of feature. Her hair was black as charred wood, and her cheeks were rosy red; but there was an evil glance in her dark eyes that mispleased him. Yet he saw that it was good that there should be a queen in Norway, and urged by his bishop, he allowed himself to be betrothed to Gudrun. It was arranged that they should be wedded at the next yuletide.

In the midwinter King Olaf gave a great bridal feast to his friends in his new banqueting hall at Nidaros. His bishops and priests were there, as also his chief captains and warmen, his scald and his saga men. His mother, Queen Astrid, was at his right hand, while at the other side of him sat Gudrun. The fare was of the best, both food and drink, and there was much merriment around the board, with singing of songs and playing of harps, making of riddles and jests and telling of stories; and of all the company the king was the merriest and the lightsomest. No story was for him too long, nor song too boisterous, nor ale too strong. As often as his drinking horn was emptied, it was filled again to the brim by his cup bearer, and always before he quaffed it he made over it the sign of the cross.

Brightly gleamed the firelight upon helmet and shield and spear, but brighter gleamed the gladness in the young king's eyes; for his realm was now assured to him, his mission was fulfilled, and his glory was complete. It seemed to him that there would now be a lasting peace in the land, with good fellowship among all his subjects, and no more bloodshed or quarrelling or discontent for ever after. He was to wed with Gudrun upon the morrow, and this, he believed, was to be the crown of his happiness.

Now, as the night wore late, and the festivities flagged, the guests rose from the board, and either departed to their several rooms or drew their cloaks about them and lay upon the side benches of the hall, and at length King Olaf was left alone at the table. Very soon he too fell asleep and lay back in his high backed chair, dreaming peaceful dreams. At his feet lay Einar Eindridson, a sturdy lad of sixteen years, whom Olaf had adopted as his favourite page and cup bearer, even as he himself had been adopted by King Valdemar. Between the folds of the silken curtains that overhung the open air spaces in the wall the light of the full moon came in, falling upon King Olaf's handsome face and long golden hair. The sapphires and diamonds studding the band of gold about his head shone out like glittering stars in the pale light. The cross of blood red rubies that hung from his neck chain rose and fell with the regular heaving of his broad chest on which it rested.

All was dark in the hall, save for that one shaft of moonlight. All was silent, save for the crackling of the dying embers on the hearth and the heavy breathing of the men who lay asleep upon the benches and about the rush strewn floor. But as King Olaf slept there came a movement at the far end of the hall, where the darkness was deepest.

Presently a woman's figure glided slowly and cautiously into the fuller light. Her black shadow moved across the floor and crept nearer and nearer to the sleeping king, until at last it halted, shielding his closed eyes. She stood before him. Suddenly her right hand went to her bosom, and she drew forth a long glittering dagger. She stood over him, holding her hand aloft, ready to strike the fatal blow.

"Your hour is at hand, proud king!" she murmured; and her voice sounded through the hall like the soughing of the wintry wind among the pines. "Your hour is at hand, Olaf Triggvison. Never shall my warm lips touch yours. Cold steel shall kiss you now."

She stepped back a pace, so that the moonlight, falling upon him, might show her where to strike. As she did so the hem of her long robe swept across the face of young Einar. The boy awoke and leapt to his feet. He saw a white arm upraised; he saw the gleaming dagger poised over his master's breast. Quick as an arrow's flight the blade flashed to its mark. But quicker still was Einar. In that instant he had caught the white arm in his two strong hands, staying the fatal blow, so that the dagger's point but struck against the ruby cross and did no harm.

The scuffling of feet, the clatter of the dagger upon the floor, and the woman's cry of alarmed surprise awoke the king. Starting from his seat he caught his assailant and held her in the light of the moon. He gazed into her pale and terror stricken face. It was the face of Gudrun.

Then Olaf besought Einar to tell him all that had happened, and Einar picked up the dagger and gave it to his master, telling him how Gudrun had attempted to slay him.

With the earliest peep of dawn Gudrun went forth upon her lonely way, and never again did she come under the same roof with King Olaf.

At this time there lived in Sweden a certain queen named Sigrid. She was the widow of King Erik the Victorious and the mother of King Olaf the Swede. She was very rich and possessed many great manors in Sweden and large landed estates among the islands of the Baltic. Many of the kings of Scandinavia sought to wed with her, wishing to share her wealth and add her dominions to their own. But Sigrid, who, by reason of her great pride and the value that she set upon her own charms, was named Sigrid the Haughty, would have none of them, although often enough she welcomed them as wooers and listened to their fine speeches and their flatteries.

One king there was who wooed her with such ardour that she resolved to rid herself of him at all costs. His name was Harald Groenske (the father of Saint Olaf), and, as he was of the kin of King Harald Fairhair, he considered himself in all respects her equal. Three several times did he journey into Sweden to pay court to her. On the third time he found that there was another wooer at her manor house, one King Vissavald of Gardarike. Both kings were well received, and lodged in a great hall with all their attendant company. The hall was a very old building, as was all its furniture, but there was no lack of good fare. So hospitable, indeed, was Queen Sigrid, that, ere the night was half spent, the two suitors and all their men were drunk, and the guards slept heavily.

In the middle of the night Queen Sigrid surrounded the hall with dry faggots and set a lighted torch to them. The hall was quickly burned to the ground, and all who were within it lost their lives.

"I will teach these little kings what risks they run in wooing me!" said the queen, as from her chamber window she watched the rising flames.

Now Queen Sigrid grew weary of waiting for the coming of a king whom she could consider in all ways worthy of her. Her eyes were lustreless, and her hair was besprinkled with gray, and yet the right man did not offer himself. But in good time she heard of King Olaf the Glorious, and of his great wealth and his prowess, and of how in his person he was so tall and handsome, that men could only compare him with Balder the Beautiful. And now she deemed that she had at last discovered one whose magnificence would match with her own. So she caused messengers to fare across the frontier into Norway to sing her praises, so that King Olaf might learn how fair she was, and how well suited to reign by his side. And it seemed that her messages had the effect that she wished.

On a certain summer day Queen Sigrid sat at her chamber window, overlooking a wide and beautiful river that lay between her own kingdom and Norway. From afar she saw a company of horsemen. They came nearer and nearer, and at last they halted at the

97

gates. Their leader entered and the queen went down to meet him, guessing that he had come upon some errand of great importance.

When he had greeted her, he told her that he had come all the way from Thrandheim, in Norway, with a message from King Olaf Triggvison, who, hearing of her great charms, now offered her his hand in marriage. And as a token of his good faith the king had sent her a gift. The gift was a large ring of gold--the same that Olaf had taken from the door of the temple at Lade.

Full joyous was Queen Sigrid at this good news, and she took the heavy ring and slipped it upon her arm, bidding the messengers take her hospitality for three days and then return to their master, with the word that she favoured his proposal, and agreed to meet him at her manor of Konghelle in three weeks' time.

Now the queen admired that ring, deeming it a most noble gift. It was most beautifully wrought and interwoven with scrolls and circles so delicate that all wondered how the hand of man could achieve such perfection. Everyone praised it exceedingly, and among others to whom Sigrid showed the ring were her own goldsmiths, two brothers. These handled it with more care than others had done, and weighed it in their hands as if they would estimate its value. The queen saw that the smiths spoke in whispers one with the other; so she called them to her and asked if they thought that any man in Sweden could make such a ring.

At this the smiths smiled.

"Wherefore do you mock at the ring?" demanded Sigrid. "Tell me what you have found?"

The smiths shrugged their shoulders.

"If indeed the truth must be spoken," said the elder of the two, "then we have found this, O queen, that there is false metal in the ring."

"Prove what you say!" cried the queen. And she let them break the ring asunder-- and lo! it was shown to be made of copper and not of gold.

Then into Sigrid's eyes there flashed an angry light.

"If King Olaf of Norway can be so false in his gifts, he will be faithless also in his love!" she cried. And she snatched the pieces of the ring and flung them furiously away from her.

Now when the three weeks of his appointment had gone by Olaf Triggvison journeyed east to the trysting place at Konghelle, near the boundary line between Norway and Sweden, and there Queen Sigrid met him. Amazed was Sigrid to see the splendour of the man who offered her marriage. Never before had her eyes rested upon one so tall and handsome and so gloriously attired. Arrived now at his full manhood Olaf looked nobler and more majestic than ever in his life before. His cloak of fine crimson silk clung to his giant frame and showed the muscular moulding of his limbs. His step was light and elastic, and, in spite of his great strength, his movements were gentle and easy as those of a woman. His hands were very large and powerful, yet the touch of them was soft and delicate; and his voice, which could be loud and full as a trumpet blast, could also be lowered to the musical sweetness of a purling brook. His forehead, where his helmet had shielded it from the heat of the sun and from the briny freshness of the sea air, was white and smooth as polished marble; but the lower part of his face was of a clear, rich golden brown. He wore no beard, but the hair was left unshaven on his upper lip and it streamed down on either side of his chin as fine as silk. When he smiled, his white and even teeth gleamed like a row of pearls between the coral redness of his lips. Queen Sigrid, as she beheld him for the first time, had no thought of the ring that he had given her, nor of its falseness.

98

King Olaf, on his part, was more than a little disappointed with the looks of the queen whose praises had been so often whispered in his ears. He had heard that she was young, yet he now saw that her hair was sprinkled with gray, that her eyes had lost the fire and fervour of youth, and that her brow was wrinkled with age. Younger and more comely was his own mother Astrid than this much exalted queen. But, having given his word that he meant to woo her and wed her, he had too much honour to draw back.

They sat together and talked over the matter of their wedding, and of how they would unite their domains and rule together over all the Swedes and Norsemen. And at last he took her hand and swore by the holy rood that he would be true to her.

Now Sigrid the Haughty was still a heathen, and she liked not to hear King Olaf swear by Christian tokens. So she turned upon him with a quick glance of suspicion and contempt in her eyes.

"Such vows do not please me, King Olaf," she said. "It is told that great Odin once swore on the ring. Will you swear by this ring to be true?" And she rose and took up the ring he had sent as a gift, which ere this time her two smiths had repaired.

"O speak not of Odin to me!" cried the king. "He is dead as the stones in the street. By no other symbol than the cross will I swear. Sorry am I to hear that you, Queen Sigrid, are still a believer in the old dead gods. Since this is so, however, there is little use in my being in this place, for I have made up my mind that the woman who weds me shall be a true Christian and not a worshipper of senseless idols hewn out of trees and rocks. Abandon these things, take christening, and believe in the one true God who made all things and knows all things, and then I will wed with you; but not else, O queen."

Queen Sigrid, astonished that any man dared to speak to her in this wise, looked back at King Olaf in anger.

"Never shall I depart from the troth that I have always held," she cried. "And although you had twice the wealth that you have and were yet more glorious than you are, yet never should I obey such a bidding. No, no, King Olaf. I keep true to my faith and to my vows; and can fare very well without you and your new religion. So go back to your bald headed priests and to your singing of mass. I will have none of them!"

Then the king rose in wrath and his face was darkened with gloom. For a moment he forgot his manliness, and in his anger he struck her across her cheek with his glove.

"Why, then, should I care to wed with thee?" he cried; "thou withered old heathen jade!"

With these taunting words on his lips he turned and strode from the chamber. But while the wooden stairway was still creaking under his tread, Queen Sigrid called after him in bitterest anger:

"Go, then, O proud and stubborn king. Go where you will. But remember this, that the insult you have offered me and the blow you have struck me shall be your death!"

So Olaf departed, ere yet he had broken bread, and he went north into Viken, while Queen Sigrid the Haughty went east into Sweden.

King Sweyn Forkbeard of Denmark had by this time regained full possession of his kingdom, and was contemplating an invasion of England which should be more complete and decisive than the attempt which he had made in company with the viking whom he had known as Ole the Esthonian. Sweyn had now, of course, discovered that this man Ole and King Olaf of Norway were one and the same person, and he began to be very jealous of the glory that was gathering about Olaf's name. A new cause for jealousy had now arisen.

Sweyn, it will be remembered, had married the Princess Gunnhild, daughter of Burislaf, King of the Wends. But in these days even now told of it befell that Queen

Gunnhild was stricken with an illness and died. King Sweyn, ever ambitious of winning great dominion, had a mind to take unto himself a new wife in the person of Queen Sigrid of Sweden. He was on the point of setting out to woo her when he heard by chance that King Olaf Triggvison was already bent upon a similar journey. Envy and jealousy and bitter hatred welled up in Sweyn's breast against his rival, and he swore by Thor's hammer that sooner or later he would lower King Olaf to the dust.

But in good time King Sweyn heard of the quarrel that had befallen between Queen Sigrid and her young Norwegian suitor. So he at once fared north into Sweden to essay his own fortune with the haughty queen. He gained a ready favour with Sigrid by speaking all manner of false and malicious scandal against the man whom she had so lately rejected. Sigrid probably saw that by marrying the King of Denmark she might the more easily accomplish her vengeance upon Olaf Triggvison. She therefore accepted Forkbeard's proposals, and they were wedded in accordance with the rites and customs of their pagan faith.

Earl Erik, the son of the late Earl Hakon, was at this time the guest and friend of Sigrid's son, Olaf the Swede King; and these three--King Sweyn Forkbeard of Denmark, King Olaf of Sweden, and Earl Erik of Lade--had each a private cause of enmity against Olaf Triggvison. It was they who, two years afterwards, united their forces in the great sea fight in which Olaf the Glorious lost his life.

CHAPTER XVIII: THE "LONG SERPENT".

King Olaf had now ruled over Norway for three years. In that brief time he had done more for the country than any king who had gone before him. He had succeeded in establishing Christianity--not very thoroughly, it is true, for during the rest of his reign, and for long enough afterwards, there was plenty of heathenism in Norway; but he did all that he could to make men Christians, as far as he knew how himself, and, by his own example of a pure and upright life, he did much to deepen the feeling that, even in a social sense, the Christian religion' offered advantages which had never before been enjoyed in the land. It was noticed almost immediately that there was less bloodshed among the people than formerly, and that the peasants lived in greater security. The doctrine of peace upon earth was set forth as one of the first principles of Olaf's mission, and he was never tired of showing that, while Odin and Thor took pleasure in bloodshed and rejoiced in war, Christ the White was a lover of peace, and accorded no merit to the manslayer.

Olaf made it a law throughout his realm that all men should keep the Sabbath holy, that they should always fast on Fridays, and that they should teach their children the Ten Commandments. He could not hope that grownup people, who had all their lives been accustomed to worship graven images, would all at once become fervent and devout Christians; but he clearly saw the importance of bringing up all the children to a full knowledge of the Christian faith, and accordingly he bade his priests give constant care to the education of the young.

What King Olaf achieved in Norway he achieved also in the outlying parts of his dominions. He sent priests into the lands of the Laps and Fins. It has been told how he sent his priest Thrangbrand to Iceland. He also sent missions to the Orkney Islands, to the Shetlands, and the Faroes, and even to so distant a country as Greenland. All these lands were converted to Christianity during Olaf's brief reign.

But it was not in religious matters alone that Olaf Triggvison exercised his wisdom and his rule. He encouraged fisheries and husbandry and handicrafts, and men who had given up their lives to warfare and vikingry now occupied themselves with useful arts and industries. Himself a rare sailor, he loved all seamen and shipmen and shipbuilders, and so that these might have work to do he encouraged commerce with the lands over sea--with

England and Scotland and Ireland, with Russia, Wendland, Friesland, Flanders, and France.

When he had been in England he had learned something of the good laws established in that country by King Alfred the Great. He strove to introduce many of these laws into his own kingdom. Like Alfred the Great, King Olaf recognized the value of a strong navy, and, so soon as he had assured himself of the goodwill of his subjects, he levied taxes upon them, and set about the work of building ships.

The great dragonship which he had taken as a prize of war from Rand the Wizard was the largest and finest vessel in the Norwegian seas at this time. The king determined to have a much larger and finer ship built, one which should surpass in splendour and equipment every vessel that had been launched in Norway or any other land throughout the ages. On the banks of the river Nid, at the place where he had built the town of Nidaros, a great forest of pine trees had been cleared, and there was timber in plenty ready at hand. There had been two most fruitful seasons, with good crops, and the country was rich. Olaf himself possessed more wealth than any monarch in all Scandinavia, and also he was fortunate in having about him a number of men who were highly skilled in the work of designing and building ships. So he had a shipyard prepared under the cliffs of Lade, and he appointed a man named Thorberg Shafting to be his master builder.

Rand's dragonship, which was named the *Serpent*, was taken as a model of the new ship that was to be made, but all her measurements were exactly doubled, for the new craft was to be twice as long in the keel, twice as broad in the beam, and twice as great in the scantling. Olaf himself helped at the work, and laboured as hard as any other two men. Whenever any difficulty arose he was there to set it right, and all knew that every part of the work must be well done, that every piece of timber must be free from rot, and every nail and rivet made of the best metal or the king would discover the fault and have it undone.

Many men were in the shipyard, some to hew timbers with their heavy axes, some to fashion iron bolts and bars, and others to spin the shining flax into the ropes that were to form the rigging. Burly blacksmiths stood at the roaring forge, wielding huge hammers; sawyers worked in the pits, making the stout beams and ribs and cutting great trunks into thin planks. Black cauldrons of boiling tar smoked and bubbled over the fires. The clattering of hammers, the rasping of saws, the whirring of wheels, and the clamour of men's voices sounded from earliest morning until the setting of the sun; and the work went on apace all day and every day, saving on Sunday, when no man was allowed to touch a nail or lift a hammer.

On a certain morning in the midsummer, King Olaf was down in the shipyard. He wore his coarsest and oldest clothes; his thick, strong arms were bared above the elbows, and his hardened hands were smutched with tar and nail rust. His head was shielded from the hot sun by a little cloth cap that was torn in the crown, and his long hair and his broad back and shoulders were besprinkled with sawdust. Save for his greater tallness and strength he looked not very different from any of the workmen about him; and indeed Kolbiorn Stallare, who stood near him in courtly apparel, might well have been mistaken for the king and the king for the servant.

Olaf had paused in his work, and was talking with Kolbiorn concerning some matter of state. As he stood thus, leaning with one elbow on the long handle of his great sledgehammer, he saw young Einar Eindridson coming towards him, followed by a woman. The woman seemed to be of middle age, and she looked weary with travel. As she came nearer, her eyes rested upon Kolbiorn as though she wished to speak with him.

"Go to her," said the king. And Kolbiorn left Olaf's side and went to meet her.

"Long have I searched for you, King Olaf," said she, drawing back the cloak from her head, and letting the sun shine full upon her face. "But I have found you at last, and now I crave your help for the mercy of God!"

"You make a mistake, lady," said Kolbiorn; "I am not King Olaf, but only his servant. Yonder is the king at work among his shipwrights. But if you would speak with him I will take you to him, for I see that you are in distress."

So he took her to where Olaf was, and when she stood near him she looked at him in disbelief, taking him to be but a workman. But when the king laid down his hammer and stood up at his full height and uncovered his head, she saw that he was no ordinary man. Her eyes went to his bare arm, where there still remained the mark branded there in the days of his bondage in Esthonia.

"By that token do I know you, O king," said she. "But you are taller and stronger than when last we met."

"In what land and in whose company was that meeting?" asked King Olaf. "Methinks I have indeed seen you before, but in what circumstances and at what time I do not call to mind."

"We met long years ago," said she. "First in Wendland, when you were a guest at the court of King Burislaf; and again when we sat side by side at the inheritance feast of King Sweyn of Denmark. My name is Thyra. Harald Bluetooth, king of Denmark, was my father, and I am the sister of King Sweyn of the Forked beard, who now reigns over all Denmark, and who has lately wedded with Queen Sigrid of Sweden."

"Right well do I now remember you," returned Olaf. "And well do I mind that, at that same feast in Denmark, you scorned me because I had been a slave."

There was a frown upon his brow and a look of mistrust in his eyes; for he guessed that the coming of this woman was some guileful trick of her brother Sweyn, whom he knew to be an enemy of his own.

"At the time you speak of," said she, "you were but a heathen viking of Jomsburg, a lover of warfare, a man who lived by plunder and bloodshed, who worshipped the pagan gods, and knew not the sweetness of a peaceful life. But now you are a king--a great and glorious king. And, what is more, you are a Christian, worshipping the true God, and doing good deeds for the good Christ's sake."

The look of mistrust now vanished from Olaf's eyes, and gave place to a look of softness and pity.

"It is because you are a Christian that I have come to you now," she went on. "For days and weeks I have travelled on foot across the mountains; and now that I have found you I crave your pity and your help, for I am in sore distress, and know of none other than you, O king, to whom I can go for shelter. At the same time that you were yourself in Wendland, and at the time when Earl Sigvaldi of Jomsburg was wedded with the Princess Astrid, and my brother Sweyn with her sister Gunnhild, it was arranged that I too should be wedded. And the husband whom Sigvaldi and Sweyn chose for me was their father-in-law, King Burislaf. Now, Burislaf was an elderly man, while I was but a little girl, and I was sorely against this matter. So I craved that they would not press me to the marriage, and they yielded so far that I was left alone for a while.

"Early in this present summer King Burislaf renewed his pleadings that I should wed with him, and he sent Earl Sigvaldi into Denmark to carry me away. So well did the Earl prevail with my brother that Sweyn delivered me into his hands, and also covenanted that the domains in Wendland which Queen Gunnhild had had should be my dowry.

"Now, already I had become a Christian, and it was little to my satisfaction that I should become the wife of a pagan king and live for ever after among heathen folk, so on a certain dark and stormy night I fled away. A poor fisherman brought me over into Norway, where I knew that the people were all of the Christian faith, and so, after much trouble and privation, I have found my way hither."

Thus Thyra spoke with King Olaf. And when she had told him all her trouble he gave her good counsel and a kindly welcome, and said that she should always have a peaceful dwelling in his realm.

Now, Olaf Triggvison knew full well that in giving succour to Thyra he was doing that which would give great offence to King Sweyn of Denmark; and that Sweyn, when he heard that his sister was here in Norway, would speedily come over and carry her back to Wendland. Nevertheless, Olaf thought well of her ways and saw that she was very fair, and it came into his mind that this would be a good wedding for him. So when Thyra had been in Nidaros some few weeks he spoke with her again, and asked her if she would wed him.

Little loth was Thyra to obey his behests, for she deemed herself most fortunate in that there was a chance of her marrying so noble a king. So she yielded to him, and their wedding was held in harvest time, and celebrated according to the Christian rites. From that time onward they reigned together as king and queen of Norway.

All through that summer King Olaf busied himself in his shipyard, and in the early autumn the great ship's hull was well nigh finished. At this time Thorberg, the master shipwright, went home to his farmstead in Orkadale to gather in his harvest, and he tarried there for many days. When he came back the bulwarks were all completed.

On the same day of his return the king went down with him to the yard to see how the vessel looked, and they both agreed that never before had they seen its equal in size and in beauty of form. All had been done as Thorberg had designed, and great praise did he win from his master. But Thorberg said, nevertheless, that there were many things that he would have improved.

But early the next morning the king and Thorberg went again to the ship. All the smiths had come thither, but they stood there doing no work.

"Why are ye standing idle?" demanded Olaf in surprise.

"Because the ship is spoiled, O king," said one of the men, "and there is no longer any good in her! Some evil minded man has been at work in the night, undoing all that we have done!"

The king walked round to the ship's side, and lo! every plank along her bulwarks was hewn and notched and deeply gashed as with an axe.

"Envious mischief maker!" cried the king in a sorrowful voice. Then as he realized the full extent of the wreckage he swore an oath, and declared that the man who had thus spoiled the ship should die, and that he who should discover the evildoer would be well rewarded.

Then Thorberg went to his side, and said he: "Be not so wrathful, O king. I can tell you who it is that has done this mischief. It was I who did it."

"You!" cried the king. "You in whom I have trusted so long? You, who have taken so much pride in the building of this ship? Unhappy man! Know this, that you shall repair this mischief and make it good, or else you shall lose your life!"

Thorberg laughed lightly and said: "Little the worse will the ship be when I have done, lord."

And then he went to the ship and planed out all the notches and cuts, and made the bulwarks so smooth and fair that all who saw what he did declared that the ship was made far handsomer than she had been before. So well pleased was King Olaf that he bade Thorberg do the same on the other side, and gave him great praise and reward.

Late in the autumn the hull was finished and painted, ready for launching. Bishop Sigurd sprinkled the vessel's bows with holy water, and as she slipped over the rollers into the sea King Olaf named her the *Long Serpent*.

There was yet much to be done before she would be ready for sea; but such work as the stepping of her two masts, fitting her standing rigging, caulking her deck planks, fashioning her cabins, and adorning her prow and stern could best be done when she was afloat.

The *Long Serpent* would not be considered a very large vessel in these modern days, but she was the largest ship known to have been built before the time of King Canute, and she was, so far as it is possible to calculate, exactly double the size of the ship in which Columbus crossed the Atlantic. Her length was not less than two hundred feet. Her breadth between the gunwales was about forty feet. It is not probable that she was very deep in the water; but of this there is no record. She was fitted with thirty-four "rooms" amidships, each room being divided into two half rooms. These half rooms accommodated eight men whose duty it was to attend to one of the long oars. Thus, there were thirty-four pairs of oars and five hundred and seventy-four rowers. Between the half rooms, and also along the bulwarks, there were wide gangways, running fore and aft. There was a large forecastle in which the warriors slept and took their meals, and abaft the main mast there was another cabin called the "fore-room", in which King Olaf had his high seat, or throne. Here he held his councils. Here, too, he had his armour chests. Thirty men lived in the fore-room.

King Olaf's own private cabin was under the "lypting", or poop. It was very splendidly furnished, with beautifully carved wood and tapestries of woven silk. Only his chosen companions and his personal servants were allowed to enter this apartment. Above it there was a large deck which in the time of battle was occupied by the king and his most valiant warriors.

The prow of the *Long Serpent*, which rose high above all other parts of the hull, took the form of a dragon's head and shoulders. This ferocious looking monster, with wide open jaws and staring eyes, was covered with beaten gold. At the vessel's stern stood the dragon's twisted tail, and this also was plated with gold. Close beside it was the handle of the steering board, which was usually held, when at sea, by King Olaf himself or his chief captain.

It was not until the middle of the next springtime that the ship was ready for sea. Then Olaf had his fair weather sails hoisted. They were as white as newly fallen snow, with a large blood red cross in the middle. Banners of silk streamed from the masthead and from the yardarms, and a most beautiful standard fluttered from a tall staff on the lypting. The midships tent, which shielded the rowers from the glare of the strong light, was striped with red and blue. The weather vanes and the dragon glittered in the sun, and the men on the decks were arrayed in their best, with their polished brass helmets and gaily coloured cloaks. King Olaf himself was most splendidly attired. He had on a newly wrought coat of chain mail, which was partly covered by a mantle of fine crimson silk. His helmet was made of burnished copper, inlaid with gold ornaments and surmounted by a gold dragon. Near to him, as he stood at the tiller, his shield was hung up. It was the same shield that he had bought from Thangbrand, bearing the image of the crucifix.

Great crowds of people assembled on the banks of the Nid. They all thought it a most wonderful sight, and they cheered lustily as, in answer to a loud blast from the king's bugle horn, the rowers began to pull. As the great vessel glided out of the river with her eight and sixty oars moving in regular strokes she looked like a thing of life. Never in all time or in all lands had such a magnificent ship been seen.

Olaf steered her out into the blue waters of Thrandheim Fiord, and then as the wind caught her sails the oars were shipped and she sped onward with such even speed that all were astonished. Not far had she gone when she came in sight of Olaf's other dragonship--the *Short Serpent*, as she was now called--which had been sent out an hour in advance. In spite of the long start that she had had, the smaller vessel was quickly overhauled and passed, as though she had not been moving. Olaf had wanted to have a race; but now he saw that this was useless; for the *Long Serpent* had proved herself to be not only the most beautiful ship to look upon, but also the quickest sailer of all vessels afloat.

Out into the sea he took her. There was a strong breeze blowing and the sea was rough. She rode easy upon the waves, both before and against the wind, and Olaf was well pleased. So, when the trial cruise was over, he returned to Nidaros, satisfied that if ever he should be drawn into a war with any foreign power he had a battleship which no enemy could equal.

Now King Olaf lived in happiness and contentment with Queen Thyra, and there was great love between them. But there was one thing which gave the queen much trouble, and over which she was for ever fretting. It was that, by reason of her flight from Wendland, she had forfeited all the possessions that had been reserved as her dowry. She felt that, here in Norway, she had no private wealth of her own such as beseemed a queen, whereas there were her great estates in Wendland and Denmark, from which large revenues were due. Again and again she spoke to the king on this matter, praying him with fair words to go and get her her own. King Burislaf, she declared, was so dear a friend of King Olaf that so soon as they met he would surely give over to him all that he craved. But Olaf always shook his head and asked her if she did not think that there was wealth enough for them both in Norway. But Thyra was not satisfied with this constant delay. Whenever her husband spoke with her she always contrived to bring in some peevish mention of her estates. She wept and prayed and pleaded so often that Olaf's patience was well nigh exhausted. It seemed that if only for the sake of domestic peace an expedition to Wendland must soon be brought about. Nevertheless, all the friends of the king, when they heard of this talk, advised him against such a journey, for they knew full well that it must end in a war with the queen's brother, Sweyn Forkbeard. On a certain day in that same spring, when it was nearing Eastertide, King Olaf was passing down the street, when by the marketplace a man met him, and offered to sell him some very fine spring vegetables. Olaf noticed that he had some large angelica heads. This was a herb very much valued in those days and eaten as we now eat celery. The king took a great stalk of the angelica in his hand and went home with it to Queen Thyra. He found the queen in her hall weeping for her lost estates.

"See here the big angelica I give thee," said he.

The queen rose and thrust the vegetables contemptuously aside, and, with the tears streaming down her cheek, cried: "A pretty gift indeed! Greater gifts did my father, Harald Bluetooth, give me when, as a child, I got my first tooth! He did not fear to come over here to Norway and conquer this land; whereas you, with all your boasted glory and your great ships, are so much afraid of my brother Sweyn that you dare not venture into Denmark to get me what belongs to me, and of which I have been shamefully robbed!"

Then up sprang King Olaf and retorted with an angry oath: "Afraid?" he cried. "Never have I gone in fear of your brother Sweyn, and I am not afraid of him now. Nay, if we ever meet, he shall surely give way before me! Now--even now--I will set sail for Wendland, and you shall have your wretched estates!"

CHAPTER XIX: SIGVALDI'S TREACHERY.

So, when Eastertide with all its religious ceremonies had passed by, King Olaf summoned a great gathering of his people, whereat he set forth that he intended to make an expedition into the Baltic, and that he required a levy from every district, both of men and of ships. He then sent messengers north and south along the land, bidding them muster his forces. The ships were to assemble in Thrandheim Fiord in the first week in summer.

Olaf paid great attention to the manning of the *Long Serpent*, and his seamen and warriors were so well chosen that it was said that the crew surpassed other men as far in strength and bravery as the *Long Serpent* surpassed other ships. Every man was picked by King Olaf himself, who determined that none should be older than sixty years, and none younger than twenty. He made only one exception to this rule. It was in the case of Einar Eindridson, surnamed Thambarskelver. Einar was but eighteen years old; but, young though he was, he was considered the most skilful archer in all Norway. With his bow, called Thamb, he could fire a blunt arrow through a raw ox hide, and not even King Olaf could aim more true or hit the mark at a greater distance. In after years Einar became a very famous warrior and lawman, and his name is often mentioned in the history of Norway. Wolf the Red was King Olaf's banner bearer, and his station was in the prow of the *Serpent*, together with Kolbiorn Stallare, Thorstein Oxfoot, Vikar of Tiundaland, and others. Among the forecastle men were Bersi the Strong, Thrand Squinteye, Thorfinn the Dashing, Ketil the Tall, and Ogmund Sandy. Thirty of the best men were in the fore-room, in front of the poop. Young Einar Eindridson was stationed in the main hold among the rowers. The complete ship's company numbered seven hundred men.

The *Short Serpent* was commanded by Thorkel Nefja, a kinsman of Olaf's; and Thorkel the Wheedler (brother of Queen Astrid) commanded the *Crane*. Both these ships were very well manned. Eleven other large ships left Thrandheim with Olaf, also some smaller vessels of war, and six that were loaded with stores. He set sail with this fleet in the early days of the summer, and Queen Thyra went with him. Southward he sailed, and as he came in turn to fiord after fiord many vikings and wealthy warriors joined him with their ships. When at length he stood out across the Skager Rack, he had a fleet of sixty longships and sixty smaller transports, and with these in his wake he sailed south along Denmark through the Eyr sound, and so to Wendland.

This expedition was not made with any warlike intent. Olaf did not expect that war would follow. But he knew that King Sweyn Forkbeard was his bitterest enemy, and that there was danger in passing so near to Denmark, and he thought it well to have a large number of battleships in his train in case of need.

He arrived off the Wendish coast without being in any way molested, and he anchored his fleet in the great bay of Stetten haven. Thence he sent messengers to King Burislaf appointing a day of meeting. Burislaf invited him to go inland and be his guest at his castle, and Olaf went, leaving Queen Thyra behind on board the *Serpent*, for she would by no means consent to come into the presence of the man whom she had jilted.

King Burislaf received him well, and gave him splendid hospitality. Olaf spoke of his queen's estates and of the revenues that were due to her. Burislaf was a just man in his own heathen way, and he answered that, since he had not got the wife that had been promised him, he did not think it right that he should enjoy her dowry. So he yielded to Olaf's claims, and at once delivered to him the full value of Queen Thyra's estates. Olaf abode in Wendland for many days, and at length returned to the coast, carrying with him a great store of gold and jewels, which, when he went on board his ship, he gave to his queen.

Thyra was now well satisfied, and never again did she attempt to taunt King Olaf concerning her estates. On the contrary, she gave him all praise for having done so much for her sake, and all her contempt of his seeming cowardice was turned to admiration of his courage.

Now, at this same time King Sweyn Forkbeard was in Denmark, living with his new wife, Queen Sigrid the Haughty. Even as Thyra had taunted Olaf Triggvison concerning her possessions in Wendland, so had Sigrid taunted Sweyn Forkbeard concerning her hatred of King Olaf of Norway. She could never forget how Olaf had smitten her in the face with his glove, and from the earliest days of her marriage with King Sweyn she had constantly and earnestly urged him to wage war against Olaf Triggvison. Sweyn, knowing the risks of such a war, turned a deaf ear to his proud wife's entreaties. But when at last Sigrid heard that Olaf had given protection to Sweyn's sister, and made Thyra his queen, she renewed her urging with increased earnestness, and so well did she succeed that Sweyn was roused to great anger against King Olaf, and he resolved to get ready his forces and abide by Queen Sigrid's counsel.

He was in this belligerent mood when the rumour reached him that Olaf Triggvison was at sea with his fleet, and was minded to make the voyage to Wendland. With this rumour also came news of the splendid dragonship that the Norse king had built.

Now, Sweyn Forkbeard was a very cautious man in the affairs of war, and he well knew that he was himself no match for so powerful a warrior as Olaf the Glorious. But he remembered that he was not alone in his desire to humble the monarch of the Norselands. His own son in law, Olaf the Swede King, had sworn by Thor's hammer to avenge the insult to his mother Queen Sigrid the Haughty, and the help of the Swede King in this war would be of great account. In addition to the King of Sweden there was Earl Erik of Lade, who was eager to take vengeance upon Olaf Triggvison for the slaying of his father Earl Hakon. Since the coming of King Olaf into Norway, Earl Erik had become famous as a viking; he had engaged in many battles both on land and on the sea. It has already been told how he fought in the sea fight against the vikings of Jomsburg. He was now one of the strongest war men in all Scandinavia, and his fleet of battleships was equal to that of either Sweyn of Denmark or Olaf of Sweden.

So when Forkbeard heard that Olaf Triggvison had entered the Baltic he sent men east into Sweden, bidding them give word to the Swede King and to Earl Erik that now was their time if they would join in battle against their common foe.

Sweyn Forkbeard was at this time very friendly with Earl Sigvaldi, the chief of the Jomsvikings, and he enlisted his help. It happened that Sigvaldi's wife, the Princess Astrid, was then staying at the court of her father King Burislaf, in Wendland. It was, therefore, a very natural thing that the earl should go thither also. Sweyn urged him to make the journey, to spy upon King Olaf's fleet, and to lay such a trap that Sweyn and his allies should not fail in their object. Earl Sigvaldi undertook this mission, and fared eastward to Wendland with eleven longships. Meeting King Olaf he made pretence to renew his old friendship with the man whom he had formerly known as Ole the Esthonian. He flattered him, praised his great wisdom, and, more than all, spoke highly of his fleet and the surpassing splendour of the *Long Serpent*. Their discourse was most friendly at all times, nor did Olaf for a moment suspect the treachery that underlay the earl's soft speeches and his seeming goodwill. Deep into the king's open heart Sigvaldi wormed his way, until they were as brothers one with the other. When Olaf hinted that he would be going back to Norway, that the weather was fair for sailing, and that his men were homesick and weary of lying at anchor, Sigvaldi made some plausible excuse and still held him back; and the time went on, the summer days grew shorter, and yet Olaf made no move.

But on a certain day there came a small fishing boat into the bay, and dropped anchor near to the earl's longship. In the darkness of the next night one of her men had speech with Sigvaldi, and gave him the tidings for which he had so long waited. These tidings were that the host of the Swede King had now come from the east, that Earl Erik also had arrayed his forces, and that these lords had joined with Sweyn Forkbeard, and all were sailing downward to the coast of Wendland. They had appointed to waylay King Olaf Triggvison in a certain channel running between the mainland and the island of Svold, and Sweyn had now sent this messenger bidding the earl to so bring it about that they might fall upon King Olaf in that place. On the next morning Sigvaldi put out one of his boats, rowed alongside of the *Long Serpent*, and stepped upon her deck. He found King Olaf sitting at his ease against the rail, carving runes upon the lid of a wooden box that he had made for the holding of the queen's jewels. Sigvaldi did not disturb him, but took a few turns across the deck and looked up into the sunlit sky. The king blew away the chips of wood that he had been cutting from the box lid and looked up.

"A fairer and finer day for sailing I have never yet seen," said he. "Why should we not heave anchor this very morning? The wind bodes well for a free run westward, and in truth, Sigvaldi, I am getting wearied of this idleness and the sight of these sandy shores."

"Let it be so by all means if you so wish it," answered the earl in a light tone of unconcern. "I, too, should be not ill pleased to be once more upon the open sea, although I shall be sorry to make an end to our close intercourse, for the sooner we sail the sooner must we part."

"The parting need not be for long," said the king. "I am hoping that you will soon see your way to coming north to Thrandheim, there to spend many happy summer months with us. And we may take a cruise in the *Long Serpent* across to the Orkneys, or north even to Iceland."

A mocking smile played about the earl's lips.

"You are ever ready with your bright plans for the future, King Olaf," he said, as he raised his great hand to stroke his bushy black beard. "But the next summer is a long while off, and it may be--who can say?--it may be that we shall not then be both alive."

King Olaf gave a playful laugh.

"Your thoughts are passing gloomy this morning," said he. "Why should you speak of death? You are still but in the prime of manhood, and are blessed with the best of health. As to a death in battle, you, who are still a believer in Odin and Valhalla, can have no fear of warlike enemies."

"It was not of myself that I was thinking," returned Sigvaldi.

"Then why should it be for me that you fear?" asked Olaf. "I am of a long lived race, and, since I am now a man of peace and no lover of bloodshed, I am not likely to be mixed up in any wars--at least, not wars of my own making. And there is but one man I know of who has any wish to wage battle with me."

"Who is that?" questioned Sigvaldi.

"King Sweyn of Denmark," answered Olaf. "And it seems that he is at this very time abroad with his hosts in search of me."

A look of alarm came upon the earl's dark face. He marvelled how Olaf had come to hear this news, and he feared also that his own schemes might end in failure.

"These are strange tidings you tell, King Olaf," he said. "One would think that, like Odin, you employed the birds of the air to bear you news."

"The bird that told me these matters was but a poor fisherman," said Olaf. "Yesternight I met him on the shore, and, seeing that he was a Dane, I had speech with him, and he said that King Sweyn, with two or three longships, had been seen bearing southward to Wendland."

Earl Sigvaldi breathed a deep breath of relief. There was still great hope of his scheme succeeding. He glanced round the bay at Olaf's great fleet, and thought of the reward that Sweyn had offered as the price of his treachery.

"Little would it avail King Sweyn to enter unaided into a battle with so well equipped and so brave a warrior as you, King Olaf," he said. "But, for my own part, I do not believe this tale. I have known the Dane King in past times, and he is far too wary to attempt so bold an attack. Howbeit, if you misdoubt that war will beset your path, then will I be of your company with my ships. The time has been when the following of the vikings of Jomsburg has been deemed of good avail to mighty kings."

Then when the earl had gone off to his own ships, Olaf turned to go below to his cabin.

At the head of the cabin stairs he was met by young Einar Eindridson.

"So please you, O king," said the lad in a halting voice, "it chanced yesternight that I had a dream--"

"Well," smiled the king, "and what of that? The people of heathen lands deem it a grave misfortune if a man cannot dream; therefore you may be accounted fortunate."

"Dreams may sometimes avert misfortune," said the lad, "and this that I dreamt yesternight may be of service to you, my master. While I slept, it seemed to me that I saw you standing at the brink of a deep well of water. At your side stood the Earl Sigvaldi. Suddenly he put his hand upon your back and pushed you forward, so that you fell into the water and sank deep, deep down, and then all was dark. I am no great reader of dreams, O king; but this one has sorely troubled me, for I fear that Earl Sigvaldi is a treacherous friend, and that he is now minded to do you an injury."

"Leave the reading of such sleeping fancies to wizards and witches, Einar," said King Olaf. "It is not for Christian folk to inquire into the future. We are in God's hands, and He alone can determine what path we shall tread. As to my good friend Sigvaldi, I will hear no word against him."

Now when Olaf went into the cabin, he found there Sigvaldi's wife, the princess Astrid, who had been for some days in companionship with Queen Thyra. Astrid warned him, as openly as she dared, that her husband was working against him. But Olaf turned aside her warnings with a jest. A strange infatuation bound him to his false friend, and nothing would shake his confidence. He resolved to abide by the earl's advice in all things.

It was yet early morning when King Olaf again went on deck. The wind blew light from the southeast, and all was favourable for departure. Loud over the bay sounded the bugle horns. Mariners cried aloud in their joy as they hoisted the yards. The sails fluttered out in the breeze, and the anchors were weighed. Gaily the ships sped out of the wide bay, and forth through the western channel past the vikings' stronghold of Jomsburg. Seventy-one keels in all there were, and the smaller vessels led the way, right out into the open sea, nor waited to know which course the king should take, for all knew that they were homeward bound for Norway, and that although there were many ways, yet they all led north beyond Denmark, and so onward into the breezy Skager Rack.

Little did Olaf see the need of keeping his fleet together. He feared no foe, and was well aware that every craft had a trusty crew who were fully able to look after their own safety. His own knowledge of these seas told him also that, however much his ships might be scattered in crossing the Baltic, they must all gather together again, as he had commanded, before entering the Eyr Sound.

Now the treacherous earl, whose craft and cunning had been busily at work throughout that morning, saw, in this scattering of the ships, the fulfilment of his dearest hopes. King Sweyn had enjoined him beyond all things to so manage that Olaf Triggvison should be separated from the main body of his fleet, so that he might thus fall into the trap that was laid for him, and be speedily overcome by the superior force that now awaited him behind the island of Svold. Sweyn Fork Beard's plans were well laid; and if Earl Sigvaldi could but contrive to lead Olaf between the island and the mainland, instead of taking the northward course across the open sea, success for the allies was certain.

The earl was careful to keep his own vessel within the close neighbourhood of the *Long Serpent*. In the wake of these two sailed the earl's ten other viking ships and a similar number of King Olaf's largest dragons, including the *Short Serpent* and the *Crane*.

The remaining portion of the king's fleet had already passed in advance, bending their course due north. Sigvaldi had tried, by delaying Olaf's departure out of the haven, to still further reduce the number of the king's immediate followers. But he knew the extent of Sweyn Fork Beard's forces, and he was content that Olaf should retain such chances as were afforded by the support of eleven of his best battleships.

Now Olaf was about to steer outward into the sea when Sigvaldi hailed him.

"Follow me!" cried the earl. "Let me be your pilot, for I know all the deepest channels between the isles, and I will lead you through them by such ways that you will come out far in advance of your other ships!"

So King Olaf, over confident and never dreaming of treachery, followed westward into the Sound, and went sailing onward to his doom.

CHAPTER XX: CAUGHT IN THE SNARE.

King Sweyn of Denmark and his allies lay with their war hosts in a large sheltered vik, or bay, on the western side of the isle of Svold. This position was well chosen, as the bay formed a part of the channel through which--if Earl Sigvaldi fulfilled his treacherous mission--King Olaf Triggvison was certain to pass into the clutches of his foes. There were seventy war galleys in all, and each vessel was well manned and fully prepared for battle. The larger number belonged to King Sweyn; but the longships of Earl Erik were in all respects superior to those of either Denmark or Sweden.

Earl Erik himself, too, was the most valiant warrior. Excepting only Olaf Triggvison there was not a braver or more daring chief in all the lands of Scandinavia. Trained from his earliest youth to a life of storm and battle, Erik had never known the meaning of fear, and it might almost be said that he had never known defeat. His own bravery and skill had inspired every one of his viking followers with the same qualities. As his men were, so were his ships--they were chosen with the main view to their fitness for encountering the battle and the breeze. His own dragonship, which had stood the brunt of many a fierce fight, was named the *Iron Ram*. It was very large, and the hull timbers at both bow and stern were plated with thick staves of iron from the gunwales down to the waterline.

For many days had these ships lain at anchor in the bay, and as each day passed the three chiefs grew more and more impatient for the coming of their royal victim. Many times and again had they sat together in King Sweyn's land tent, discussing their prospects and planning their method of attack. Their purpose was not alone to wreak vengeance upon King Olaf for the supposed wrongs that each of the three had suffered at his hands. The idea of vengeance, indeed, stood only second to the great hope of conquest and of personal gain, and they had made this secret bargain among themselves, namely, that in the event of Olaf Triggvison being slain, they should each have his own third share of

Norway. To Earl Erik were to be given all the shires along the western coast from Finmark to Lindesness, with the exception of seven shires allotted to Olaf the Swede King. All the shires from Lindesness, including the rich district of Agder, to the Swedish boundary, were to be taken by Sweyn Fork Beard; excepting only the realm of Ranarike (to this day a part of Sweden), which was to be given to the Swedish king.

It was further agreed among the three chieftains, concerning the expected battle, that he who first planted foot upon the *Long Serpent* should have her for his own, with all the wealth that was found on board of her; and each should take possession of the ships which he himself captured and cleared of men.

Touching this same arrangement Olaf Sigridson was not well content, for he knew that both Erik and Sweyn were better men than himself, and that in contending for the prize he would have but a sorry chance if either of his companions should enter the battle before him.

"It seems to me," said Sweyn, on a certain morning when they were talking this matter over, "that the fairest way of all would be that we should cast lots or throw the dice; and let it be that he who throws the highest shall be first to attack King Olaf's own ship."

So they brought out the dice box and each cast his lot in turn. Earl Erik threw a two and a five. Then the Swedish king took up the dice and he threw two sixes.

"No need is there for a third to throw!" he cried. "Mine is the first chance, and, by the hammer of Thor, the *Long Serpent* shall be mine also!"

But King Sweyn had still to take his throw.

"There are yet two sixes on the dice," said he, "and it is easy for the gods to let them turn up again."

He made his cast, and there were again two sixes. But one die had broken asunder, showing a three as well as the two sixes. Thus Sweyn was the victor, and it was agreed that his ships should take the centre of battle and lead the attack upon the *Long Serpent*.

When this matter was decided the three chiefs went up upon the heights of the island, as they had done every morning since their coming to Svold, and stood there with a great company of men. They looked eastward along the line of the Wendic coast, and as they watched they saw a great number of ships upon the sea, bearing outward from Stetten haven. The weather was very bright and clear, and the sunlight, shining upon the gaily coloured sails and upon the gilded prows, made a very fine sight.

Earl Erik noticed with some concern that the fleet was making due north. But Sweyn said: "Wait, and you will see what our good Sigvaldi will do when he comes into sight!" So they waited and watched.

In about an hour's time they saw many larger and finer vessels appearing. But they were yet too far off to be clearly recognized. Sweyn was very silent for a time, and he kept his eyes fixed upon the ships, noting their every movement. At last he cried aloud:

"Now I can see that Sigvaldi is doing as we bade him. No longer do the ships stand outward into the main. They are bearing westward for Svold! Let us now go down to our ships and not be too slow in attack."

So they all went down to the lower land and Sweyn sent boats out to bid the shipmen weigh anchor and prepare for battle as quietly as might be.

Now the channel through which Sigvaldi was to lead the Norsemen was full wide, and deep, but it had many turns and twists, and before the ships could enter the bay, where their enemies awaited them in ambush, they had need to pass round an outstretching cape. On the ridge of this cape, and hidden by trees, King Sweyn and his companions took their stand, knowing that although they might wait to see the whole of

King Olaf's fleet pass by, they would still have ample time to board their ships and be in readiness to meet their victim ere he entered the bay.

It was not very long before they saw a large and splendid dragon sailing proudly into the channel. It was the ship of Eindrid of Gimsar.

"A great ship, and marvellous fair!" cried King Sweyn. "Surely it is the *Long Serpent* herself!"

Earl Erik shook his head and answered: "Nay; though this ship is large and fine it is not the *Long Serpent*."

Shortly afterwards they saw another dragon, larger than the first; but the dragon's head had been taken down from the prow.

King Sweyn said: "Now is Olaf Triggvison afraid, for he dares not sail with the head on his ship!"

"This is not the king's ship," returned Earl Erik with confident denial; "for by the green and red striping of her sails I know that her captain is Erling Skialgson. Let him pass on! If, as I believe, he is himself on board, we shall be better served if he and his band are not found among those with whom we are to fight this day."

One by one, in irregular order, the great ships of the Norse chieftains sailed by, and with each that passed, King Sweyn or Olaf of Sweden cried aloud: "Now surely this one is the *Long Serpent*!" But Earl Erik the Norseman recognized every one, and told her captain's name.

Presently Earl Sigvaldi's viking ships went by, holding close inshore; and at length the earl's own dragon, with a red banner at her prow, by which token King Sweyn understood that all was going as had been intended. Following close behind came the *Crane*.

"Now let us hasten on board!" cried King Sweyn, "for here comes the *Serpent* at last!"

But Earl Erik did not move.

"Many other great and splendid ships has Olaf Triggvison besides the *Long Serpent*," said he, "yet only nine have sailed past. Let us still wait."

Then one of Sweyn's Danish warriors who stood near gave a hoarse mocking laugh and said:

"We had heard that Earl Erik was a brave and adventurous man. But now it is clear that he has but the heart of a chicken, for he is too cowardly to fight against Olaf Triggvison and dares not avenge his own father's death. Great shame is this, to be told of through all lands, that we, with all our great host, stand here, while Norway's king sails out to sea past our very eyes."

Erik became very angry at hearing these taunting words.

"Go, then, to your ships," said he; "but for all your doubts of my courage you shall see before the sun goes down into the sea tonight that both Danes and Swedes will be less at their ease than I and my men!"

As they moved to go, yet another of King Olaf's ships hove in sight.

"Here now sails the *Long Serpent*!" cried the son of Queen Sigrid. "Little wonder is it that Olaf Triggvison is so widely renowned when he has such a splendid ship as this!"

All turned to watch the great vessel as she floated by. Her gilded dragon glistened in the sunlight; her striped red and blue sail swelled in the breeze; crowds of stalwart men were on her decks. No larger or more magnificent battleship had ever before been seen on these waters.

King Sweyn Fork Beard cried aloud in his exultation:

"Loftily shall the *Serpent* carry me tonight when I steer her north into Denmark!"

112

Then Earl Erik added with a sneer:

"Even if Olaf the Glorious had no larger ship than the *Short Serpent*, which we now see, methinks Sweyn with all his army of Danes could never win it from him without aid."

King Sweyn was about to give an angry retort when Earl Erik pointed towards the headland from behind which all these ships had in their turn appeared. And now did Sweyn at once understand how greatly he had been mistaken in what he had expected of King Olaf's famous dragonship, and how much his fancy had fallen short of the reality. He stood in dumb amazement as the towering prow of the *Long Serpent* glided into view, shooting long beams of golden light across the sea. First came the glistening dragon head, and then a long stretch of gaily painted hull; next, the tall mast with its swelling white sail, and, in the midst of the snowy expanse, the blood red cross. The dense row of polished shields along the bulwarks flashed in the sunlight. Sweyn marvelled at the ship's great length, for the stern did not appear in sight until long after he had seen the prow. His companion chieftains murmured their astonished admiration; while fear and terror crept into the breasts of many of the Swedes and Danes, who felt that for some of them at least the great ship carried death.

"This glorious vessel is worthy and fitting for such a mighty king as Olaf the Glorious," declared Earl Erik, "for it may in truth be said of him that he is distinguished above all other kings as the *Long Serpent* is above all other ships."

All unconscious of the guiles of Sigvaldi, King Olaf steered his ship in the earl's wake. At the first he took the lead of his ten other dragons, Sigvaldi sailing in advance. But as they neared the island a thing happened which caused him to fall back to the rear. Young Einar Eindridson, ever full of sport and play, had perched himself astride of the yardarm, and there, with his longbow and arrows shot at the seagulls as they flew by. Presently he espied a large bird flying over from the westward. Its wings and body were perfectly black. Slowly it came nearer and nearer, as though it would cross the *Serpent*'s bows. Einar worked his way along to the end of the yard, and, steadying himself, fixed an arrow to the string. As the bird came within easy bow shot the lad took aim. But as he drew the string he saw the great dusky bird open its stout beak. He heard a hoarse croak, and knew it to be the croak of a raven. Now the croaking of a raven was held in those times to be a sound of very ill omen; it was also considered that the man who killed one of these birds was certainly doomed to meet with speedy misfortune. Einar slackened his bow, and the arrow slipped from his fingers. In trying to catch it, he dropped his famous bow, Thamb, and it fell into the sea. Now Einar treasured that bow beyond all his worldly possessions. Without an instant's hesitation he stood up upon the yard and leapt into the sea.

King Olaf, standing at the tiller, had seen all this, and he quickly put over the helm and, bringing the *Serpent* round head to wind, lay to while a boat was launched. Einar and his bow were rescued. But meanwhile the *Long Serpent* was overtaken by all her companion ships; and so it was that she was the last to enter the straits.

Earl Sigvaldi still held on in advance. But it was noticed that when he came abreast of the cape whereon the three chiefs had stood, he lowered his sails and steered his ships nearer inshore. The Norsemen suspecting nothing, followed his example, and very soon King Olaf's fleet gathered closer together. But when Thorkel the Wheedler came up with the *Crane* he shouted aloud to Sigvaldi, asking him why he did not sail. The earl replied that he intended to lie to until King Olaf should rejoin him. So Thorkel struck sail also. But the ships had still some way on them and the current was with them. They drifted on until they came to a curve in the channel which opened out into the bay where the host of King Sweyn and his allies waited in ambush.

Now by this time the *Short Serpent* had come alongside of Sigvaldi, and her captain, espying some of the enemy's fleet, questioned the earl concerning them.

"Strangers they all are to me," answered Sigvaldi with an evil look in his eyes. "But whoever they be, it seems that they are not altogether friendly to us. I see their red war shields from where I stand, and it looks very much as though a battle awaited us."

Then Thorkel Nefja had his oars brought out, and he steered the *Short Serpent* round against the stream and went back with all speed to meet the king.

"What do I see?" cried King Olaf. "Why have the ships struck sail? And what is the meaning of your coming back?"

"It is because a great host of war galleys are lying in the farther bay," answered Thorkel. "It is the host of King Sweyn of Denmark, for I saw the banner on one of the longships, and it was like unto the banners that Sweyn Fork Beard carried at the time when we were with him in England. Turn back, I implore you, O king! Turn back by the way we have come! For our fleet numbers but eleven keels, while our foes have fully two score of dragons!"

The king stood on the lypting of the *Long Serpent* as he heard these tidings. He turned to his mariners.

"Down with the sails! Out with the oars!" he cried with a loud voice that could be clearly heard across the waters; and the men quickly obeyed.

Still holding the tiller, Olaf kept his ship's prow ahead as before.

"Never yet have I fled from a battle," he called out to Thorkel Nefja. "And although Sweyn Fork Beard had thrice two score of warships, I would rather fight him than turn tail like a coward hound. God rules over the lives of all Christian men, and why should we fear to encounter King Sweyn and all his heathens? Let our cry be 'Onward, Christ men; onward, Cross men!'"

Now when the *Long Serpent*, sweeping quickly along with all oars at work, came nigh to her companions, Olaf saw that Earl Sigvaldi and his vikings had passed on beyond the cape, while his own captains had turned their prows about and were rowing back against the current.

"Why do ye take to flight?" roared Olaf in an angry voice of thunder. "Never will I fly from any earthly enemy. He is no worthy king who shuns his foes because of fear. Reverse your ships and follow the *Long Serpent*, be it to glory or to death!"

And now, taking the lead, he arrayed his ships in order, with the *Short Serpent* and the *Crane* together in his immediate wake, and his eight other longships following close behind. Proudly, and with all his banners flying, he sailed into the bay. Before him, at about a mile's distance, he saw the seventy warships of his foes. Their vast number and their compact battle array might well have struck fear into the heart of one who had but eleven galleys at his back. But not for an instant did Olaf Triggvison shrink from the unequal encounter. He brought his vessels to a halt, but it was not from hesitation. It was only that, taken wholly unawares, he had need to prepare for the coming battle. Taking down his great war horn from the mast, he blew a resounding blast. His warriors understood the call, and they hastily donned their armour, brought their arrows and spears on deck and stood at their stations with a readiness which showed how well their royal master had trained them.

Olaf himself went below into his cabin. He knelt for a time before the crucifix in silent prayer, and then, with his stout heart well prepared for all that might happen to him, put on his finest armour and returned to the deck.

As he stood beside his fluttering banner--a snow white banner with its blood red cross--he could easily be distinguished from all who were near him. His tall majestic figure

114

was crowned with a crested helmet of pure gold. Over his well wrought coat of mail he wore a short tunic of scarlet silk. His shield, with its jewelled image of the crucified Christ shone in the sunlight and could be distinctly seen by his awaiting foes.

Some of his companions warned him of the danger of thus exposing himself and making himself a mark for his enemies. But he answered proudly that he wished all men, both friends and foes, to see that he shunned no danger.

"The more I am seen," he said, "and the less fear I show in the battle, the more shall I inspire my brave friends with confidence and my foes with fear and terror."

As he spoke, he saw that King Sweyn with his ships was rowing slowly out into the mid bay to meet him, leaving two detachments in his rear. There was no sign of haste on board of any one of the ships, for all men knew that there was a long day's fight before them, and that it was well to make all their preparations with slow caution.

For some time after he had come on deck King Olaf was more intent upon observing his enemies than in arraying his own small armament. He had seen from the first that it would be his place to assume the defensive, and he had given the order for his ships to be drawn up in line, broadside to broadside.

This order was being carried out as he now stood watching the advance of his enemy's battle.

"Who is the captain of the host now drawing up against us?" he asked of Bersi the Strong, one of his chieftains who stood near him. "By the standard on his prow methinks I should know him well."

"King Sweyn of the Forkedbeard it is, with his forces from Denmark," was Bersi's answer.

"That is even as I thought," returned Olaf. "But we are not afraid of those cowards, for no more courage is there in Danes than in wood goats. Never yet were Danes victorious over Norsemen, and they will not vanquish us today. But what chief flies the standards to the right?"

"Those, lord, are the standards of Olaf the Swede King."

"The son of Queen Sigrid the Haughty stands in need of a little practice in warfare," said Olaf. "But for the harm that he can do us, he might well have stayed at home. And his heathen Sweden, I think, would find it more agreeable to sit at the fireside and lick their sacrificial bowls than to board the *Long Serpent* under the rain of our weapons. We need not fear the horse eating Swedes. But who owns those fine ships to the left of the Danes? A gallant man he must be, for his men are far better arrayed than the rest and much bolder of aspect in all ways."

"Earl Erik Hakonson is the owner of them," answered Bersi.

"He is the noblest champion who will fight against us today," said Olaf, "and from him and the high born men that I see upon his decks we may expect a hard battle. Earl Erik has just cause for attacking us, and we must not forget that he and his crews are Norsemen like ourselves. Now let us make ready!"

Then the king turned to his own ships. The eleven dragons had been ranged side by side as he had ordered, with the *Long Serpent* in the middle and the *Crane* and the *Short Serpent* at either side of her. To right and to left of each of these four ships were placed. This was a very small force, compared with the overwhelming numbers of the enemy, and as Olaf glanced along his line he sorely missed the fifty of his fleet that had gone out to seaward. Nevertheless he did not allow his men to see that he was in any way anxious.

The seamen were now lashing the ships together stem by stem. Olaf saw that they were tying the beak of the *Long Serpent* on a level with the other prows, so that her poop stood out far behind. He called out loudly to Ketil the Tall:

"Bring forward the large ship. Let her prow and not her stern stand out. I will not lie behind my men when the battle begins!"

Then Wolf the Red, his standard bearer, whose station was forward in the bow, mumbled a complaint:

"If the *Serpent* shall lie as far forward as she is longer than your other ships, then there will be windy weather today in her bows."

The King answered: "I had the *Serpent* built longer than other ships, so that she might be put forward more boldly in battle, and be well known in fighting as in sailing. But when I chose her crew, I did not know that I was appointing a stem defender who was both red and adread."

This playful taunt ruffled Red Wolf, who replied insolently: "There need be nothing said, lord, if you will guard the poop as well as I shall guard the forecastle."

The king had a bow in his hand. He laid an arrow on the string and turned it on Wolf, who cried:

"Shoot another way, king, and not at me but at your foes, for what I win in the fight I win for Norway, and maybe you will find that you have not over many men before the evening comes."

The king lowered the arrow and did not shoot. When the men had finished lashing the ships together he again took his war horn and blew a loud blast upon it that echoed and re-echoed along the rocky shores of the island. As he turned to put the horn aside he saw that Queen Thyra, alarmed by the growing tumult, had come up on deck.

She looked out upon the bay, and seeing the enormous hostile fleet that was closing in upon Olaf's diminished force she burst into tears.

Olaf went to her side and laid his hand on her shoulder.

"You must not weep," he said gently. "Come, dry your tears; for now you have gotten what was due to you in Wendland; and today I mean to demand of your brother Sweyn the tooth gift which you have so often asked me for."

CHAPTER XXI: THE BATTLE IN SVOLD SOUND.

King Olaf stood on the poop deck of the *Long Serpent*, a conspicuous figure among his fighting men, with his gold wrought helm towering high above the others' heads. From this position he could survey the movements of his foes, command the actions of his own shipmen, and direct the defence. From this place also he could fire his arrows and fling his spears over the heads of his Norsemen. His quivers were filled with picked arrows, and he had near him many racks of javelins. The larger number of his chosen chiefs--as Kolbiorn Stallare, Thorfinn the Dashing, Ketil the Tall, and Thorstein Oxfoot-- had their stations forward on the forecastle deck or in the "close quarters" nearer the prow. These stood ready with their spears and swords to resist boarders, and they were protected by the shield men, who were ranged before them at the bulwarks with their shields locked together. At various points of vantage groups of archers had been placed, the best marksmen being stationed before the mast, where no rigging or cordage would mar their aim. At this part stood Einar Eindridson throughout the whole battle. Loud and shrill sounded the war horns from both sides. Nearer and nearer King Sweyn of Denmark drew onward to the attack. The wind had fallen, the sea was calm; the sun hung hot and glaring in a cloudless sky, flashing on burnished helmet and gilded dragon head. King Olaf's prows were pointed towards the north, so that the enemy as they came down upon him had the strong midday sunlight in their eyes. King Sweyn Fork Beard opened his attack with a shower of arrows directed at the stem defenders of the *Long Serpent*. King Olaf's archers at once replied in like manner. This exchange of arrows was continued without ceasing while Sweyn's ships came onward at their fullest speed. Then, as the

Danes drew yet closer under the Norsemen's prows, arrows gave place to javelins and spears, which were hurled with unerring aim from side to side.

Sweyn's men turned their stems towards both bows of the *Long Serpent*, as she stood much further forward than any others of Olaf's ships. Many who could not approach this coveted position turned their attention to the *Short Serpent* and the *Crane*. And now the battle raged fiercely. Yet the Norsemen stood firm as a wall of rock, while the Danes, assailed by a heavy rain of spears and arrows from the *Serpent's* decks, began to lose heart ere ever a man of them was able to make his way through the close bulwark of shields. Olaf's prows were so lofty that they could not be scaled, while the defenders, from their higher stand, had full command over their foes. Thrand Squint Eye and Ogmund Sandy were the first of the Norsemen to fall. These two leapt down upon the deck of King Sweyn's dragon, where, after a tough hand to hand fight, in which they vanquished nine of the Dane King's foremost warriors, they were slain. Kolbiorn Stallare was very angry at these two having broken the ranks, and he gave the order that none of the Norsemen were to attempt to board the enemy's ships without express command.

Sweyn's ship lay under the larboard bow of the *Serpent*, and Wolf the Red had thrown out grappling hooks, holding her there. She was a longship, of twenty banks of oars, and her crew were the pick of all the warmen of Denmark. Sharp and fierce was the fight at this side, and great was the carnage. While Kolbiorn and others of Olaf's stem defenders kept up an incessant battle with their javelins and swords, King Olaf and his archers shot their arrows high in air so that they fell in thick rain upon the Danish decks. Yet the Danes, and the Swedes from the rear, were not slow to retaliate. Although they found it impossible to board the *Serpent*, they nevertheless could assail her crowded decks with arrows and well aimed spears, and the Norsemen fell in great numbers. In the meantime Sweyn's other ships--not one of which was larger than the smallest of King Olaf's eleven dragons--made a vigorous onset upon Olaf's left and right wings. The Norsemen fought with brave determination, and as one after another of the Dane ships was cleared of men it was drawn off to the rear, and its place was occupied by yet another ship, whose warriors, fresh and eager, renewed the onset. All along Olaf's line there was not one clear space, not a yard's breadth of bulwark unoccupied by fighting men. The air was filled with flying arrows and flashing spears and waving swords. The clang of the weapons upon the metal shields, the dull thud of blows, the wild shouts of the warriors and cries of the wounded, mingled together in a loud vibrating murmur. To Earl Sigvaldi, who lay with his ships apart at the far end of the bay, it sounded like the humming of bees about a hive. Not only at the prows, but also behind at the sterns of Olaf's compact host, did the Danes attempt to board. The Norsemen, indeed, were completely surrounded by their foemen. King Olaf fought from the poop deck of the *Serpent* with no less vigour than did Kolbiorn and his stem defenders at the prow. He assailed each ship as it approached with showers of well directed arrows. Then, as the stem of one of the Danish longships crashed into his vessel's stern, he dropped his longbow and caught up his spears, one in either hand, and hurled them into the midst of his clamouring foes. Time after time he called to his followers, and led them with a fierce rush down upon the enemy's decks, sweeping all before him. Seven of King Sweyn's vessels did he thus clear; and at last no more came, and for a time he had rest. But a great cry from the *Serpent's* forecastle warned him that his stem men were having a hard struggle. So he gathered his men together and led them forward. Many were armed with battleaxes, others with spears, and all with swords. Calling to his shield bearers to make way for him, he pressed through the gap and leapt down upon the deck of Sweyn Forkbeard's dragon.

"Onward, Christ men, Cross men!" he cried as full three score of his bravest warriors followed close at his back. And he cut his way through the crowd of Danes, who, led by Sweyn himself, had been making a final rally and preparing to board the *Serpent*. King Sweyn was wounded in the right arm by a blow from Kolbiorn's sword. Kolbiorn was about to repeat the blow when several of the Danes, retreating aft, crowded between him and their king. Sweyn drew back, and crying aloud to his men to follow him, turned tail and led them over the bulwarks on to the deck of a ship that was alongside of him. This ship, which had not yet been secured by the Norsemen's grappling irons, he now withdrew to the farther shores of the bay. As he thus retreated from the battle he sounded his horns, calling off those of his ships that were not yet altogether vanquished. Tired, wounded, and despairing, he owned himself no match for Olaf the Glorious. He had made the attack with five and forty fully manned warships, and yet all this great force had been as nothing against the superior skill and courage of the defenders. Thus it befell, as Olaf Triggvison had guessed, that the Danes did not gain a victory over the Norsemen. While the Danes were in full retreat the Swedes hastened forward to renew the attack. The Swedish king, believing that Olaf Triggvison must certainly have suffered terrible loss at the hands of the Danes, had the fullest hope that he would take very little time in turning the defeat of King Sweyn into a victory for himself. He had already, from a distance, kept up an intermittent fire of arrows into the midst of the Norse ships, and it may be that he had thus helped to reduce King Olaf's strength. He now rowed proudly upon the left wing of the Norse fleet. Here he divided his own forces, sending one division to an attack upon Olaf's prows, and himself rowing round to the rear. Many of the disabled Dane ships barred his way, but he at last brought his own longship under the poop of the *Long Serpent*. This interval had given the Norsemen a brief respite in which to clear their disordered decks and refresh themselves with welcome draughts of cooling water which their chief ordered to be served round.

Vain were the Swede king's hopes. When he advanced upon the *Serpent* Olaf Triggvison was ready to meet him, refreshed by his brief rest, unwounded still, and with his warlike spirit burning eager within him.

"Let us not lose courage at the sight of these heathen devourers of horse flesh!" he cried as he rallied his men. "Onward, my brave Christians! It is for Christ's faith that we fight today. Christ's cross against Thor's hammer! Christian against pagan!"

Then, when the anchors and grappling hooks were fastened upon the Swede king's ship, Olaf hastened to the rail and assailed her men first with javelin and long spear, and then with sword. So high was the *Serpent*'s poop above the other's stem that the Norsemen had to bring their weapons to bear right down below the level of their sandalled feet, and whenever the Swedish soldiers, emboldened by seeing an occasional gap in King Olaf's ranks, tried to climb on board, they were hewn down or thrown back into the sea.

At last Olaf of Sweden came forward with a strong body of swordsmen and axemen, intent upon being the first of the three hostile princes to plant his foot on the deck of the *Long Serpent*. Olaf Triggvison saw him approaching, and again calling his Norsemen to follow him, he leapt over the rail and landed on the enemy's deck. The son of Queen Sigrid stood still on his forecastle. His face suddenly blanched, but he gripped his sword, ready to encounter Norway's king. Here the two Olafs met and crossed swords, and a desperate duel ensued. Scarcely had they made half a dozen passes when Olaf Triggvison, with a quick movement of his wrist, struck his opponent's sword from his grasp and it fell on the deck.

"Too bold is Queen Sigrid's son," cried Olaf, "if he thinks to board the *Long Serpent*. Now have I got you in my power and might put an end to you and your worship of heathen idols. But never shall it be said that Olaf Triggvison struck down a foe who was unarmed. Pick up your blade, proud King of the Swedes, and let us see who is the better man, you or I."

So when Swedish Olaf stood again on guard, the two crossed swords once more.

"Now will I avenge the insult you offered my mother!" cried Olaf Sigridson, "and you who struck her on the cheek with your glove shall be struck dead with a weapon of well tempered steel instead of foxskin."

"Guard well your head," returned Triggvison, "lest I knock off your helmet. The man who taught you the use of the sword might have been better employed, for in truth he has taught you very little."

"He has taught me enough to enable me to slay such a man as you!" cried the Swede, gathering his strength for a mighty blow.

"That remains to be proved," retorted Olaf Triggvison. "Wait! you have got the wrong foot foremost!"

But without heeding, the Swede king brought down his sword with a great sweep, aiming at Olaf Triggvison's head. As with a lightning flash Olaf raised his sword to meet the blow. His opponent's blade was broken in two halves, while at the same moment he fell severely wounded upon the deck.

"Swedish sword blades are good," said Olaf Triggvison, "but the swords of the Norsemen are better."

He thought that he had made an end of the King of Sweden. But some of the Swedish soldiers who had been watching the duel rushed forward, and, raising their fallen king, carried him off on board another of his ships, while Olaf Triggvison went aft along the crowded decks, and men fell beneath his blows, as the ripe grain falls before the mower's scythe. It happened to the Swedes, as to the Danes, that notwithstanding their superior numbers they found that they were ill matched in skill and prowess with the Norsemen. Their picked champions were speedily killed or wounded, their best ships were disabled, and although they had indeed reduced Olaf Triggvison's forces by about half, yet they had not succeeded in boarding any one of his ships, much less in carrying any of them off as prizes. As King Sweyn had retreated, so did King Olaf of Sweden. His ships were called off from the combat and withdrawn out of range of the Norsemen's arrows. He had won no fame by his daring attack, but only ignominious defeat, and he was fain to escape alive, albeit very badly wounded.

Thus Olaf Triggvison had made both the Danes and the Swedes take to flight, and it had all befallen as he had said.

And now it must be told how Earl Erik Hakonson fared in that fight. True to the agreement which he and the two allied kings had come to over their dice throwing on the morning of that same fateful day, he had stood apart from the battle while Sweyn had vainly striven to make a prize of the *Long Serpent*; and during the midday and until the retreat of King Sweyn he had engaged no more in the conflict than to direct his arrows from afar into the thick of Olaf Triggvison's host. Now, Earl Erik was wise in warfare, and a man of keen judgment. He had fought with his father in the great battle against Sigvaldi and the vikings of Jomsburg, and from what he had seen on that day of Olaf Triggvison's prowess, and from what he had since heard of Olaf's warfare in England and other lands, he had made a very true estimate of the man who now fought in defence of the *Long Serpent*. He had also seen Sweyn Forkbeard in the thick of battle, and Olaf of Sweden no less. He was, therefore, well able to judge that neither the king of the Danes nor the king of the Swedes was capable of overcoming so brave and mighty a warrior as the king of the Norsemen, or of wresting the *Long Serpent* from the man who had built her and who knew so well how to defend his own. Pride in his own countryman may have had some share in the forming of this opinion. But Earl Erik had fought against the men of every land in Scandinavia. He had a firm belief that the men of Norway were braver and bolder, stronger in body, more skilful in the use of their weapons, and had greater powers of endurance than any of their neighbours. And it may be that in this he was right. He at least saw cause for thinking that the only men who could succeed in vanquishing King Olaf's Norsemen were the Norsemen of Earl Erik Hakonson. Earl Erik's vikings and berserks, eagerly watching the fray, had seen how the Danish ships had one after another been driven off, disabled and defeated. They had watched every movement of the tall and splendid form of the Norse king as he fought in his shining armour and his bright red tunic on the *Serpent*'s lypting. For a time they had not been certain whether Olaf Triggvison was at the stem or on the poop of his great dragonship, for it was seen that at each of these important points there was a tall chief whose prowess and whose attire alike distinguished him from all other men; and these two champions so resembled one the other that it was not easy to tell which was Kolbiorn Stallare and which King Olaf. But Earl Erik had not a moment's doubt. He would have known Olaf Triggvison had a score of such men as Kolbiorn been at his side. Earl Erik was the eldest son of the evil Earl Hakon who had fled from Thrandheim at the time of Olaf's coming into Norway, and been slain while taking refuge at the farmstead of Rimul, and Erik had naturally hoped that on his father's death he would succeed to the throne. Olaf Triggvison had shattered all his plans of future glory; and during the five years that had already passed of King Olaf's reign he thirsted for such an opportunity as now presented itself, not only of avenging his father's death but also, it might be, of placing himself upon the throne of Norway. His only uneasiness at the present moment arose from his fear lest King Olaf should be overcome in the battle ere he had himself encountered him face to face and hand to hand.

While the King of Sweden and his forces were engaged with their attack upon Olaf's centre of battle, Earl Erik adopted a plan which, although seemingly more hopeless, was in the end more successful than any that had yet been attempted by either the Danes or the Swedes. He saw that while the *Long Serpent* continued to be supported on either side by five strong and well manned dragonships she was practically unassailable. Her poop and her prow were the only points of her hull that were exposed, and these towered so high above the bulwarks of all other vessels that to attempt to board her was both useless and dangerous. Herein lay the secret of Olaf's successful defence, the proof of his forethought and wisdom in building the *Serpent* so much larger and higher than all other vessels in his fleet. Earl Erik, indeed, had observed that every ship that had approached her, either fore or aft, had been in its turn completely cleared of men or forced to withdraw out of the conflict.

Urging his rowers to their fullest speed, Erik bore down with his ships upon the extreme of King Olaf's right wing. The heavy, iron bound bow of the *Ram* crashed into the broadside of Olaf's outermost longship, whose timber creaked and groaned under the impact. Vikings and berserks leapt down upon her decks, and now Norseman met Norseman in a terrible, deadly combat. The king's men were well nigh exhausted with the long day's fighting under the hot sun; their bronzed faces streamed with perspiration, their limbs moved wearily. But, however, tired and thirsty they were, they could give themselves no respite. Every man that fell or was disabled by wounds left a gap in the ranks that could not be filled. The earl's men were fresh and vigorous; they had waited for hours for their chief's orders to enter the fray, and now that those orders had been given to them they fought with hot fury, yelling their battle cries and cutting down their foemen with ponderous axe and keen edged sword.

So fierce was the onslaught that many of Olaf's men, for the first time that day, fell back in fear and clambered over the bulwarks of the next ship. Very soon the decks of the first longship were completely cleared of defenders. Then Earl Erik backed out with the *Iron Ram*, while the seamen on his other ships cut away the lashings that had bound Olaf's outermost vessel to her neighbour, and drew the conquered craft away into the rear, leaving the next ship exposed.

Again Earl Erik advanced with the *Ram* and crashed as before into the exposed broadside of the outermost ship. As before, the vikings leapt on board and renewed the onset. Five of the viking ships lay with their high prows overshadowing the broadside bulwarks, and their men swarmed and clamoured upon the decks from stem to stern, clearing all before them. Again the lashings were cut and the conquered longship was withdrawn.

Two of King Olaf's dragons had now been captured by Earl Erik. It was not very long ere yet two others followed; and then the *Short Serpent* was exposed, even as her four companions had been. At this juncture Earl Erik paused, for he saw that Thorkel Nefja's decks were densely crowded with men who had retreated from vessel to vessel before the onslaught of the vikings. With the caution which long years of viking work had taught him, the earl decided that the *Short Serpent* might best be assailed by means of arrows, fired from a safe distance, until her numbers had been sufficiently diminished to warrant his attacking her at closer quarters. So he arrayed six of his ships near hand and set his archers to work, and for a long while this method of assault was continued.

There was no lack of arrows on the *Short Serpent*, or indeed, on any other of King Olaf's battleships. But it was noticed by the earl's vikings that the larger number of the shafts that were shot at them by the defenders were of Danish or Swedish make, and by this it was judged that the king's men were using the arrows that had been fired upon them by their enemies.

Leaving his six ships where he had stationed them, Earl Erik now rowed the *Iron Ram* round to the left wing of Olaf Triggvison's array. Four of his best longships followed him. He passed astern of the king's fleet. As he rowed by under the poop of the *Long Serpent* he saw the majestic figure of the King of Norway, looking brilliant in gold and scarlet as he stood in flood of the afternoon sunlight, sword in hand and shield at breast. The eyes of the two bravest of Norse warriors met. Waving his sword in mock salute, Earl Erik cried aloud:

"Short will be Olaf's shrift when Erik boards the *Long Serpent*!"

King Olaf saw that near to where Erik stood, on the *Iron Ram*'s forward deck, the image of the god Thor was raised, and he cried aloud in answer:

"Never shall Erik board the *Serpent* while Thor dwells in his stem!"

"A wise soothsayer is the king," said Earl Erik to one of his warriors as he passed onward astern of the *Crane*. "And I have been thinking, ever since this battle began that the great luck of Olaf may be due to that sign of the cross that we see on all his banners and shields. Often have I felt a wish to turn Christian, for it seems to me that all Christian men have something noble and honest about them--a greatness which we heathens can never achieve. Now do I swear upon the hilt of my sword"--he raised his sword hilt to his lips--"that if I win this battle and take the *Long Serpent* for my prize I will straightway allow myself to be christened. And, to begin with, I will have that image of Thor thrown overboard into the sea. It is ill made and cumbrous, and a figure of the cross will take less room in our stem and bring us more luck withal."

121

So speaking, Earl Erik stepped forward and, gripping the idol in his strong arms, flung it over the bulwark. Then he lashed two spars together, a long plank crossed with a shorter one, and raised this rough made crucifix high in the stem of the *Iron Ram*. By this time his vessel had passed beyond the extreme of King Olaf's left wing. He bade his rowers stop their rowing on the starboard side. They did so, and the ship turned about. Then at fullest speed he bore down upon the king's outermost dragon, crashed into her side and renewed his onslaught.

Erik dealt with the left wing as he had done with the right, and one after another of the four ships was cleared and unlashed. And now the *Long Serpent* lay with only two companions, the *Short Serpent* at her starboard and the *Crane* at her larboard side.

Already the *Short Serpent* was greatly crippled. Her commander, Thorkel Nefja, had fallen, and the larger number of her men had retreated on board of Olaf's ship, driven thither by the vikings of the six vessels that were now ranged close against her. Earl Erik now made a vigorous attack upon the *Crane*. He boarded her with a vast crowd of his vikings. On the mid deck he encountered her captain, Thorkel the Wheedler, and the two engaged in a sharp hand to hand fight. Regardless of his own life, Thorkel fought with savage fury. He knew how much depended upon his preventing Erik from boarding the king's ship. But he had already received a severe wound from a javelin across the fingers of his right hand, and he was full weary from the heat and long fighting. His assailant speedily overcame him, and he fell, calling upon God to save the king. As Thorkel had fought, so fought his men--desperately, furiously, but yet weakly, and at last both the *Crane* and the *Short Serpent* were cleared; their lashings were unfastened, they were withdrawn to the rear, and King Olaf's great dragonship stood alone among her foes.

CHAPTER XXII: THE DEFENCE OF THE "LONG SERPENT"

The sun was sinking lower and lower to the sea; light clouds were gathering in the western sky. But there would yet be three hours of daylight, and Earl Erik deemed that this would be ample time in which to win the *Long Serpent*. His own decks were thickly strewn with dead; his men were weary and athirst, and he saw need for a respite from fighting, if only for a very brief while. Also he saw on coming nearer to King Olaf's ship that it would be no easy matter to win on board of her; for the *Iron Ram* was but a third of her length, and her highest bulwarks reached only to a level with the oar holes in the *Serpent*'s wales.

Erik blew his horns for a short truce. His ships were drawn off, and for a time the battle ceased. In this interval the combatants on both sides rested themselves and took food and drink. King Olaf had his decks cleared of the dead, sent the wounded below into the shelter of the holds, and arrayed his men anew. He was himself unwounded still, but his silken tunic was tattered, so that the links of his coat of mail showed through. His helmet was battered by the many spears and swords that had struck upon it, and his shield bristled with broken arrows.

When he had freshened himself and got together a new supply of arrows and spears, he mounted to the poop deck, and there, standing in the sunlight, looked around the bay. The water was strewn with wreckage, an arrow floated on every wave. Small boats had been put out to pick up the men who had fallen, or been thrust overboard from the ships. All was silent now, save for the suppressed cries of the wounded and the hoarse voices of the chiefs who were giving rapid orders to their men for the renewal of the fight.

Earl Erik's ships, among which there were also some of the Swedes and Danes, stood off from the *Serpent* at a distance of an easy arrow's flight. They surrounded the *Serpent* like a pack of eager wolves held at bay; and the most eager of all men there present was Earl Erik.

When he had prepared his men he said to a chief who stood near him--Thorkel the High, it was, brother of Earl Sigvaldi:

"Many fierce battles have I fought; but never before have I found men equally brave and so skilled in warfare as the men fighting for King Olaf today; nor have I ever seen a ship so hard to win as the *Long Serpent*. Now, as you are one of the wisest of men, Thorkel, give me the best advice you know as to how that great ship may be won."

"I cannot give you sure advice," Thorkel answered: "but I can say what seems to me the best; and I would say that you would do well, when we presently come alongside, to take heavy timbers or such like weighty things, and let them fall across the gunwale of the *Serpent*, so that the ship will lean over. You will then find it easier to board her, for she will be brought down by the weight to a level with our own bulwarks."

"The advice is good," said Erik, "and I will follow it."

As he spoke, there came the loud blast of King Olaf's war horns, calling to his foes to come on.

The *Iron Ram*, and other ships, to the number of fifteen, then closed in about the *Serpent*, and, as they advanced, the archers on their decks opened battle by shooting their arrows high in air, so that they fell into the midst of Olaf's men in an unremitting shower. Olaf's warriors, one and all, raised their shields above their heads and held them there while the rain of shafts pattered upon them with a loud drumming noise that could be heard far across the bay. Many of the men were killed and many more wounded by this terrible hail, and when at length the shooting ceased, every shield was found to be closely bristled with arrows.

Earl Erik bore down upon the *Serpent* with the *Iron Ram*, whose heavy stem struck her amidships with tremendous force, so that the men on her decks were thrown off their feet. The good ship creaked in all her beams, but no great damage was done. Erik shipped his oars and drew his vessel close alongside, and at once his men began to heave great planks and logs of wood over the *Serpent's* gunwale. In this work they were speedily stopped, for Olaf's spearmen and archers on the deck of the foreroom assailed them with their weapons in such wise that they dared not continue. Not to be outdone, Erik had all his long oars brought on deck, and with these he made a bridge from the top of his foreroom across to the *Serpent's* gunwale. In this work he lost many of his men, who were shot down by Einar Eindridson and others of the king's best marksmen. But a gangway was made, nevertheless, and the chief difficulty was surmounted.

Not yet did Earl Erik attempt to board King Olaf's dragon. He sent many of his best men on board, armed with axe and sword. Most of them crossed the gangway to certain death; but many of the king's men also fell, both from wounds and from sheer exhaustion. It was amidships that the toughest fighting went on, and it was here that the larger number of the defenders met their death. But at the foreroom and the stem of the *Serpent* the fray was also of the fiercest. Company after company of the vikings clambered on board, for so fully were the king's men occupied in guarding their own lives that they could give little heed to their foes, who seemed to come from every point, not only from the *Iron Ram*, but also from other ships that were now drawn close in against the *Serpent's* hull. For every viking or Dane or Swede who fell, there were ten ready to take his place. The clang of weapons was now at its highest. Spears and arrows flew in the midst, not aimed at random, but each at its own particular mark, and each carrying death on its keen point.

King Olaf, surrounded by a burg of shields, flung his spears and shot his arrows with untiring vigour; but often he paused to watch how the battle fared or to give some new order to his men. He saw that his stem defenders were quickly becoming fewer and fewer, and that those who yet remained wielded their weapons with slow and heavy strokes. In a momentary lull of the conflict he left his own post and went forward.

"Why do you raise your weapons so slowly?" he cried. "I see they do not bite!"

Bersi the Strong replied: "Our swords are both dull and broken, lord."

The king then went into the foreroom, unlocked the high seat chest and took therefrom many bright and sharp swords which he carried out in his arms and put down among his men. As he bent over the weapons and picked out a very fine one to give to Bersi the Strong, Kolbiorn saw that blood flowed out of the sleeve of his coat of mail. Others saw the blood; but no one knew where the king was wounded. Then Olaf strode back to the lypting deck and once more surveyed the battle from on high. He saw that his stem defenders, to whom he had served new weapons, had now become so furious that they leapt upon the gunwales in order to reach their foes with their swords and kill them. But many of Earl Erik's ships did not lie so close to the *Serpent* as to afford any hand to hand fighting. The vikings were still cautious of Olaf's champions. Still, many of the king's men thought of nothing but going constantly forward, and in their eagerness and daring they seemed to forget that they were not on dry land. They went straight overboard, and several sank down with their weapons between the ships. Olaf was very angry at their want of care, for he now deemed every man of more value than ten had been at the beginning of the battle. Nevertheless, it was easy to see that the greater loss was on the side of Earl Erik. Olaf's archers and spearmen dealt such destruction that the victory for Norway seemed to become more possible with every moment.

Now Earl Erik had found very soon that his gangway of oars was by no means satisfactory, because while his men were crossing they became so fully exposed to King Olaf's marksmen that of every three who started only one succeeded in gaining a foothold on the *Serpent's* deck. Many hundreds of men--vikings, Swedes, and Danes--lost their lives on this bridge. So when Erik saw that King Olaf was gaining the upper hand of him he got his berserks to take down the oars and to fling them over the *Serpent's* nearer gunwale, together with all logs of wood, spars, ballast stones, and other weighty things that could be found. And as the weight increased so did the *Serpent* lean over, until at last her bulwarks were almost on a level with those of the *Iron Ram*.

While the vikings were at this work a constant rain of arrows and javelins was showered upon them by King Olaf himself and his marksmen on the poop, and as Erik saw his best men falling he half repented having taken them from the fight. But when the great obstacle that had baffled him so long was overcome, he rallied his vikings, and placing himself at their head, led them on board the *Serpent*. And now ensued one of the sharpest combats that had been seen that day.

Olaf's voice sounded loud above the tumult, calling to his chiefs in the bow to leave their station and resist the boarders in the waist. Wolf the Red, Ogmund Sandy, and Thrand Squinteye had already fallen, and Ketil the Tall and Vikar of Tiundaland had been sent below seriously wounded. But there still remained Kolbiorn Stallare, Thorstein Oxfoot, Bersi the Strong, and Thorfinn the Dashing; and these champions gathered a score of men about them, and hastening aft to the midships deck, turned against Earl Erik and made a very hard resistance.

Bersi the Strong encountered the earl hand to hand, their swords clashed, a few blows were exchanged and dexterously guarded; then Bersi fell. Thorfinn the Dashing took his place, and while the earl and he were fighting their hardest, Thorstein Oxfoot and Kolbiorn engaged with four of the earl's vikings. Kolbiorn felled two of them and turned to a third. Then Thorstein Oxfoot's sword was struck from his hand. Thorstein doubled his fist and struck his opponent on the cheek. The viking stumbled, and

Thorstein snatched up the half of a broken oar and wielding it above his head rushed among the vikings, belabouring them right and left. When King Olaf saw this he called aloud to Thorstein in a loud voice of command:

"Take your weapons, man, and defend yourself with them fairly. Weapons, and not fists or timber, are meant for men to fight with in battle!"

Thorstein then recovered his sword and fought valiantly.

There was still a most fierce fight going on between the earl's men and Olaf's champions. Kolbiorn vanquished the third viking he had engaged with, while Earl Erik was pressed back and back by Thorfinn the Dashing. Then Thorfinn caught sight of King Olaf, and at a sign from the king he lowered his blade and drew back a pace. Before Earl Erik could understand, a javelin whizzed past his left ear and buried its point in the bulwark behind him. He turned to see who had flung the javelin and saw King Olaf standing by the poop rail poising a second spear. The king flung his weapon, taking good aim; but this spear missed its mark as the first had done. King Olaf bit his lip in vexation, but as the earl turned quickly to beat a retreat on board the *Ram*, Olaf flung a third javelin after him. It struck the crest of Erik's helmet, but did no harm.

"Never before did I thus miss a man!" cried the king as he watched his enemy's retreat. "Great is Earl Erik's luck today. It must be God's will that he now shall rule in Norway; and that is not strange, for I see that he has changed the stem dweller on the *Iron Ram*. I said today that he would not gain victory over us if he had the image of Thor in his stem."

Now young Einar Eindridson had by this time taken up his position in front of the poop deck, where he found he could command a better sweep of the *Iron Ram*'s deck, and so pick off Earl Erik's champions. Einar saw the vexation in King Olaf's face, and when he got a good chance he levelled his aim against Earl Erik. He drew his bow. The arrow flew from the string and went straight to its mark. But in the same instant the earl suddenly moved round his head, so that the arrow, meant for his bared temple, only grazed his ear.

"Shoot me that tall, beardless youth!" cried the earl, pointing at Einar. "Full fifty of our best men has he slain with his arrows this day!"

Finn Eyvindson, to whom Erik spoke, aimed an arrow at Einar just as the lad was bending his bow for a second shot at the earl. The arrow hit Einar's famous bow in the middle and broke it with a loud snap.

"What was it that broke?" asked King Olaf.

Einar answered sadly as he dropped the pieces of his bow:

"Norway from thy hands, my king!"

"So great was not the breach, I hope," King Olaf said. "Take my bow and shoot with it instead."

Einar seized the king's bow and straightway drew it right over the arrowhead, bending it almost double.

"Too weak, too weak is the king's bow," said he, casting it aside. Then, for the first time that day, he took his shield and sword and rushed into the fray. No man in all King Olaf's host had slain more men in that battle than Einar with his arrows; and now the lad made himself no less distinguished with his sword.

Earl Erik presently saw that the sun was sinking nearer and nearer to the line of the sea. The number of his men had become woefully small, and yet, as he believed, Olaf Triggvison was still unwounded, undaunted, and as full of confident hope as he had ever shown himself to be. So the earl decided to make one more effort after the victory and to risk his all in a final hand to hand encounter with the King of the Norsemen. Gathering all his available men together he prepared to make a rush upon the *Long Serpent*'s deck.

King Olaf, seeing the earl's design, called his men aft, and ranged them in a compact body in front of the poop deck, ready to meet their foes.

At the same time Kolbiorn Stallare went up to Olaf's side, and the two, so much alike in size and dress, stood shoulder to shoulder, with their shields before them and their swords in their hands. A row of shield bearers stood in front of them. Then, with wild yells, the vikings, led by Earl Erik, rushed upon the mid deck.

As it had been throughout the whole day's battle, so was it now. King Olaf's men were greatly outnumbered; it was a conflict of skill and endurance against overwhelming odds. This final contest, while it lasted, was fierce and terrible. In a short time, however, many of King Olaf's champions fell. Brave and strong though they were, they could not withstand the furious onslaught of the ambitious and valiant Earl Erik. For a moment Olaf Triggvison was tempted to rush down and join the poor remnant of his men. He pressed forward to the stairs; but Kolbiorn Stallare drew him back.

"Wait, lord!" he cried; and then he whispered in Olaf's ear, and they both strode slowly aft to the rail. Here King Olaf turned and spoke to one of the shield bearers.

"How many of our men now remain?" he asked.

The man counted.

"Twelve are still left," he answered.

In a little while the king repeated his question.

"There are now but six," was the answer.

And then there came the sound of hurried feet upon the stairs, and Einar Eindridson rushed upon the upper deck, followed by three of his shipmates, and pursued by Earl Erik and a great crowd of clamouring vikings.

"Death to King Olaf!" cried the earl, in a voice which, in the silence that suddenly fell upon the ships, could be heard far across the bay. In that moment King Olaf and Kolbiorn leapt upon the rail, paused there amid the red light of the setting sun, and then, raising their shields above their heads, threw themselves over into the sea.

A cry that was half a groan escaped Earl Erik's lips. Flinging his sword aside, he went to the rail where King Olaf had stood. He looked down into the sea. Shadows were creeping over it. For a moment he saw the two swimmers. So much alike were they, each with his flowing gold hair, his crested helm, and his tattered red silk tunic, that it was impossible to tell which was the king. Presently one disappeared. The other was assailed by arrows and spears, but instantly he turned over and held his shield above him.

"It is the king! It is Olaf the King!" was the cry and boats were put out to rescue him. But Einar Eindridson kept his eyes upon the waves until at last, in the midst of a bright beam of sunlight far away he saw the shield of King Olaf appear, with its glistening image of the holy cross. And when the word went round that the rescued man was Kolbiorn Stallare and not the king, the lad pointed outward upon the sea and all looked in amaze upon the shining crucifix as it rose and fell with the motion of the waves.

The tale is told that the king, as he swam beneath the cover of his shield, stripped off his armour and, making his way to the land, went away on a pilgrimage to Rome. But the young grew old, and the world went on, and never again did King Olaf the Glorious come back to his realm in Norway.

Made in United States
Orlando, FL
05 February 2023